NO SUBSTITUTE FOR MYTH

NO SUBSTITUTE
FOR
MYTH

Carolyn J. Rose

No Substitute for Myth
Copyright © 2015 Carolyn J. Rose

www.deadlyduomysteries.com

ISBN: 978-0-9837359-9-1

This novel is a work of fiction. Names, characters, places, incidents, and dialogues are products of the author's imagination and are not to be construed as real. Any resemblance to actual events or persons, living or dead, is entirely coincidental.

Cover design by Dorion D. Rose, Broken Cork Photography

Interior design for print edition by Boulevard Photografica/Patty G. Henderson

Digital editions (epub and mobi) produced by Booknook.biz

Skyler – thanks for an idea
Lori – thanks for your support
Tristan – thanks for making us smile

Chapter 1

Myth.

The word conjures stories of how the earth was created, tales of gods and goddesses, sagas about ancient-world heroes, or legends featuring strange beasts.

It also brings to mind urban fables, stories shared on playgrounds and in college dorm rooms. Maybe you've heard the one about the killer stalking lovers' lanes, the man with a hook where his hand once was.

In the Pacific Northwest, the word often evokes images of Bigfoot, and sparks debate about whether he's real.

And, given my cynical nature, the word also makes me think of beliefs and sayings passed down through generations, sayings that may sound logical, but often aren't.

Practice makes perfect.

That's one of them.

If the person practicing has talent and ability and is aiming for perfection, the goal might be achieved. But if that person is Allison, the teenage daughter of my live-in love, drug cop Dave Martin, the odds decrease. And if what's being practiced is the art of meal preparation, you can bet the farm no amount of practice will result in anything you'll want to taste more than once.

Still, when my neighbor Muriel Ballantine suggested members of the Cheese Puff Care and Comfort Committee dish up weekly cooking lessons, I uttered not a single peep. As Dave often says, Mrs. B is a force of nature. "You can't change her course, you can only reckon with how she'll change *your* course."

Besides, arguing would lead to a one-sided discussion of what Mrs. B sees as my biggest character flaw. "You're too negative, Barbara, too pessimistic. Negativity is a magnet for bad luck and people who mistreat you."

To escape the lecture, I avoid even hinting that my elementary school science lessons with magnets proved negativity should actually attract good luck and positive people. Mrs. B, a former Las Vegas showgirl and widow of a man who pretended to be a mobster to seem dangerous and exciting, wouldn't buy that. She'd only laugh and point to what she considered proof of her theory—events of my recent past. I'd been downsized from my job, swindled by my ex-husband, targeted by a drug dealer, suspected of murder, and nearly killed by a woman aiming to advance her husband's political career.

And besides, who am I to deprive Mrs. B, Sybil, Verna, and other members of the Committee? Let them experience close encounters with kitchen chaos. They'd soon discover Allison was shaky on the concept of sanitation, scoffed at following directions, saw no need for exact measurements, and believed she already knew everything. Like Dario O'Brien, who had volunteered to teach Allison to drive, they'd find out the hard way.

Despite nerves of titanium honed by years of working for shady operators in Las Vegas and Hollywood, Dario developed a facial tic and gnawed his nails after only three driving lessons.

But the main reason I said nothing to warn them off was because Allison needed supervision during the long summer days when Dave and I had to work. Leaving her alone in the condo was fraught with peril. On a recent evening she spilled a gallon jug of tea on the sofa, dribbled nail polish on the carpet, and poured laundry detergent into the dishwasher. All while I was just down the hall.

Dave had considered burning vacation and personal time to ride herd on her, but we voted that down. Asking for anything beyond a refill for his stapler would make him far too visible to the cop shop brass. Since a debacle involving the acting police chief, an off-base politician, my bombastic sister, and thousands of women taking it to the streets, Dave had been trying to fly under the radar.

As for me, I have as many vacation days as worms have legs. Substitute teachers in the Reckless River School District don't get benefits, and they don't get paid unless they work. It being late June, school was out for the summer. So, with checkless months looming, I'd agreed to tackle the job of office manager at the auto repair shop formerly owned by the drug dealer who held my dog hostage.

Said dog, a ten-pound mutt named Cheese Puff with more attitude than Allison on a bad-hair day, hadn't lost sleep over the incident. Neither would my work schedule inconvenience him. Mrs. B and other members of the Committee could be counted on for feeding, walking, and pampering. While I soothed customers apoplectic about their repair bills, he'd be on outings with his adoring

3

posse. And by "outings" I don't mean strolls along the Columbia River that flowed by my condo complex. I mean excursions to restaurants, museums, plays, and festivals. No one faced with Mrs. B's sapphire eyes and a few greenbacks slipped discreetly from her purse had ever upheld a no-dogs-allowed rule.

Yet.

But back to Allison.

Her grades at the end of her sophomore year hadn't prompted Dave to alert the media. In fact, the string of Ds broken only by a C- in theater, resulted in a long lecture and an up-by-the-bootstraps summer educational enrichment plan. That relied on visits to area museums and points of interest with members of the Committee, an informal course in interior design taught by our friend Paulette, reading the daily paper, keeping a current events notebook, and receiving math tutoring from her boyfriend Josh. Cooking classes and weekly chores rounded out the program.

Allison described it as torture. "The only thing that could make this worse," she whined, "would be if Iz gave me a lecture on women's rights twice a day."

That sounded like the ultimate threat if all else failed to penetrate Allison's self-absorbed teenage brain. If you want consciousness raised, audiences energized, or rabble roused, my older sister is the one to call. Iz—that's short for Indigo Zephyr, a name she picked for herself—revels in giving speeches and issuing commandments. But while she's long on opinion, she's short on the ability to realize when she's driven a topic into the ground. I can count the number of genuine conversations we've had on the toes of one foot.

To my great joy, she and Penelope were at a lodge in Wyoming, enlarging their spiritual selves, broadening their awareness of nature, and discovering their totem animals. A glance inside the glossy brochure indicated the spiritual enlargement process involved more than enjoying the view while lounging on a porch or soaking in a hot tub. The print beneath the photographs mentioned hiking, cold water swims, and 24 hours of fasting.

Fasting!

Just hearing the word made my stomach rumble. I'm a grazer. I seldom go more than two hours without a little something to tide me over to the next meal, snack, or appetizer. Fat cells in those ten pounds I can't seem to shed lobby hard for munchies, and my brain rationalizes that eating a little now will help me eat less later on.

Iz has older and more determined fat cells, plus an ability to rationalize the average dictator would envy. After 120 minutes of deprivation with 1,320 more to go, she'd gnaw bark off trees.

That image made me positively giggly as I crawled out of bed early on the first Monday of summer vacation. I grabbed a quick shower, pulled on jeans and a T-shirt, and waved to Dave, Cheese Puff, and Lola. As I anticipated, Dave and Cheese Puff didn't interrupt their snoring to return the wave. Cheese Puff had no excuse, but I gave Dave a pass because he'd been out until 3:00 AM on a drug bust. Lola, a drug-sniffing Golden Retriever had been with him every step of the way, but *she* managed to open one eye and thump her tail.

Downstairs I scorched a piece of whole wheat bread, hit it with the last of the peanut butter, and washed it down with OJ while scanning the headlines. Same old same old. War, disease, inflation, and politicians doing back-door favors for their cronies and then issuing denials.

I was about to grab my purse and boogie when I spotted this headline: "Bigfoot in Reckless River?"

No way.

A Sasquatch sighting.

Not deep in the Cascade Range, but right here in the city.

Granted, Reckless River is, as cities go, pretty puny. But it's only a bridge away from Portland, Oregon. I wasn't about to check with the Census Bureau, but I'd bet a second piece of toast there were way more than a million people hanging out in the vicinity.

I scanned the article, skipping over phrases like "claimed to have seen" and "dimly lit area" and "found no tracks or other evidence." The gist was that a woman walking her dog in a park—barely half a mile from the chair on which my cheeks were planted at this moment—spotted a tall and shaggy creature digging through trash cans. When her dog barked, the creature loped away into the night.

Not "ran away," but "loped away."

Loping implied long but relaxed and easy strides. Casual. Loose.

What it didn't imply—at least to me—was fear.

So the creature that loped off was covering ground, but not at top speed. Exactly the way I imagined Bigfoot would vacate the area if he was concerned, or even a little worried, but not panicked.

Either the woman—who asked that her name not be used—was a proponent of descriptive verbs, or . . .

"Good grief," I mumbled while chewing the last bite of toast. "Talk about myths."

Bigfoot didn't have the status of Pegasus or the Minotaur, but he was—at least in my mind—in a league with the Loch Ness Monster.

I snagged my purse from the end of the counter, snatched the sack containing my personal mug and tiny cuplets of flavored creamer, flipped the car keys from their hook, and headed for the parking lot. If Bigfoot existed, why didn't people stumble across more tracks? Or find skeletons? With all the cell phones and cameras out there, even deep in the wilderness, why weren't there more recorded encounters?

I didn't have the answers.

What I had was another question: Given the human-nature desire for 15 minutes of fame, would I want to remain anonymous if I spotted a tall, shaggy creature, "loping" past my condo?

CHAPTER 2

When I pulled into the parking lot at Start 'er Up Auto Repair 15 minutes before opening time, one bay door was raised and a car hoisted on the hydraulic lift. Larry Tate was underneath it, doing something with a wrench, frowning in concentration. Most people appear older when they frown. Not Larry. He looked like a toddler in need of a hurry-up visit to the nearest restroom.

I felt a stab of anxiety. Customers might take advantage of his youth, demand better deals, negotiate for freebies, and in general walk all over him.

Well, not on my watch.

At least not if those customers were fairly small, alone, and not packing heat. I'm brave. But I'm not stupid.

Okay, not completely stupid.

Still, I had a year of experience as a substitute teacher, a year of giving unruly teens THE LOOK. Most of the time that steely squint had some effect. It wouldn't hurt to practice on customers until school started again.

I drove around behind the shop to a small dirt lot and parked beneath a spreading maple tree. Nearby, a warped and weathered picnic table hunched on a cracked concrete slab—both in need of pressure washing or a direct hit from a meteorite. Beyond, the ground sloped to a strip of tall grass that gave way to a wetland bristling with cattails. When I got out of the car, a red-winged blackbird conked out a single note, trilled his brief song, then took flight toward a stand of young poplars on the bank of a stream. The stream, protected by a greenbelt on either side, meandered through Reckless River, feeding into the Columbia not far from my condo. A trail ran along it and narrow wooden bridges crossed here and there. If I got an early start, I could walk to work or ride my bike.

I snickered, grabbed my sack, and tucked my car keys in my pocket. Early starts weren't what I was noted for. Last-minute arrivals were pretty much my speed—an irregular speed characterized by panicked bursts of energy.

I headed for the front of the shop, then returned and locked the car. There was nothing in it to steal, and the vehicle itself was worth only as much as a scrap metal dealer might fork over, but as a recent newspaper article pointed out, car thefts were on the rise. According to Dave, the population of tweakers was growing and even *my* car could feed a habit for a few days. No point in making it easy to steal.

Granted, the car was only a few feet from the shop, but just a single small window—in the restroom— overlooked the rear lot. And the greenbelt, so attractive to bicyclists, runners, and walkers, was also a draw for others. Living in makeshift tents hidden in the brush, they used the trails to reach social services, parks, highways, and the corners where panhandlers hung out with cardboard signs.

Another reason to drive to work. I was all for helping those hit by hard times, but I was also all for not making myself a target by walking or biking alone through an isolated area.

And then there was the creature that loped off through the park. If he stuck to the shadows, the greenbelt trails gave him a way to get around town without being noticed. And the wooded area provided secluded spots to lurk while waiting for prey to wander by.

I glanced over my shoulder at the tall grass and trees, wondering what kind of prey Bigfoot preferred. Ducks? Muskrats? Pizza delivery guys? Substitute teachers?

The creature in the park hadn't attacked the dog that barked at it or the woman who held the leash. Perhaps it hadn't been hungry. Or perhaps canine and companion weren't on the menu.

The article hadn't mentioned whether it growled or postured in an aggressive manner before it loped off. Was this creature a gentle soul? Was he more into flight than fight?

But in any case, Bigfoot was, well, big. No, make that BIG.

And BIG could be scary. Especially when you're alone. And especially at night.

Musing about how an encounter with the Footster might proceed—and how fast I might proceed in the opposite direction—I strolled through the open bay door and inhaled the scents of old grease, fresh oil, and cleaning solvent.

"Changing my oil." Larry slipped a rag from the top of a stack of pristine squares of red cloth and wiped his hands. He wore a smudge across one cheek, but I didn't mention it. After all, it might make people take him more seriously.

"Wouldn't inspire confidence if I blew out my own engine." He tucked the rag in the rear pocket of gray work pants that matched the shirt with his name stitched on the pocket in red.

I put on a show of enthusiastic nodding, pretending I knew exactly when I last changed the oil in my car. On the third nod I realized I did. Larry took care of that a few months ago when my car was hauled in having an automotive near-death experience. "I'll get coffee going and check for messages."

Larry smiled. "Doug said I could count on you to hit the ground running."

Unless there's a sale on cheesy snacks, running is something I try to avoid, but I gave him a smile. "I hope you'll settle for a fast walk."

"I'll settle for whatever kind of locomotion works for you."

Not something he'd want to say to every employee on the first day, but I appreciated the vote of confidence. Besides, I didn't think of myself as a true employee. I hadn't applied for this job, hadn't even considered applying. Doug, Larry's future brother-in-law and a teacher at Captain Meriwether High School, convinced me to hold the fort until Larry found someone to take over booking customers, filling out bills, and collecting money.

But at least I'd get paid. Doug was helping out for free in the interest of getting the business going, getting his sister married to Larry sooner, and putting an end to the drama of wedding planning.

"Anything I need to know?"

Larry opened the door to the office and ushered me inside. "Uh, yeah, uh, we didn't get around to organizing your area. It's kind of messy."

Messy would have been an improvement.

I'd checked out my work area—cramped, crowded, and crying out for a complete makeover—a few weeks ago. Since then, conditions had deteriorated. I groped for a response, and stuck with the same silence I delivered when I opened last year's Christmas present from my sister.

(For the record, that was an autographed picture of Iz leading a crowd of women onto a football field in protest. I didn't know what that protest was about, but didn't for one moment think it involved whether the ball was deflated.)

"Sorry it's such chaos." Larry scuffed one shoe on the gray linoleum floor, shoved sandy hair out of his eyes, and pointed to stacks of cardboard boxes placed at the perfect angle to impede progress toward the restroom, the copy machine balanced atop a file cabinet, or the door to the parking lot. "Doug put the old records in those boxes. I was going to organize the desk, but we got a bunch of deliveries and . . ."

"It's cool."

The tall desk had about eight square feet of surface, but that was piled with computer manuals, bank deposit bags, boxes of paper clips, grungy coffee cups, an aging coffeemaker, a sack of coffee, filters, a container of synthetic cream granules, a tattered address booklet, a phone book shedding pages, and a welter of pens and pencils.

"It's fine." I forced a smile that was all teeth and a laugh that sounded a lot like cause to employ the Heimlich maneuver. "If I organize it, I'll know where everything is."

"Doug said you like a challenge."

And it would be a challenge to refrain from asking Doug why he couldn't at least have hooked up the printer. Or why he hadn't set the coffeepot and creamer on the tiny table hunkered between the two chrome-and-vinyl chairs that furnished the waiting area opposite the desk.

"I cleaned the restroom," Larry volunteered with another scuff at the linoleum. "But then my mom did it over. She said you'd have enough to deal with the first day without gagging your guts out, and I should stick to fixing cars." He glanced toward the shop. "If you're okay, I'll get mine off the lift before a customer shows up. *If* a customer shows up."

"I'm good. And I'm sure we'll have plenty of customers."

After Larry flashed a hopeful grin and departed, I yanked open the bottom drawer to stash my purse, but had second thoughts when I caught a whiff of the nest of greasy take-out menus inside. A wet dog rolling in barbecued roadkill had nothing on that stench. First step: disposing of the menus, cleaning out the drawers, and spraying the desk with industrial-strength germ killer.

Fortunately, there was plenty of that stashed in the tiny restroom which was clean enough to meet even Paulette's standards. I snagged the spray bottle and a handful of paper towels and made a mental note to send Larry's mother flowers—on the repair shop's account.

In a few minutes I had plastic cups, spoons, and creamer on a small tray and the coffeepot set up and gurgling. I inhaled the revitalizing aroma of Colombian roast, then clicked on a small fan mounted between the tiny windows above the waiting area seats, and went to work on the desk. Deciding on a sort-later policy, I dumped the contents of the drawers into a box and sprayed and wiped with a vengeance. In half an hour, I had the top cleared and polished, the keyboard degreased, the printer hooked up, and the computer running.

Not long after he recruited me for the job, Doug copied the billing program and installed it on my home computer so I could check it out. It was a simple system but had quirks, one of which was a tendency to dump information at random. I wrote "Save Often" on a sticky note and slapped it at the top of the screen.

A large window behind my desk gave me a view of the work area. As I cleaned it, I saw two young men join Larry in the garage. Must be Mark and Denny, I thought. One, tall, dark, but hardly handsome, lowered the lift. The other, short, freckled, and younger, puttered around the workbench while Larry backed his car out.

The coffeepot spit a final burst of hot water into the filter and I hustled over to fill my mug. Adding a dash of French vanilla flavored creamer from my personal stash, I climbed into the tall chair behind my desk. Getting up took some effort, but the chair was comfortable and well-padded with an adjustable backrest and a bar to hook my heels on.

Surveying my domain, I sipped coffee. So far, this was no more stressful than starting a day of subbing at Captain Meriwether High School. In fact, given that this room wasn't packed with hormone-driven teens, it was almost—

Whomp!

The door from the outside banged against the stack of boxes. "That young man says he's in charge," a querulous voice wheezed. "All I can say is he better know what he's doing."

I spun the chair toward the door and a man who looked like an oversized grouchy garden gnome. He had

14

receding gums and a hairline to match. A scraggly white beard, laced with bits of egg yolk and assorted crumbs, hung to the middle of his chest. A few strands tangled in the faded red suspenders that lifted the waistband of beige slacks several inches above his waist and revealed a pair of gray socks sagging over the tops of muddy brown work boots.

"He claims he's got three years of experience, but he don't look like he's been out of high school more than a week."

Gnome Guy turned to survey the shop through my freshly polished window. Together we watched Larry raising the hood of a truck that looked like it had served hard time in a desert prone to paint-stripping sandstorms and 200-pound tumbleweeds.

"If he messes up my engine or charges me more than is right, I'll sue his shorts off." Gnome Guy turned to eye me from beneath bristly brows. "Sue your panties off for good measure, Missy."

I strained my lips into a smile while holding on to three snappy comebacks: "Good luck with that, Buster," "The last guy who called me 'Missy' has his nose in a cast," and "I'm not wearing any."

(For the record, not true. My grandmother would have been proud of the underwear I'd stepped into earlier— clean, white, possessing wide elastic, and without a single hole.)

Why did the first customer have to be a caricature of a codger? Was Mrs. B right about the attraction thing? *Was I a magnet for problem people?*

He snapped his suspenders, tangling more strands of his beard. Freeing them with sidelong jerks of his chin, he loosed a tumble of crumbs from breakfasts past. "Well? Cat got your tongue?"

I decided to pretend the last few moments hadn't happened, and match his attitude with enough smarmy charm to raise his blood sugar level to the danger zone. Beaming on a toothy smile, I tapped a few keys and brought up a client-information form. "Good morning. Thank you for choosing Start 'er Up Auto Repair to service your vehicle. I understand you've already spoken with Mr. Tate about the work we'll be doing and a rough idea of the cost, so let me get a few details and your sig—"

"Not yet, Missy." He coughed into a crumpled green handkerchief. "I ain't signing one damn thing until I see what kind of job that young feller's doing on my tune up."

I broadened my smile a few millimeters. "And a wise decision that is."

"Told him I intended to sit right out there and keep a close eye on him. He claims there's a state rule about customers being in the shop on account of they might get hurt. That's a bunch of mommy-state bull crap for people too stupid to breathe through their noses."

He snapped his suspenders again, opened the door to the garage, pulled one of the customer chairs into the doorway, and dropped into it with another cough and a spit for good measure. "I'll park it right here until he's done."

His tone implied that would happen whether I liked it or not, but he didn't trust implication alone. "Don't you even think of telling me to move."

Time to drop the synthetic smile. "I wouldn't dream of telling you to move." I reached for the phone. "I'll have someone with more authority do it."

Chapter 3

Gnome Guy scowled.

"It's probably another mommy-state rule, but that door has to remain closed." I waved a hand in front of my face. "Fumes, you know. When the guys rev up those engines, the door is the only thing standing between this office and a toxic cloud of carbon and chemicals."

As if I scripted it, Larry cranked the truck's engine. It sounded like a double-door refrigerator falling down a long flight of metal stairs. A cloud of exhaust the color and density of Mississippi mud spewed from the tailpipe.

Even I could tell that truck needed far more than a tune up.

My cantankerous customer's scowl deepened.

"If you're not worried about what you'll be inhaling or what you might be cited for in the way of obstruction, then stay right there." I slipped from the chair and grasped my mug. "As for me, I'm going outside where the air is cleaner. I'll make my calls from there. Hope I don't spill hot coffee as I squeeze behind you to get to the other door."

17

When Doug turned up later in the morning, I had a new filing system set up and the desk drawers cleaned out and organized. I'd managed those tasks in spite of Gnome Guy.

He'd closed the door to the garage and moved his chair beside the small table, then devoted himself to complaining about the quality of the coffee while emptying the pot. Having exhausted that topic, he moved on to a running commentary on vehicles he used to own and how they don't make things like they used to. The commentary started from the top each time Larry came in to confer with him about new problems he'd discovered.

Doug set a box of generic chocolate chip cookies beside the coffeepot and handed me a weighty white paper sack that gave off the enticing aroma of butter, cinnamon, and sugar. "Any problems? I mean, besides the mess we left for you?"

I slid my gaze toward Gnome Guy who was dropping clusters of fresh crumbs into his beard as he chomped two cookies. "Nothing a little child psychology couldn't handle."

Doug glanced over his shoulder. "Shoulda bought more cookies," he said in a low voice.

"And encourage him to stay longer? Or return tomorrow?"

"Good point." He dropped his voice to a whisper. "I'll look forward to your report at the end of the day."

"If he doesn't drive me out of here before then, I'll give it to you." I peeped into the sack to confirm my guess that it contained a cinnamon roll the size of a large grapefruit. "In the meantime, I'll expect further tribute."

At 4:45, Larry came in from the shop juggling slips of paper, wrappers, and flattened cardboard boxes. Denny—or maybe Mark, there hadn't been time for introductions—followed, dragging an enormous black plastic sack that rattled with each step. Larry dumped his load on my desk. Mark—or maybe Denny—left his at the feet of the man least likely to be named customer of the year.

Gnome Guy stood with a grunt and a belch and yanked the sack open. "What the hell is this? There's nothing wrong with these parts. Why'd you change them out?"

While Gnome Guy worked up a head of steam, Denny—or maybe Mark—reached into the sack and held up a black hose cracked like a lake bed during a lengthy drought and a belt worn to a fraying strip no wider than my pinkie. He followed those exhibits with a plastic jar containing half an inch of what looked like tar.

"That was in your oil pan," Larry said. "Do you want to see what was in your radiator? Or what was left of your brake pads? Or your shocks and struts?"

I beamed at Larry like he was a star pupil. If he could handle this customer, my worries about him being taken advantage of were out the window.

Gnome Guy glowered and rooted around in the sack.

"Every part we removed is in there. And every label or wrapper or box for the new parts is here." Larry stirred the heap on my desk. "We'll copy the receipts and attach them to your bill."

Gnome Guy slapped a protective hand over the rear pocket where I imagined he kept a wallet stuffed with greasy bills dating from the Nixon Administration. "How much?"

"We'll know in a minute." Larry handed me a strip of cardboard with penciled notations.

It was the fifth such row of words and numbers I'd seen today and I was getting the hang of reading his scribbles and filling in the correct columns on the computer spreadsheet. I brought up the account in Gnome Guy's real name: Elmer Buttress. Belching like a man who spends the day swilling coffee and devouring cookies is prone to do, my least favorite customer sorted through the labels and packaging while I worked.

When I was finished plugging in repairs and numbers, Larry checked over the form on my screen and nodded.

I saved the report and sent the job to the printer which hummed and coughed out four pages. Larry stapled them together and, with a bow and a flourish, handed them to Gnome Guy.

He flipped to the bottom line on the final page and crumpled the printout in a tightening grip.

I sucked in a breath and braced for the explosion.

Larry didn't flinch.

Gnome Guy's face turned the color of cheap red wine. Then he eyed the sack, squinted at the bill, and pointed to the empty cookie box. "Those tasted like crap. So did the coffee."

"Then it's a good thing we didn't bill you for them," Larry said in a matter-of-fact tone.

I choked on a laugh.

Gnome Guy gave us both the evil eye, then dug into his front pockets. Instead of the bulging wallet I expected, he brought out a dozen greenish cubes and scattered them on the desk.

It took me a moment to figure out they were bills, folded and shaggy with pocket lint. I unfolded one and was face-to-face with Benjamin Franklin. Larry unfolded a second and there was Grant. A few more Franklins and another Grant or two and the repair bill was covered.

Larry gathered the remaining cubes and handed them back to their owner. I dug a few dollars and some change from the petty cash box and counted bills and coins into Gnome Guy's hand. He counted with me, lips moving, then wadded the change into his pocket with the green cubes.

I manufactured a smarmy smile to prove he hadn't worn me down. "Thank you for choosing Start 'er Up Auto Repair. We appreciate your business and hope to see you again."

Not!

I stuffed the wrappers and boxes and labels into a second plastic sack. Then Larry signaled to Mark and Denny, and they hustled the bags out to the idling truck. After walking around, peering underneath, and cocking his head to listen to the engine, Gnome Guy was on his way, parts rattling and clanging in the bed, but not a trace of smoke issuing from the exhaust pipe.

When he was out of sight, Larry slumped against the desk. "I owe you one. Heck, I owe you two."

"Shucks, it was merely your basic baptism by fire." I printed another copy of the bill and slipped it and the copied receipts into a manila folder with Gnome Guy's name printed on the tab. "If my name was Elmer Buttress and I looked like a giant garden gnome with hemorrhoids, I might be grouchy too."

5:00 PM came, the last customer departed, and Mrs. B twinkle-toed in with Allison, Cheese Puff, and a picnic hamper. The hamper was mounded high with what I had no doubt were calorie-laden treats. Mrs. B was dressed in what, for her, amounted to casual attire—creamy linen slacks, a pale green silk blouse, a single strand of pearls, and only three diamond rings. Allison wore cutoff jeans and a red tank top that matched her flip-flops and nail polish. Cheese Puff sported a new collar—a wide black leather band with shiny silver studs. I guessed one of the Committee members bought it thinking it would make him look tough or perhaps protect his neck if he got into a fight.

Cheese Puff—who resembles an orange feather duster with legs—makes up in attitude what he lacks in size, and is prone to snarling at far larger dogs he encounters on the river trail. Most of those big dogs seem amused by his combativeness, but others bark in a way that says "Bring it!" So far, those aggressive dogs had been securely leashed, but I feared one day the Puffster would bare his teeth at the wrong hound—like the huge mutt from the condo complex up the river.

That creature's build and bristling hair made him look like a cross between a hyena and a hay wagon, and I'd never seen him on a leash. Rumor had it the mutt's owner, a high-powered attorney, claimed he was a free-range canine and it would be against nature to tether him. Rumor also had it the owner was lawsuit happy and politically connected—which so far made condo residents try to avoid the dog and potential confrontations with the owner. They'd been urging condo manager Bernina Burke to approach the owner on their behalf. Bernina, however, was dragging her feet, claiming *she* hadn't seen the dog acting in a vicious manner, and couldn't act on what amounted to hearsay.

Mrs. B greeted Larry with a hug and a kiss that left a circle of tangerine colored lipstick on his cheek. "Shall we celebrate the first day of our business enterprise?"

"Otherwise known as the longest day in business history thanks to the customer from hell," I muttered.

Mrs. B shot me one of her don't-be-negative glances and I put a cork in it, saving comments about Gnome Guy for Dave. Larry lowered the bay doors, the guys washed up, and we all adjourned to the picnic table behind the shop. While Cheese Puff sniffed along the edge of the tall grass and left pee-mail messages, Mrs. B spread a blindingly white tablecloth on the weathered table, set it with equally white napkins, and dealt out thin china plates with gold leaves around the rims. Allison brought forth champagne, tall crystal flutes, sparkling cider, finger sandwiches, and chocolate-covered strawberries in a silver bowl.

Mark and Denny eyed the stains on their uniforms.

"A little dirt won't hurt anything," Mrs. B said.

Mark and Denny didn't seem convinced, but Larry shrugged and took a seat in the center of the bench facing the auto shop. Allison and I sat on one side of him, with Doug on the other. Mrs. B poured champagne—giving Allison a splash—and took her place between Mark and Denny, facing the greenbelt.

The table shuddered and rocked as we reached for goodies but, to my surprise, didn't splinter into a pile of kindling.

In about two minutes Mrs. B established that Mark was the older and taller of the two and preferred to work on cars made in the USA. Denny confided that his girlfriend probably knew more about cars—and everything else—than he did, but said he didn't mind and actually kind of liked that.

Mrs. B ignored Mark's frown, gestured toward the wetland and the trees beyond, and moved on to a new topic. "Isn't this lovely? It's almost like being out in the country. It's positively revitalizing. What a wonderful place to eat a leisurely lunch or take a little break between customers."

Larry shot me an if-only glance, but said nothing to dim her fantasy. A man intending to repay his loan quickly wouldn't take many breaks—little or otherwise. And if he wanted a leisurely lunch, he'd wait for the weekend.

I raised my champagne flute and clinked it against the others. "To success."

"To many satisfied customers," Mrs. B added. "May they return again and again and again."

Larry slipped me another glance. "Except for one," he mouthed.

Color me jaded, but I wasn't at all surprised by what I found when I got home. The summer schedule listed Monday as laundry day. That called for Allison to sort, wash, dry, and then fold or hang clothing in the appropriate closets. The summer schedule, however, hadn't included a start time. So, naturally, she'd put the project off—except for building a mountain of laundry in the kitchen. The pile blocked the folding doors to the pantry and thus to the washer and dryer. It also blocked the refrigerator where I'd hoped to find a diet cola to dilute the champagne I'd imbibed. Even a little bubbly could deliver a screaming headache if I didn't add more liquid to my system along with a jolt of caffeine.

"I had to do my nails," Allison said when I pointed out the problem. "At least I got all the dirty clothes downstairs."

"At least." Stressing the second word, I kicked aside a tangle of jeans and T-shirts and opened the refrigerator wide enough to fish out a cold aluminum can. "Now how about getting it sorted and starting the first load?"

"Couldn't I do it later? I want to go to the pool."

Of course.

I popped open the cola and gulped down half the contents. Then I set the air conditioning down a couple of degrees.

"It's summer vacation," Allison added. "I'm supposed to be having fun."

I kicked off my shoes, flopped on the sofa, and watched Cheese Puff digging a nest at the top of the laundry pile. "You're also supposed to be earning that increased allowance you lobbied for."

She parried that with her own brand of logic. "But Dad hasn't paid me yet."

"In the real world we get paid *after* we do the work."

"That's stupid." She booted a sock to the top of the heap. Cheese Puff levitated from his nest and scampered to his favorite chair. "I should at least get some money *before*. Then I'd work harder."

I pointed at the clock. "Stupid or not, if that laundry isn't finished by midnight, Cinderella, you're going to turn into a girl with a very unhappy father. He might decide you don't deserve to be paid at all."

Allison pouted, kicked a pair of Dave's gym shorts, and draped herself across the heap. "But Josh is coming over when he gets off work."

"Maybe he'll help you with the laundry."

25

"But he'll be all hot and tired," she wailed. "Working at Krammee's is brutal."

Krammee's was one of many fast-food joints catering to those more concerned about speedy service and low prices than nutrition or calorie count. Its menu challenged the definition of "edible" as well as the limits of the human digestive system. The signature selection was a trio of burgers, each sized to be "krammed" into your mouth whole, bun and all.

(For the record, I can't imagine any reason I'd be inclined to do that. Due to word-of-mouth reviews and health department scores, I'd never eaten there.)

On the plus side, the restaurant was locally owned and operated and the chamber of commerce regularly lauded Woodrow Krammer for creating jobs and giving back to the community. That giving back, in my opinion, seemed to be largely in the form of campaign donations and turning out for civic events designed to net him maximum media coverage with minimum effort.

"Josh should totally walk away when his shift is over, but no, he even does extra stuff. Like buying that little rake thing to bust up the ice cubes when the soda machine jams. They didn't even pay him for it 'cause he didn't ask Mr. Krammer before he spent his own money on it."

Allison made a gag-me gesture, then plunged on. "Last night he had to clean the grill and mop the floor after they closed. He says he's the only one who does it right and gets up all the grease in the corners, but he only gets paid for half an hour and it takes him like forever."

"Forever" to a girl going on 16 might mean only an extra five minutes, but I didn't mention that. I didn't make poor-baby sounds, either. Although I felt sorry for Josh and vowed to have a talk with him about possible recourses regarding money owed for the rake, I'd already engaged too much with Allison's laundry-avoidance drama. It was time to feign lack of interest and let her decide to girl-up and tackle her task, or skate off and face the consequences.

Yawning, I set the cola on the coffee table and rested my arm across my eyes. Cheese Puff, recognizing a nap about to happen, bounced from his chair and sprawled on top of me. I scratched his ears and he rewarded me by grunting and licking my chin. Allison, meanwhile, whined on about oppressive rules, unreasonable expectations, and adults who couldn't remember being kids. I closed my eyes and imagined she was a mosquito.

CHAPTER 4

When I woke up, the washer was chugging and the laundry heap had migrated. That freed the refrigerator and the cabinet where I keep cheesy snacks, but blocked access to the stove.

"Good thing we had those finger sandwiches and strawberries," I told Cheese Puff. "There will be no cooking tonight."

He flashed me a doggie smirk that implied there wasn't much cooking done on *any* night, then jumped down, trotted to the sliding glass door, and scratched. "No, you're not going to Mrs. B's," I told him. "You have kibble in your bowl."

He eyed the stack of laundry, barked once, and pawed at the door again.

I spotted the problem—dirty clothes avalanching across the kibble and into the water bowl.

"All right." I unkinked myself and trudged to the door. Who knew that sitting in a chair all day and following up with a nap would make my muscles as stiff as old leather?

I slid open the door and Cheese Puff pranced through and crossed the deck to Mrs. B's condo. I followed and found her lounging in a chair with a martini glass at hand and sheets of music spread on her lap.

"The Puffster is annoyed. He craves adoration and sustenance. There's dirty laundry in his dinner bowl."

"The poor little prince." Mrs. B shoved the papers to the floor and headed inside for the cabinet where she keeps a supply of designer dog treats. Forget run-of-the-mill kibble, this stuff is priced beyond what I'd spend on a meal for myself. Without a backward glance at me, the woman who'd found him shivering in the rain and given him a home, Cheese Puff followed my neighbor.

"I'll be at the pool," I said.

Neither of them acknowledged me.

"As if anyone cares," I added, wondering once again why Cheese Puff didn't abandon me and move in next door where his every whim was catered to. Perhaps he felt an obligation. Or a twinge of guilt. Or even pity.

Nah.

More likely it was because he was infatuated with Lola. Despite his lack of certain male parts and her lack of certain female ones, and despite the fact that she was a foot taller and outweighed him by more than 50 pounds, it had been love at first sniff.

I retraced my steps, picking up the pace when I detected the thudding of an overloaded washer trying in vain to reach spin speed. Hurdling the heap of laundry, I skidded against the washer, flipped up the lid, and bellowed for Allison.

"I'm upstairs," she yelled in a drama-laden tone. "I chipped my nail polish on that stupid machine."

Muttering about a few things I'd like to chip, I plodded upstairs to my bedroom, pausing to deliver an update to the closed door of her room—the door posted with a KEEP OUT sign. "I stopped the washer. It's overloaded."

"What does that mean?"

"It's too full."

"It is not. I got the lid closed."

I opened my mouth to respond, decided further conversation wouldn't be healthy, and reminded myself I'd foreseen a fiasco. Then I delegated. "When your polish is dry—and that better be soon—ask Mrs. B or one of the other Committee members to help you."

"Help me do what?"

"Take some of the clothing out and redistribute the load."

"Huh?"

Sheesh.

"Just don't leave it until your father gets home."

That happened about an hour later. I was in the deep end of the pool, where I'd vowed to be every day until it closed for the season and I returned to aerobics classes at the rec center. I was wearing a flotation belt and doing a slow cross-country move with a twist. It was designed—according to my water aerobics instructor—to work my waist. So far working had made no difference, but Paulette assured me I was turning fat into muscle and swore this exercise worked for her.

(For the record, Paulette has only about four ounces of total body fat to use the exercise on, but I like her in spite of her trim figure.)

"I regret to inform you," Dave said, "that Allison will still be with us even if you stay in the pool all night." He tossed a towel on the pool deck and cannonballed in, splashing me and soaking the towel. Surfacing, he nuzzled my neck.

I felt not a trace of stubble, not even around the dimple in his chin. "What's with the close shave?"

"Not every undercover assignment is in the scumwad section of Reckless River. You wouldn't believe what you can buy at one of the local bridal shops."

"Let me guess. A little something to help the bride and her maids diet to a smaller size."

"A *lot* of something," Dave confirmed. "Major something. The lieutenant was thrilled."

The lieutenant possessed a poker face any Vegas player would covet. "How could you tell?"

"A corner of his mouth twitched. Twice."

I unsnapped my flotation belt and tossed it onto the pool deck. "How'd you make the bust?"

"Luck and Lola. The shop is around the corner from the fried pie place."

"The place where you found the caterpillar in your food last winter?" Despite the heat, I shuddered. "The place you said you'd never eat at again?"

"Um, yeah." He flushed and ducked underwater for a moment. "I, uh, see, uh, they sent me a bunch of coupons for free pies."

"A *bunch* of coupons?"

"Twenty." He flushed a deeper red. "I guess they were glad I didn't take the caterpillar and the remains of the pie to the health department."

"I thought you told me you were going to."

"I was. But, I, uh, lost it."

"Lost the caterpillar? Or the pie?"

"Both." He ducked under again and emerged a few feet away. "I, uh, left the bag in the car while I went in to a gas station to make a pit stop. I think Lola ate it."

"Ewwww."

"She's a dog. It was protein."

"Double ewwww."

"The crust was probably worse for her than the caterpillar. Anyway, I ate six pies since I got the coupons. I haven't found anything weird."

"Yet."

Dave went under again and surfaced doing a backstroke so clumsy it made him look like he was having convulsions.

"Eating there is the culinary equivalent of Russian roulette," I told his churning wake. "Sooner or later your luck will run out and—" I clamped my lips shut and willed my mind not to think about what manner of vermin might be fried inside a lard-laden crust.

He made the world's sloppiest turn at the end of the pool and returned. "So, back to your question about how I made the bust. Last week there was no room in the lot at the fried pie place, so I parked in front of the bridal shop and Lola and I got out and she did her I-smell-drugs thing. If she wasn't a dog, and if she wasn't always right about what she sniffs out, I would have accused her of messing with me. Instead, I hooked up with an officer I happen to know got engaged last week. She couldn't believe her assignment was to shop for something to wear on an aisle walk."

He mimed putting a gun to his head. "If I have to sit through another two hours of talk about fabrics and bodices and tiaras, I'll shoot myself. When we decide to get married, could we make it a casual wedding?"

Part of me wanted to kiss him and say I'd marry him wearing a brown paper bag. Another part of me wanted to haul myself out of the pool and run. I'd like to believe the third time down the aisle would be the charm, but more likely that third time thing was a myth.

"Not that we'll have any say about what we wear." He put the finger gun to his head again. "Mrs. Ballantine will take charge."

True. She wouldn't be able to help herself, being a force of nature and all. "We could elope. In the middle of the night."

"If we want to get away without members of the Committee spotting us, it will have to be not only night, but a dark and stormy night. A night with a power outage and a tornado warning that has everyone huddling in their bathtubs."

Good point. Given erratic sleep patterns due to TV viewing, reading habits, tendencies to snack in the wee hours, the assorted ailments of age, and a broad interest in the comings and goings of their neighbors, Committee members' watchfulness could out-perform that of some professional security guards. "Speaking of stormy, what about Allison and that pile of dirty clothes?"

"Jim's on it."

Jim, somewhere in his 70s and with a beard like Father Christmas, was the only male member of the Cheese Puff Care and Comfort Committee. To say he had a checkered past was to put it mildly, but these days he was clean-living, level-headed, and responsible. "He's not *doing* the laundry, is he?"

"Nope. He's kicking it in Cheese Puff's favorite chair and drinking a beer." Dave shook his head, sending water droplets flying. "The man is a motivational genius. Who knew all you had to do to get Allison moving was to threaten to read her diary?"

"Now that's a megaton threat." I wiped water from my eyes. "Wait, doesn't she keep her diary locked in a box in her closet?"

"Except when she leaves it on the stairs. All Jim had to do was scoop it up and riffle the pages. Presto, instant impetus."

"OMG. And Josh is coming over soon."

"Yeah, and Jim has offered to stage a dramatic reading on the deck if the laundry isn't finished before he arrives." Dave choked out a laugh. "Allison has washers going at Mrs. Ballantine's, at Sybil's, *and* at Verna's. I haven't seen her move this fast since the day she went to try for her learner's permit."

"A day that will live in infamy." I paddled for the steps. "I've got to see this to believe it."

Dave yanked one strap of my swimsuit and pulled me to him. "How about we spend a few minutes without my difficult daughter or your demanding dog or our various and sundry friends and neighbors?"

He punctuated that last sentence by nuzzling my neck once more. "How was your first day on the job?"

"Longer than a day at high school and with its own brand of stress." Between nuzzles and a few kisses, I filled him in on the mess in the office, Gnome Guy, and the in-charge version of Larry.

"Well, the mess is straightened up and Larry seems to have the helm. The rest of the summer should be a cakewalk. I mean, the odds of running into Gnome Guy again are about the same as getting involved in another murder case or finding Bigfoot using the pool as a bathtub."

Little did he know.

When the condo security lighting blinked on, we abandoned the sanctuary of the pool and found Josh on the deck with Mrs. B and Cheese Puff. A trio of scented candles cast light on the sheet music she'd been studying earlier. She tapped the papers with her forefinger while Josh picked out a tune on an electric guitar—a tune that seemed to be a fusion of hard rock, high-speed collision, and power-line overload.

"Interesting mix of sound." Dave dropped into a chair beside Mrs. B. "For your act?"

Mrs. B shook her head, her silvery hair glinting in the candlelight. "No, I haven't decided on that yet. Josh has given me so many pieces to consider and directions to go that I can't make up my mind."

Josh grinned, tucked his shoulder-length hair behind his ears, and squirmed inside the too-large catsup-colored Krammee's uniform shirt. Musical taste aside, he was a great kid—responsible, reliable, an A student, and a good example for Allison, who was none of that. Their romance was proof Mrs. B's theory of attraction was faulty. But, as I said earlier, there was no point in bringing that up.

"Don't you have a deadline to commit to the program and present a preliminary plan for your act?" I perched on the end of Mrs. B's lounge chair. "Isn't it next week?"

She waved that pesky thought aside, diamonds glittering. "It's more of a suggested benchmark than a deadline."

That wasn't what I'd heard from Dario O'Brien a few days ago. For months Mrs. B had been putting off a decision on when she'd appear on the Las Vegas reality show *Still Got That Strut*. Dario, who held a title like Chief

Assistant to the Assistant Chief in Charge of Assistants, regularly pleaded with her to firm up the details of her act, give him a definite commitment, and sign a contract. But Mrs. B, who outshone other showgirls of her day—a day she referred to as "back then" without providing a specific year—apparently wanted to make sure she could still make an impression before she touched her pen to the dotted line.

"I created my legend by making men wait," she told us with a breathy laugh. "There's no reason to change my strategy now."

Dave raised one eyebrow to signify the obvious—waiting could get old. "If it's the music that's holding you up, why not go with a medley?"

Josh thrashed a couple of chords that echoed in the closing darkness. Mrs. B cocked her head, thinking. "No. I like medleys to be collections of familiar tunes, not fresh and original music."

She patted Josh's shoulder. "But you'll want a medley for the overture for your project."

"Cool." Josh strummed a softer chord, one that almost didn't make me want to cover my ears. "An overture."

Dave and I exchanged glances. He mimed a coin flip, then pointed at me, indicating I should ask. "Overture for what project?"

"Josh is writing a rock opera," Mrs. B said with pride.

"A rock opera," Dave echoed with a mix of amazement and apprehension. "What's it about?"

"The soul-sucking experience of working as a wage slave, shoveling fast food into sacks for customers without health consciousness or taste buds." Josh attacked his guitar, producing a tortured wail. "Mrs. B said I should write what I know."

36

"Makes sense," Dave agreed. "If you need a song about fried pies, I can help."

"How many songs have you written?" I asked.

"A bunch. There's 'Grease Fire Friday' and 'Spit On The Special' and 'The Clogged Artery Blues' and—"

"My favorite is the one about losing your heart at the drive-up window." Mrs. B clasped her hands. "It's so sad when the girl drives off and you think you'll never see her again because you wrote her a note on a napkin but forgot to put it in the sack with her burgers."

"Poignant," Dave said.

"Positively worthy of a Shakespearean sonnet," I added.

"I guess." Josh blasted another chord into the darkness.

"Stop assaulting that guitar," a deep voice shouted from down the way, "or I'll come over and assault you."

CHAPTER 5

"Some people should learn to appreciate music," Mrs. B called in a sharp voice.

"And some people should learn to tell music from high-volume mayhem," the deep voice responded. "Cut the noise or I'll call the manager. Or come over there. Or both."

Mrs. B patted Josh's arm. "I apologize for such rude behavior. That man is new here. I'll speak to him tomorrow."

"It's okay. My dad says stuff like that all the time."

"Only because he hasn't recognized your talent. Someday he will." Mrs. B removed Cheese Puff from her lap, drawing a grunt of protest. "But I've taken too much of your time. After all, you came to see Allison. So we'll shut the concert down."

She headed for her door. "Much as I'd enjoy passing the time with Bernina Burke should that man make good on his threat to call her, I'm tired. See you all tomorrow."

When her door closed, Dave and I laughed in a hollow kind of way. The condo complex manager had come a long way toward being human, but if she paid us a visit as a result of a noise complaint, we'd see her dark side. Bernina no longer blamed me for *all* the recent unfortunate incidents involving my ex-husband, Jake Stranahan, but she still had a crush on the smarmy con man and she feared I retained feelings for him.

And I did. All as negative as the bank balance I was left with after our divorce.

Bernina, however, saw little beyond Jake's handsome face and buff body. Sadly, that was pretty much what had affected my own good sense. I chalked marriage to Jake up to temporary insanity, hormones, and loneliness caused by the death of my first husband. An avid birder, Albert had been trying to get a closer look at a puffin when he lost his footing and plunged from a cliff on the Oregon Coast.

With Josh in the lead and Cheese Puff dragging behind, we trooped inside and found Allison folding T-shirts and piling them in three stacks on the dining room table. "This job sucks," she said by way of greeting. "Sucks, sucks, sucks, sucks, sucks."

Dave rolled his eyes. "Tell us how you really feel."

"There's too much laundry!"

I surveyed the stacks of T-shirts. "And it appears most of it is yours."

"So?"

I raised my hands in surrender. "Just sayin'."

Allison folded the final shirt and launched into a new complaint. "Jim had no right to touch my diary. And totally no right to tell me I couldn't have it until I finished the laundry. My diary is private. All my thoughts and feelings are in there."

I refrained from commenting that it seemed all her thoughts and feelings were out here and being shared whether we were interested or not. Instead, I turned to Josh and gave him a take-care-of-this-and-you'll-be-rewarded look.

He picked up on it in a nanosecond, pulled Allison into a hug, and kissed the top of her head. "I'm sorry you had such a hard day, baby."

"Ick." Allison broke free. "You're still wearing your uniform. You smell like old grease. And you should have been here an hour ago."

"I didn't want to take time to change. Besides, I told you I'd be late. I had to wash the windows."

"Blah. Blah. Blah. Nobody else takes as long as you do."

"Nobody else does it right." Josh put some steel into his voice.

I turned a thumb up, noting that Dave did the same. Go, Josh.

"But you don't get paid for the extra time," Allison whined. "And when you got off you didn't come here first. You went to see Mrs. B."

"I did come here first. Jim said you were at Sybil's and you had to finish the laundry before we could hang out."

"Jim." Allison stomped her feet and wheeled on Dave. "I hate Jim. I hate him. Tell him he can never come over here again."

"You're out of luck there," Dave told her. "Jim's a member of the Committee."

"So?"

"So Committee members are like family. The Committee has been helping Barb and Cheese Puff for a long time. And now they're helping you and me. They have rights and privileges that can't be revoked."

"What does that mean?"

"It means don't waste your energy fighting a battle you can't win." Josh took her arm. "Save some for a walk along the river. The ice cream place is open late. I'll give you only one math problem to work, and I'll buy you a double cone even if you don't get the answer right."

Allison's frown softened, but she pulled away. "I'm not going anywhere with a guy in a Krammee's shirt. Those things are ugly."

As a general rule, Allison and I weren't on the same page when it came to fashion, but this time I agreed with her. The polo shirt managed to be both clingy and loose and the slick fabric made me wonder if there was a label inside warning against wearing it near an open flame. Or out in the hot summer sun.

Dave tossed Josh a gray T-shirt from the top of his stack of clean clothing. "Problem solved."

Josh unbuttoned his shirt, peeled it from his skin with a swish of synthetic fabric and a crackle of static, and pulled Dave's over his head.

"Great," Allison said. "That's all bagged out, there's a hole under the arm, and you can't even read what it says on the front cause it's all peeling."

"Harsh words for my favorite workout shirt," Dave said. "Plus it's a classic. That band broke up a decade ago."

Every time he wore the shirt he reminisced about the last concert of Spurned Ambition and the Determinators, the concert where they smashed their guitars across their amps, mooned the audience, and torched their tour bus. I don't remind him the guitars were held together with tape and wire, the audience was Dave, three friends, and their manager, and the bus was more of a van. Nor do I mention how grateful I am that they recorded only one album—if four songs can be considered an album.

"Turn it inside out," I suggested.

Josh did. "Better?" He walked around the kitchen like a hip-sprung model on a catwalk.

Allison sighed long and loud. "Okaaaaay. But you have to stay where the wind doesn't blow the grease smell at me. If that stink gets in my hair I'll smell worse than the Krammee twins."

"Deal." Josh led her to the door and the sound of her flip-flops faded into the distance. But not before she called out. "There's a message from Jake on the machine."

"Great." While Cheese Puff leaped onto his favorite chair, I crossed to the machine and hit the little button that erased the message, wishing I could do the same with most of my memories of my ex, especially the ones involving other women.

Dave raised an eyebrow.

"No, I'm not going to listen to it." I folded my arms across my chest. "He called because he wants something. Jake *always* wants something. Usually money."

"Jail's not a health spa. He could be hurt."

True. But the bottom line was that Jake was in jail by choice—his choice. Faced with too much freedom, Jake tended to screw up. "Let him call Bernina."

"Jim says Bernina is screening Jake's calls."

"Goody for her."

"And not shelling out more than $20 a week for his jail account, no matter what he promises to do when he gets out."

"Double goody." Call me petty, but it would be a blistering day in Antarctica before I warmed to Bernina. "Change the subject."

"Got it." Dave collapsed on the sofa. "If Josh wasn't already Allison's boyfriend, I'd consider paying him to take the job. But there's no way I could pay him enough."

I crumpled at his side. "Who are the Krammee twins?"

"They're Woodrow Krammer's teenage daughters. According to Josh, they're vicious harpies. They work in the restaurant."

"I'm surprised I haven't run into them at Captain Meriwether High School."

"They go to private school in Portland. A really strict private school. Woodrow Krammer leans so far to the right he's almost horizontal. His wife spends her days doing good works for her church and the community." Dave leaned closer. "Mostly, I've heard, to avoid spending time with him or her daughters. They're smart girls, but in a scheming kind of way. And they think rules are for everyone else."

"You do realize those last sentences could be used to describe your daughter."

"But Allison's not—"

"Malicious. Or hurtful. She's selfish and she doesn't mind inconveniencing others or even annoying them, but she knows when to stop. Deep down, she has a moral core."

"Sometimes it's really deep down, but thank you for seeing it." Dave gave me a lingering kiss that made coping with Allison worth it. "Anyway, regarding the Krammee twins, you didn't hear it from me, but these girls have firsthand knowledge of the workings of law enforcement and the legal system. Shoplifting is their hobby, although they've been known to make off with odds and ends from unlocked vehicles and unwatched handbags."

Plenty of teens, pressured to own the brands of clothing and gadgets their peers flaunted, succumbed to the temptation to shoplift. But if Krammer was as successful as he made out, economics wasn't a factor. "Kids reined in too tight sometimes mistake trouble for freedom."

"Yeah." Dave nodded. "Maybe that explains it. Or maybe Brooklyn and Manhattan are just bad to the bone."

"Brooklyn and Manhattan?"

"They were born in New York."

"I never would have guessed."

Dave caught my earlobe between his teeth. "Remind me again what it is I like about sarcastic women."

"We're the only ones who can put up with your daughter?"

"There's that. And a lot of other things." Dave kissed me and slid his hands beneath the long T-shirt I'd put on over my bathing suit. "Why don't we dash upstairs and I'll display a little gratitude?"

"Only a little? After what I've been through today, I deserve more than a little."

He glanced down and grinned. "It appears you're in luck. My gratitude seems to be growing."

Tuesday's paper made no mention of further Bigfoot sightings. I headed off to work feeling a little cheated, the way you do when you're sure there's one more cookie wrapped in foil and stashed behind the frozen peas in the freezer, but there isn't, and you're not sure whether someone else found it, or you ate it and don't remember.

(For the record, this can happen. And it often does. Several times, after a stressful day of subbing in the band room, I've found myself eating ice cream out of the carton

44

with no awareness of having opened the freezer, and no knowledge of what I may have devoured before I got to the ice cream.)

But, anyway, Gnome Guy didn't appear and the day went by without accident or injury—until I got home. That's where I found Allison on the sofa with gauze wrapped around both hands. A pile of broken glass and steaming noodles lay on the floor in front of the open oven. Verna and Sybil hurled accusations like harpoons.

Every time I saw them together I was reminded of those vaudeville comedy teams—one member tall and thin and possessing a dollop of intelligence, the other short and round and in need of more than a few brain cells.

"I *know* I told her she needed oven mitts to take the casserole out," Sybil insisted.

"And I know you didn't," Verna claimed. "You forgot to tell her to chop and sauté the onion, so why should I believe you remembered the oven mitt information."

"Well, *you* forgot to tell her to drain the tuna and grease the casserole dish."

"And *you* bought the wrong kind of cheese for the topping. That stuff wouldn't melt if you took a blowtorch to it."

It appeared that by dropping the casserole, Allison spared us a dining experience right up there with eating raw groundhog dipped in a horseradish and Limburger cheese sauce. But that was the last thing Sybil and Verna needed to hear, especially since I had a suspicion Allison engineered this fiasco.

I dropped my purse on an end table, drawing their attention.

"You know I wouldn't hurt Allison for the world." Flapping her hands, Sybil fluttered around the dining area like a butterfly on speed.

"Then why didn't you remind her about the oven mitts?" Verna sniped, her tanned cheeks dark with rage.

"I was about to remind her when I had to run to the little girls' room." Sybil halted and fanned herself with a potholder. "I thought *you* would keep an eye on things."

"Well, you should have said something." Verna turned to me, spreading her long fingers in appeal. "I was in the pantry rearranging. I thought everyone knew you shouldn't keep onions so close to potatoes."

Aiming for only minimal sarcasm, I apologized for my woefully lacking knowledge of vegetable storage rules, and promised to do better. Allison, meanwhile, said nothing. In fact, so far she hadn't uttered a single attention-seeking moan or whimper.

Strange behavior. Out-of-character behavior. Behavior that made me certain there was a lot more to this incident. Especially since it seemed neither Verna nor Sybil had witnessed the crashing casserole.

"Thank goodness she didn't lift the dish too far or she would have burned more than the tips of her fingers," Sybil said.

I surveyed the culinary wreckage. It was all on the floor, not a bit on the open oven door. I turned to Allison, recalling that she was no stranger to oven mitts. In fact, she used a pair the other night when she made brownies. "How did you get the casserole dish past the oven door and so far out onto the floor?"

She chewed her lower lip and then raised her chin, playing the brave patient. Or should I say overplaying? Allison, already a natural drama queen, recently acted in a school play and lately seemed to think of herself as having the lead in a production of her life—a production she wrote as she went along.

"I can't remember," she said in a breathy Marilyn Monroe voice. "Maybe I started to lift it and felt it burn me and pulled away?"

"I've done that," Sybil said.

"It's a natural reaction," Verna agreed.

"I think I'll be okay to go with the Committee on the boat to Astoria tomorrow. But I won't be able to cook until I heal." Allison raised her bandaged hands. "And I really, really, wanted to make meatloaf on Thursday."

I guessed she wanted to make meatloaf about as much as I wanted to make a date with Gnome Guy, but I kept my lips zipped. If I questioned her story, Sybil and Verna would take her side and shoot me down. Worse, they'd trot next door to inform Mrs. B. Having her own experiences with Allison, Mrs. B might consider the clues I'd spotted. But she also might dismiss what amounted to flimsy evidence and deliver yet another lecture on my negative attitude.

There was nothing to do but help clean up the mess and order a pizza.

I was inhaling the aromas of cheese, sauce, and a host of toppings when Mrs. B tapped in wearing silver stiletto heels and a blue and green feathered costume. It made her look like she was being attacked by a flock of parakeets. "What do you think?"

"It's unique." Allison grasped at one of the few safe answers.

"Um, interesting," I added, grabbing at another.

"Be honest," Mrs. B instructed. "Does it make me look fat?"

Uh oh. The most loaded question of all.

As I combed my mind for an answer, my gaze swept across the calendar on the side of the refrigerator and the notation on today's date. "Eeek."

Mrs. B planted her fists on slender hips. "What does that mean?"

I pointed at the calendar. "It means I forgot that Iz and Penelope are landing in 25 minutes."

"Then you'd better get your skates on, dear. You know how your sister hates to be kept waiting."

As I raced for the door, Mrs. B said she'd take the pizza to her place to keep warm and whip up a salad and dessert to go with it.

Chapter 6

Traffic on the way to the airport was, as always, pure joy—if your definition is creeping along at five miles an hour, inhaling fumes, and watching drivers breaking the rules about cell phone use. Of the two who weren't talking or texting, one had a book propped on the steering wheel and the other was laying out quilt pieces on the dashboard.

Dreading the usual lecture from Iz about giving more thought to others and organizing my time better so those particular others didn't have to cool their heels, I took the first empty space I spotted in the parking garage. Afraid to glance at my watch, I hurtled from my car, sped across the skyway, and charged to the waiting area where the concourse fed into the terminal. Travelers streamed past as I mopped sweat from my forehead and flapped my arms to dry my pits, all the while gasping like a beached sturgeon.

My heart rate was nearing normal—or as normal as it can be if an encounter with my sister looms—when Penelope emerged from the concourse, tanned and smiling, her blond hair in stubby braids. Iz wasn't by her side. She wasn't anywhere in sight.

"She went to San Francisco," Penelope said before I could ask. "Things didn't go well in Wyoming. She cut out two days early. Took the rental car and left me to find a ride to the airport."

"I'm sorry." I put my arm around her narrow shoulders. Trim and tiny, Penelope could easily work as a model for teen clothing or play a department-store elf, but she was an electrician by trade, and in big demand. Despite her petite frame, pastel blouses, and pressed jeans, Penelope always pulled her own weight and then some. "I know how much you were looking forward to the experience."

"I was." Her shoulders slumped, then straightened. "I should have told Iz not to come. She wasn't committed. She went to make me happy."

No wonder things went wrong. Making other people happy was foreign territory for Iz, territory a long way from her home turf in Self-Centered Land. "Was it the fasting that got to her?"

"No." Penelope smiled. "Iz told the organizers about the shooting and said her doctors advised her not to go more than a few hours without food or she might have a setback. When she headed off for her fast, she had more granola bars stashed in her cargo pants than I could eat in a week."

"The hikes?"

Another head shake. "She insisted her doctor said she shouldn't walk more than a few hundred yards, so she skipped every hike. And, really, she probably shouldn't exert herself until she heals."

"The cold water swims?"

"Sinus and ear infections." Penelope laughed and stepped onto the escalator descending to the baggage claim area. "I wasn't aware she'd gone to a doctor until she pulled out the note and a bottle of pills."

Penelope's tone implied what I was thinking—the note was forged and the pills were bogus. I gripped the moving handrails and followed her, making sure I got my feet on the correct side of the yellow line and not on the gap between steps. I have a fear of being chomped by escalators or plunging down cascading stairs when the steps separate.

"I wasn't upset," Penelope said. "In fact, I expected it. Iz doesn't think much of any program unless she's running it. And she believes most rules are for others."

Seems I was hearing that a lot lately. "So what went wrong?" I dismounted from the escalator with a jump and a skip and a stumble. "I mean, it's not my business, but if you want to talk about it, I'm here for you."

"I appreciate that." Penelope squeezed my hand. "And I appreciate you."

"Ditto." And not simply because she deflected my sister's discourse and demands. Penelope was an all-round champion in a lot of departments, and I'd make a supreme effort to keep her as a friend. That effort would be easier if Iz didn't return from San Francisco and insist I side with her because of that old blood-is-thicker-than-water saying. "You've been good for Iz."

"And she's been good for me." Penelope led me to the third in a row of luggage carousels. "Even if you find that hard to believe."

"I try not to think about things that are hard to believe. I let them be what they are. Especially relationships. If they work, they work."

"Until they stop working." Penelope rested one foot—in a cute leather boot—on the edge of the carousel as it lurched to life. Suitcases and duffel bags emerged through a portal, moving with jerky motions like legless, armless, headless zombies.

"I hope this is a detour and not a dead end. I mean, I know small and stupid things split couples apart, but this. . ." She flipped her hand, batting the idea aside. "I had to laugh even while I was crying."

I didn't know what this petty and stupid thing was, but I *did* know my sister. Although she'd never own up to it, there were plenty of times when the petty shoe fit her the same way that glass slipper slid onto Cinderella's foot. "I bet Iz didn't laugh. And that made things worse."

"Yeah." Penelope reached for a burgundy suitcase adorned with a bright yellow ribbon, swung it from the carousel, and popped up the handle. "This is it."

"I thought there were four suitcases when I dropped you off."

"Three of those belonged to Iz." She rolled the suitcase toward the escalator. "A foam pad. Her special pillow. Provisions."

"Of course." If it had been up to my sister to lead pioneers west into the Louisiana Purchase, the edge of the frontier would still be within a few miles of the Mississippi.

Penelope thumped her suitcase onto the escalator. "Her excuses and modifications and cheating didn't bother me much. After all, she's still recovering from getting shot. Besides, she didn't knock my experiences. So it was okay until the day we meditated and waited for our totem animals to appear."

"That's the part Iz said would confirm that her totem animal was an eagle because she soars above everyone else." I let three steps go by, heard the rumble of rolling suitcases close behind, gripped the moving rail, and landed with both feet in the center of a step. "Uh oh. It wasn't an eagle, was it?"

"Not even close."

"Another bird?" I hoisted myself a step closer to Penelope. "A duck or a chicken?"

"If only."

Penelope strode smoothly from the escalator. I waited a second too long, stutter-stepped, and caught my toe on the carpet. A man close behind gripped my elbow, got me steady, then zoomed past towing a suitcase the size of a dishwasher. I yelped my thanks and jogged to catch up with Penelope. "Worse than a chicken?"

"Much worse. And not a bird."

That cancelled turkey vulture and shrike. I reeled off a short list of North American wildlife with Iz's most conspicuous qualities. "Grizzly? Wolverine? Weasel?"

Penelope shook her head with each guess. We reached the end of the skyway and I pointed to the rear of the parking garage. "I give up."

"Skunk."

I halted. Swallowed. "OMG."

"It's actually a pretty good totem animal," Penelope said in a rush. "It represents self-reliance and strength, intuition, distinctiveness and presence."

I laughed and started walking. "Skunks have presence all right."

"Yes. And Iz got 'presence' all over her."

I halted again. "She got sprayed?"

"Up-close-and-personal sprayed."

"Tell me." I unlocked the trunk. "Tell me the whole story. Every tiny detail. I promise not to laugh."

Penelope rolled her eyes.

"Okay. I promise not to laugh so hard I spit up."

She heaved the suitcase into the trunk. "She'll be furious that I told you."

"She's usually well on her way to furious when she gets out of bed in the morning," I pointed out as I unlocked doors. "Besides, she abandoned you in Wyoming. Which, considering the length of time skunk scent lingers, probably was a bonus."

"I hadn't thought of that." Penelope grinned and buckled herself in.

"Did anyone get video? I know people who would pay to see it. And if we post it on the Internet, it might go viral."

Penelope's grin broadened, but then she shook her head. "There was no one near when it happened. We were spread out along a stream and around a lake, maybe a quarter of a mile apart."

Dang.

"I bet she tried to stomp that skunk into the terrain."

"She probably wanted to. She took some of the spray in the face. I don't know how she managed to get to the lodge, let alone drive to the airport." Penelope rolled down her window. "I bet the rental company trashes the car. And how they let her on a plane is beyond me. Unless she stopped somewhere to shower. A dozen times. With industrial-strength soap."

Chuckling, I threaded my way out of the parking garage and to the airport access road. "I don't have a lot of experience with skunks, but I thought they sprayed only if they were startled. Or threatened."

54

"My guess is the skunk wandered to the stream to get a drink and saw Iz, or maybe smelled her, and got frightened," Penelope said. "See, the idea was that we each went to a specific place where we were supposed to lie down and listen to a recorded guided meditation with our eyes closed. When it ended, we were told to open our eyes and watch for an animal to appear. I spotted a chipmunk right away."

"That's a perfect totem animal for you."

"I know." Penelope was quiet for a moment. "Maybe Iz wasn't by the stream when she got sprayed. Maybe she left her spot to climb to where she could see the sky and make sure there *was* an eagle flying around before she claimed she'd seen one."

I didn't think much of that theory. Looking for a bit of truth to bolster a lie wasn't something Iz was prone to do. Most people didn't dare question her.

Penelope braced one hand on the dash as I took the turn onto the freeway ramp. To say my shock absorbers were mushy was to give them far more credit than they deserved. The best thing about the job at the repair shop was a deep discount on parts and service. But given all the other demands on my paycheck—living expenses, student loan, nerve medicine in the form of the occasional bottle of rum—only a discount that sliced away 90% would be deep enough to cover everything my car needed. And, despite the "emergency surgery" Larry performed earlier in the year, it still needed a lot.

"Or maybe she tried to scare the skunk off," Penelope theorized, "before the guy who was leading the exercise came by to see how she was doing and spotted it."

Far more likely. I got an image of Iz shouting, charging at the skunk, or throwing rocks. Once again I wished someone had been on the scene with a camera or cell phone.

"We'll probably never know exactly what happened," Penelope said.

I accelerated up the ramp. Well, to be accurate, I pressed the gas pedal and we inched up the incline with a series of chugs and bumbles and jerks. Penelope eyed the speedometer, but didn't express doubts that we'd arrive in Reckless River before midnight.

"Well, we'll know what *didn't* happen," I said. "Whatever Iz claims did."

"If she says *anything*. She may edit the incident from her life," Penelope said. "Along with me."

No matter how delighted *I* might be to be edited from my sister's life, this wasn't the time to mention it. Instead, I insisted Penelope join us for dinner. A dose of sympathy from Mrs. B would do her a world of good. And Penelope's tale of Iz in the wilderness would go a long way toward distracting Mrs. B from seeking further comments on her costume.

The next morning, armed with a slice of leftover pizza and an apple for lunch, I tooled around behind the auto repair shop to find Larry stooped over and studying the dusty ground. "Drop something?" I called.

"No. Come here and look at these." He made a circling motion with one arm. "Come around to my right so you don't step on them."

"Don't step on what?"

"You'll see."

And in a moment, I did. The prints of naked feet were enormous—maybe 20 inches long. They were broad, too. The toes were elongated and squared off rather than slanting from large to small like the toes on my feet. And each print was pressed deep into the dirt of the lot. "Wow. I wonder who left those."

Larry peered over his shoulder at the greenbelt. A breeze tousled the leaves, creating flickering shadows. "I wonder *what* left those."

What?

As in something not a human? As in something like—

CHAPTER 7

"Bigfoot?"

Feeling like I'd landed face first in a reality show, I gripped Larry's arm. "You think Bigfoot was here?" Allison would have been awed by my melodramatic delivery.

"Something really heavy with big feet was here." Moving like a crab, Larry followed the tracks to the asphalt apron in front of the shop. "Unless this is a hoax. Remember how Doug laughed when you told him about the Bigfoot article in the paper? Maybe he decided to mess with your head."

"He went to a lot of trouble if he did—using two footprint forms and brushing away his own tracks when he was done." I knelt to study the impressions. "Wait. These tracks aren't all alike. Some are partial prints, like he was moving faster, going up on the ball of his foot. It would be tough to make impressions like this with a plaster cast."

"If I'd known you were a Sasquatch specialist when I hired you," Larry teased, "I might have been tempted to pay you a decent wage."

"You can't afford to pay me a decent wage." I stood and dusted my jeans. "You should call the newspaper."

"You're kidding, right? They'll think I'm a nut job."

"Maybe. But maybe they'll jump on it because of what that woman saw in the park a few days ago. And if the paper goes with it, the TV stations won't be far behind."

"And we'll have a pack of TV reporters clogging the parking lot with their news trucks."

"Exactly. It'll be great."

Larry scratched his left ear. "It will?"

"It's publicity. Free publicity."

He progressed to scratching the other ear. "I don't know, Barb. People aren't going to bring their cars to me because I saw strange tracks in the parking lot."

"Maybe not, but a lot of people will come to get a look at those tracks. And while they're looking, Doug and I will hand out business cards and maybe coupons for a few dollars off a brake job."

Larry frowned. "The discount thing is okay. But what if Doug made these tracks?"

"Let's find out." I headed for the shop. "If he didn't, I'll call the *Reckless River Roundup* and give them the first shot."

Larry tagged along at about the same speed I hit when trolling the snack aisle in search of something that promises half the calories and twice the faux-cheese taste. "What if someone else made the footprints?"

I turned to face him. "As long as you or someone connected with the business didn't do it, and you have no knowledge that it's a hoax, then you're good. If we get reporters interested in the tracks, it will be up to them to figure out how to present the story. Maybe they'll bring in Bigfoot experts."

Larry gaped. "There are experts on a creature that might not exist?"

Apparently Larry didn't watch reality TV—or at least not the programs I did. "There are experts on *everything*. Listen, the worst that can happen is that we all look silly. What do we have to lose except a little self-respect?"

Larry thought that over while he unlocked the door to the shop. "Okay, I guess it can't hurt. I'll move my car and block the side of the building so Mark and Denny don't pull in there and mess up the tracks. You check with Doug."

Even when I threatened to quit, leave him in charge of the reception desk, and bribe Gnome Guy to bring his truck in daily, Doug disavowed any knowledge of the tracks. That cleared the deck to dial the paper.

Despite my pep talk to Larry, I felt a tad ridiculous passing along information to the woman who answered the phone. Perhaps it was my imagination, but it sure sounded like she sighed before she told me she'd leave a message for Stan Stewart. And perhaps I also imagined that she chortled like a wicked witch when she referred to him as "the reporter on the Bigfoot beat."

I'm an expert at being put off, brushed off, and blown off, so I took out a little insurance. She'd given me a name and the paper's website gave me an e-mail address. I scampered outside, snapped a couple of cell phone shots of the prints, and sent them to Stan Stewart.

Twenty minutes later he called.

"Tell me about these tracks." His tone exhibited the same lack of interest mine did when Allison explained why she needed three new pairs of flip-flops to supplement the two dozen in her closet. Having once been a radio talk show producer and knowing the perils of appearing too enthusiastic, I recognized where he was coming from, adopted an all-business tone, and spit out the salient points. "The prints are at least 20 inches long and about six inches across. It appears that after a few steps he quickened his pace and perhaps broke into a run."

"A run?"

"Or a lope. The heel prints are fainter. The toe imprints are deeper."

"Hmmm."

"The tracks came from the greenbelt."

"Hmmm."

I could almost hear his interest draining away. Time to put on the pressure. "I'm a big fan of your editor's take on local politics." That statement happened to be true. Said editor and I shared similar ideas about politicians, namely that many of them had hidden agendas. "So I haven't called anyone else. Yet. But if you're not interested, I'll see what the TV stations think. Or maybe I'll put the pictures on the Internet."

"Let me run this by management," he said with about 12% more enthusiasm. "If they sign off on it, and if I can free up a few minutes, I'll come by later on."

After I hung up, I did a brief end-zone happy dance and trotted into the shop. Doug was just coming in from an examination of the prints and I gave him a high-five. "I had to dangle an exclusive, but I've got a reporter on the hook."

"Cool," Larry, Denny, and Mark harmonized.

"I'll get doughnuts," Doug said. "What kind do reporters like best?"

"Free," I told him. "And plenty."

"I listen to Rick Rivers' show a lot," Mark said. "Want me to call and tell him?"

"Yeah," I snarled. "Call him 10 minutes after hell freezes over."

"But—"

"If the reporter bites, we'll honor the exclusive until tomorrow," Doug said. "But even if he doesn't bite, I say let Rick Rivers find his own news. If he *can* now that Barbara isn't running down stories for him."

"Yeah," Larry agreed. "And besides, anyone who downsizes my friend doesn't deserve to have a story fall in his lap."

"Wow." Mark's eyes widened. "You worked with Rick Rivers? What's he like when he's not on the air?"

The words "egocentric lying scumball" leaped to mind.

"He's not what you'd expect." Doug sanitized it for me. "He doesn't live up to those principles he talks about."

Mark got the dejected expression of a kid who put a tooth under his pillow and found it still there in the morning.

"We can talk about that later," Doug said. "Are we agreed that we keep quiet about those footprints until the story runs in the paper or goes up on their website?"

"I'm down with that," Denny said.

"Yeah. And I'm taking Rick Rivers off my radio presets." Mark patted my shoulder. "I was downsized once. It sucked listening to that bull about how sorry they were and how it was the fault of the economy. Heck, the shop was doing great with people fixing their old cars because they couldn't afford new ones."

"It's better to be fired for screwing up. At least then you know why you got the axe." Denny flushed and ducked his head. "Not that I think you screwed up, Barbara."

"Thanks. I shouldn't take being downsized personally, but—"

"It hurts," Doug said.

"Especially since you're such a good worker," Larry added.

I was so touched I didn't mention his opinion was based on exactly two days of seeing me in action. Feeling the need to live up to his praise, however, I hustled into the office, shoved the last of the boxes of old files under the desk, and wiped down the restroom.

As I finished, the door from the parking lot opened and a young man with wiry brown hair and a scruffy beard slouched through. Despite the heat, he wore a baggy brown corduroy jacket, a long-sleeved blue shirt, jeans reduced to thread at the knees, and leather sandals patched with silver tape. The outfit screamed "I'm a reporter. A *newspaper* reporter. A *real* reporter. Not a big-hair TV type."

"Stan Stewart," he said without offering a hand to shake.

"Barbara Reed." I zipped through the door he'd left open, talking as I went. "I know you're pushed for time, so I won't waste it. Larry spotted the tracks."

I pointed to the third bay where Larry, his head and torso under the hood of a black car, looked like he was being devoured by a killer whale. "Let me know when you want to talk to him and I'll get his attention. The tracks are this way."

A few minutes later Stewart and a photographer—a lanky woman with black hair knotted on top of her head— were circling the lot, following the trail of paper floor mat protectors Larry had laid beside the footprints.

"They're certainly big," Stewart mused. "And they come out of the greenbelt." He headed down the slope and skirted the cattails. In a moment he called for the photographer.

I hauled myself onto the picnic table to follow their progress along the edge of the swale.

"The grass is crushed here." Stewart pointed to the ground. "Looks like he sat or maybe laid down, waiting. And there's some long reddish brown hair caught on a blackberry cane." He motioned for the photographer. "Get a close-up of that."

While she snapped photos, Stewart returned to the parking lot, dug a cell phone from his pocket, turned away, and reported to someone up the journalistic food chain. Pretending disinterest, I watched the photographer as she worked her way out of the marsh and got wide shots of the greenbelt. Meanwhile, I eavesdropped for all I was worth, gleaning that Stewart's boss liked the story a lot and wanted him to flesh it out with interviews and background on Bigfoot. I also gleaned that, sure enough, his boss wanted an expert to study the tracks.

"Is the guy I talked to the other day the only expert around?" Stewart asked in a tight voice.

From the way his knuckles whitened as he squeezed the phone, it appeared he didn't care much for the expert and wasn't looking forward to another encounter. Naturally, I couldn't wait to witness their meeting.

"Coffee?" I asked in a bright voice as he stuffed the phone into the sagging pocket of his jacket. "It will take me five minutes to make a fresh pot. And we have some dynamite doughnuts."

Stewart frowned. The photographer didn't. "I could do serious damage to a doughnut," she said.

64

"We've got all kinds," I volunteered, taking on the role of Ms. Helpful Citizen. "Custard filled, jam filled, chocolate covered, glazed. And some of those fat cakey ones with pink icing and sprinkles."

"Any apple fritters?" she asked in a wistful voice.

"Only two or three."

Eyes gleaming, she left Stewart in the dust and headed for the office. He glanced at the tracks, turned his gaze to the sky as if asking for divine intervention, then dug the phone from his pocket and glared at it.

Taking my exit cue, I scurried off to turn hot water and ground beans into coffee and chat with the photographer. Midway through her second fritter she allowed that Stewart wasn't a bad guy, just a guy with ambition who thought he wasn't climbing the newspaper reporting pyramid fast enough. Given competition from the Internet and other sources, the pyramid wasn't what it used to be. Stan Stewart was lucky to have a job, even a job in Reckless River.

The last of the water was gurgling through the coffee filter when he trudged in, snatched a glazed doughnut, and slumped into a chair. "The Bigfoot buff is on the way," he said with the same enthusiasm the rest of us might employ when saying "I'm due in front of the firing squad in ten minutes."

The photographer grimaced, polished off her second fritter, and filled a cup.

Stewart sprawled in the chair, masticated the doughnut like a cow chews its cud, and cast his gaze to the ceiling.

I almost felt sorry for him. If he hadn't been able to pry higher-power intervention out of a clear sky, no way could he manage it through the ancient acoustical panels of the office ceiling. I poured coffee and closed his fingers around a cup.

The photographer drained her brew, cast a longing glance at the last fritter, and gathered her gear. "Gonna get some exteriors."

Stewart nodded, swallowed the doughnut, and went to work on the coffee like a man with a robotic arm and wooden lips.

Obviously, nothing I said would improve his state of mind, so I got busy designing flyers and coupons for Larry to consider.

Ten minutes later the door from the outside swung wide, slamming into Stewart's foot. He yelped, spilled the dregs of his coffee on his shirt, and emitted a string of inventive and colorful curses.

I noted a few I'd like to have on hand if my ex-husband emerged from jail and oozed into my life again. But as I reached for a pen and pad to jot them down, I was stunned into temporary paralysis.

There in the doorway was Elmer Buttress, better known—at least to me—as Gnome Guy.

CHAPTER 8

I willed myself to breathe and then to blink.

Gnome Guy was still there.

I blinked again.

Still there.

Despite the fact that he looked exactly as he had on Monday, right down to the egg in his beard and the scowl on his face, he wasn't a figment of my imagination.

Resigned to my fate, I was about to ask, with fingers crossed, if he was having problems with his truck, when he slammed the door and launched into a lecture aimed at Stewart. The text was fool's errands and wasting a busy man's valuable time.

Hold the phone!

Gnome Guy was the Bigfoot expert?

I blinked for a third time as he enlarged on his lecture, accusing Stewart of not having sense enough to keep his feet out of the way of a door.

Feeling giddy with relief because Gnome Guy wasn't here on automotive business, I cowered behind my computer screen and pretended deep interest in my flyer. Stewart, meanwhile, sat as if cast in bronze. When Gnome

Guy fizzled out, the reporter stood and, without a word, led the way to the back parking lot.

Larry, Mark, and Denny stopped what they were doing to watch Gnome Guy pass. Denny crossed himself. Twice.

The second they were out of sight, I trotted into the restroom, stood on the toilet cover, eased the tiny window open, and peered out. Gnome Guy made disparaging sounds as he approached the footprints. Stewart wedged his hands in his pockets, but said nothing. Having used the same tactic on my sister, I knew there was often more power in the unspoken word than in a heated response.

Gnome Guy tromped along Larry's paper trail, shaking his head. Stewart tipped his chin and looked to the sky once more.

Gnome Guy halted, retraced his steps, and crouched with a crack and pop of knee joints. Stewart's lips moved in what I guessed was silent invocation of a higher power that so far had proven to be less than interested in the course of his life.

Gnome Guy dug a magnifying glass from his pocket and studied the print from heel to toes. Stewart kept up his one-sided silent conversation with the sky.

Getting down on his well-padded belly, Gnome Guy took a closer look, and said something I couldn't hear. Stewart's jaw dropped like a cartoon character catching sight of the falling safe hurtling toward him.

I hugged myself, started to do a victory dance, remembered where my feet were less-than-firmly planted, and jumped to the floor.

The clock was ticking down to our 15 minutes of fame.

That evening, after erasing another message from Jake without listening to it, I made dinner—BLTs and fresh strawberries add up to dinner in my book. Allison, meanwhile, examined the "wounds" on her hands and claimed she really wanted to help cook and clean up, but shouldn't get the burns wet. I suggested she could do additional chores when she healed, and retreated to the tiny office at the end of the hall to escape a deluge of whining and moaning. There I scoured the newspaper's website searching for a hint of the Bigfoot story.

Nothing.

Half an hour later, Dave ambled in with a beer and a triple-decker sandwich constructed from the B, L, and T I left for him. "I thought I'd eat in here with you." He set the sandwich on his desk and sank into a beat-up swivel chair he'd found dumped by the side of a road.

"Because you can hardly hear Allison's moaning and complaining from here?" I asked.

"Well, yeah, but there are other reasons I'd rather be with you."

"Such as?"

He leered. "Such as reasons I'd prefer to discuss later, upstairs."

"Let me get this straight, you only want to *discuss* these reasons?"

"Nope. Discuss, demonstrate, and do it all again."

I shivered with anticipation. "Better eat your sandwich. You'll need sustenance."

While he demolished the sandwich, I filled him in on the day's adventure, including the reappearance of Gnome Guy. "And you said the odds of running into him again were about the same as getting involved in another

69

murder case or finding Bigfoot using the pool as a bathtub."

"That's because I didn't know he was a Bigfoot expert and you'd find Bigfoot tracks." Dave swung his feet to the corner of my desk, resting them on a stack of envelopes. "What's all that stuff?"

"Bills I have to pay. And don't change the subject. We're talking about your bogus prediction."

He thumped his feet to the floor, sat up, and sorted through the envelopes, peering into a few. "Some of these are due soon."

"Thank you for the bulletin. I'm already painfully aware of that fact."

"Sorry." Dave set the pile aside and cupped my face in his hands. I had no choice but to look into his eyes unless I closed mine. And I didn't. Dave had great eyes, eyes like pools of melted milk chocolate. "I didn't mean to question your system. I'm happy you're handling the bills. I've had a lot on my plate with the move and the police department upheaval. But if ends don't meet, I need to know. Okay?"

I nodded but didn't mention ends hadn't met for a year. The only way I could get them close was to run a credit card balance that made me sweat and hold off on mailing payments until the day before my paycheck hit the bank.

Dave was now kicking in on rent, utilities, and groceries, but it was a myth that two could live as cheaply as one. I mean, that might be possible if one of the two was, say, an inanimate object or perhaps mummified. But in the real world, in *my* world . . .

"Would it take some pressure off if I knew more about what we have and what we owe every month?" Dave massaged my temples with his fingertips. "We could set up a spreadsheet and work out a budget so it's all in black and white. That way I'll know if I need to cut corners, pack my lunch, or tell Allison to forget about new flip-flops."

He tapped the stack of bills. "I definitely think I should kick in more than we decided on. Allison has Josh over a couple of times a week and they eat like locust. Plus, she drains the hot water heater every time she takes a shower."

Which was at least twice a day in warm weather.

"So your utilities have to be a whole lot higher than before. I should pay three-quarters of the water and electricity bills and a bigger share of the garbage fees. And kick in a lot more for groceries. What do you think?"

What I thought was YES. I'd considered everything he mentioned, but hadn't brought it up. I didn't want to seem pushy or greedy but, most of all, I didn't want our relationship to be tainted by on-going discussions of money. That might raise the specter of Jake and the negative emotional baggage from being duped, deluded, and defrauded. "I think that would be great."

"Okay. Let's look at how it breaks down." He handed me a yellow pad. "We'll start on paper. List your income and your monthly expenses."

"*All* my expenses?"

"Well, not each individual bag of cheesy snacks you feel compelled to buy." He flashed an indulgent grin that made me want to hug him close while delivering a kick to his shin. "Just round off."

Armed with a pencil and a yellow pad of his own, he sat at the desk angled next to mine, alternately scratching his head and scratching numbers on the paper.

I shielded my pad with my arm as I started to work, rounding up amounts for the mortgage, property tax, insurance, condo fees, utilities, and vet bills. On one hand, I was glad Dave had initiated the budget talk. I'd never asked what he made, but I figured it was way ahead of my pay and included benefits. He knew I struggled to stretch a maximum of about $2000 a month—on those months when school was in session and I worked every day—to cover rent, food, car expenses, a skimpy health insurance program, and payments on my student loan. On the other hand, I dreaded the moment when Dave saw the size of my loan and realized I'd be paying on it for approximately—give or take a few months—the rest of my life.

It wasn't that I'd lied about my financial bottom line. I knew that a long-term relationship with me meant a long-term relationship with my debt. If he asked, I would have told him.

But he hadn't.

Was that because he wanted to keep his head in the sand? Or because it hadn't occurred to him?

I went with choice number two. Mix a stressful job with a teenage daughter, then factor in a new relationship and living arrangement. Dave was lucky to remember to tie his shoes.

I opened the top drawer of my desk, raised the tray that held pens and pencils, and checked the number on the slip of paper beneath it.

My stomach flipped and my heart pounded. Forget the rest of *my* life. If I ever had children, they'd be paying on this until their children had children.

Not that I planned to have children—at least not any time soon, no matter what Mrs. B hoped. This mountain of debt coupled with daily close encounters with Allison added up to powerful incentive for using birth control.

"How are you coming?" Dave asked.

"Almost finished." Giving myself points for not having car payments and buying most of my clothes at thrift stores, I hauled in a breath and wrote the monthly student debt payment in tiny numbers. As if that might make the amount appear smaller.

Sheesh.

That was right up there with doing everything to look thinner except losing weight.

"Maybe we should do the rest another night." Dave turned his yellow pad over and rubbed his eyes. "It's getting late."

"It's barely 8:30. We should be finished by 9:00."

He yawned and flexed his shoulders, then scooted his chair beside mine and breathed in my ear. "Or we could put this aside and be upstairs in a few minutes."

Warmth tingled along my spine. I imagined us upstairs with the door locked. I imagined unbuttoning and unzipping and—

No.

Before any of that, I had to tell Dave about my debt. He deserved to know. And I needed to know how he'd react, and how we'd go on after that.

"It will take only a few minutes to plug in the numbers." I kissed the soft skin on his neck where his sprouting stubble ended. "Once we're done I'll be able to relax."

He sighed and laid his yellow pad beside mine. "Okay. Let's do it."

Keeping an elbow planted on my loan number, I brought up the budget spreadsheet on the computer. Dave read off the figures for our incomes and I filled them in, thrilled to note that his monthly income was significantly more than mine.

"Now expenses. You first."

I shook my head. "No, let's do yours first."

He hesitated, then read off a string of numbers. I plugged them into the chart. When he stopped, I did a quick bit of addition in my head. Even paying a little more on the mortgage and utilities, Dave had about half his income left at the end of the month. Subtract the cost of food, his car, and Allison's many wants and needs, and he should still have a good chunk.

Then I noticed his finger tapping a number at the bottom of the page, an amount written, like the one for my student debt, in tiny numbers.

Squinting, I made it out: $500.

I felt a mix of relief and joy. Dave had an obligation he hadn't wanted to tell me about. Now we'd both come clean. We'd bond. Obligations would make our relationship stronger.

Unless that sum represented a gambling debt, restitution for a crime, or worse.

I squelched the suspicious part of my brain. The sum had to be a loan. Like mine. For courses he'd taken. Or medical expenses.

Sure, that was it, a loan.

But, wait. What if that loan was from a loan shark? To cover a gambling debt or drug habit?

My stomach flipped.

Dave cleared his throat. "Barbara, I haven't been honest with you about . . . about Allison's mother."

My stomach executed a second flip, one an Olympic gymnast would have been proud of. I swallowed the acid taste of fear, sucked in a breath, reached for his hands, and pasted on what I hoped was a passable you-can-tell-me-anything expression.

"She . . . she isn't my ex."

What?

Gritting my teeth, I held my dinner down, held my expression in place, and held back from whacking him with my keyboard.

"And she didn't run off to Miami with another guy."

CHAPTER 9

Jaw aching, I nodded. Forget the keyboard. I'd hit him with the desk. As soon as I heard the whole sordid story.

"I should have told you a long time ago." Dave squeezed my numb fingers. "I should have known you'd understand."

I slid my hands from his grip, rolled my fingers into fists, and rolled my chair as far from him as space allowed. "I *might* understand. *If* you were telling me something specific, instead of *not* saying stuff that's making me extremely tense."

My voice rose to glass-shattering range when I hit the final words.

Dave winced.

Cheese Puff and Lola came on the run.

"What's the matter," Allison yelled from the living room.

Dave winced again. Nothing like having both women yelling. "Barbara thought she saw a mouse."

"Yeek," Allison screamed. "I hate mice. Keep it away from me."

The dogs milled around, threading themselves between our chairs. Lola's tail whacked my desk. Cheese Puff yipped in annoyance when I folded my arms across my chest and refused to pick him up.

"There's no mouse," Dave called. "Everything's fine."

"Fine?" I hissed. "You think this situation is fine? You're not divorced and your wife isn't in Miami and I'm . . . we're . . . I don't even know what we are!"

He stood and closed the door. "What we are is the same as what we were two minutes ago."

"No, we're not. Because two minutes ago I didn't know you were married."

"I'm not." He sat and stretched a hand toward me.

I batted it aside. "You said Allison's mother isn't your ex."

"She's not my ex because we were never married."

As I parsed my way through that sentence, I opened the mental file labeled "Dave's Life Before We Met" and found no details of a wedding, years of marriage, or issues fought out in divorce court. "But . . . ?"

"Allison thinks we were. It's . . . complicated."

"Complicated, schlomplicated! I'm so sick of that expression I could barf in my shoes." I thumped a fist on my desk, making the keyboard jump.

Cheese Puff and Lola stopped milling, stared at me with their ears laid flat, then tumbled over each other in a rush to escape my wrath. Finding the door closed, they slunk behind Dave.

"Okay, it's not complicated," he said in that smugly soothing voice most women loathe. "It's just—"

"What? A heap of lies? A pile of crap? A bunch of baloney?"

For a long moment he said nothing, then he let out a breath. "You're right. I mean, you're right that it's not complicated, or at least that I shouldn't try to use that as an excuse. I should have been honest with you right from the start, especially since you were up-front about Jake."

Relationship points for me. I made a note to use them later. If we *had* a later.

Dave hung his head. "But I was . . . well, embarrassed. No, I was disgusted with myself. And I thought you'd be disgusted, too."

I wasn't disgusted yet, but the more he talked around this subject, the more I suspected I might be. "Let's get it over with. Start at the beginning. Tell me how you met—"

I realized he never told me her name and I'd never asked. That was strange behavior for me, a woman who lived on the border between curious and nosy. But I guess compared to everything else going on in our lives—murder cases, protests, a drug dealer holding Cheese Puff hostage—it hadn't seemed to matter. "Tell me how you met whatever her name is."

Dave stood, opened the door to let the dogs out, peered down the hallway, then closed the door and sat on the edge of his chair. "Rayanne. I met her at a bar, in Seattle. I was up there for special training. A bunch of us were celebrating a big bust. If I hadn't had so much to drink, it might have been different."

He paused, swallowed, hung his head lower, and gripped his knees.

I knew what was coming, a closing-time horror story. I had at least one I'd like to have surgically removed from my brain, but I wasn't about to bring it up to make him feel better.

78

"Anyway, by the time I realized the kind of person she was—the people she ran with and what she was into—she was pregnant with Allison. I . . . I wanted to change my name and move to Mongolia." Dave raised his head, his eyes steely. "But that baby . . . I couldn't walk away from my baby. So I asked her to marry me."

If I wasn't already there, that last part would have sucked me deep into the sea of love with Dave Martin. Forget candy and flowers and poetry. Give me a man who faces up to his responsibilities.

I scooted my chair closer and covered his hands with mine. "But she refused?"

"She said she didn't like me enough." His eyes clouded and he sucked in another breath. "She told me I cramped her style and she was getting an abortion and getting gone."

Dave flipped his hands and gripped mine. "I wanted her out of my life more than I ever wanted anything, but I couldn't let her throw that baby away. So I did the only thing I could think of to change her plans—I arrested her."

Whoa!

"On what charges?"

"Possession of cocaine. Intent to distribute. Anything else I could think of. She had Allison in prison."

Double whoa!

"When she got out I gave her a choice. She could give me full custody of Allison and live her life the way she saw fit, or share custody and know that if she wasn't clean, sober, and the best mother on the planet, she'd find herself behind bars again."

"Courtesy of a network of cops keeping tabs on her?"

He nodded. "I never had to test that. I gambled that having a baby cramped her style more than I did. Within a week she was at my door willing to sign anything in exchange for $25,000. I borrowed from everyone I knew."

Dave glanced at the closed door. "The woman Allison remembers as her mother is my sister. She lived with us for a few years until she married an Army colonel and moved to the other side of the globe. When Allison got older, I came up with the moved-to-Miami story."

It all made sense, except . . . "If you paid Rayanne off, why are you sending her money?"

"In the fall she got out of jail in Missouri. She's been busted at least four times over the years for drugs and assault and robbery and forging checks. Anyway, she claimed she was a new person and wanted to get to know her daughter and make up for the years she lost."

Was it possible to make up for lost years? I thought of the way my parents checked out of my life, and the emptiness and sense of being cheated I still felt, would always feel. "Do you think she's changed?"

"No. Not yet, anyway. I mean, I'd like to think it's possible for people to change—for her to change—but saying so doesn't make it true. I told her I was open to negotiation if she could get a job and stay clean and out of trouble for a year."

"And?"

"And she blew up."

"Which pretty much proved she hadn't changed?"

"It was all the proof *I* needed." Dave rubbed his eyes. "I reminded her she signed away her rights. And she threatened to get a lawyer and make me eat the contract. I got pissed—big mistake—and wished her luck. She escalated and threatened to kidnap Allison."

He thumped a fist on his desk. "I had to stop her. You know how fragile Allison was then."

Fragile was a word that only scratched the surface. Last fall I'd discovered Allison cowering under a shrub in the rain, crying her heart out because she believed Dave didn't love her. Peeling away the drama, I determined Dave had been worried, upset, and annoyed because she'd gone off with a friend, missed a dentist's appointment, and didn't return his calls.

If a long-lost biological mother had added herself to the emotional stew, there was no telling what Allison might have done. The grass always seemed greener around the parent who wasn't reminding you to do your homework and get to bed at a reasonable hour. "So you're paying her to stay away. Where is she now?"

He shrugged. "I don't know. She was in St. Louis when she called the first time. Then Tucson. Then Denver. I wire money."

The grass along the highways a long-lost biological mother traveled might seem not only greener, but far more interesting than the stuff growing around our condo complex. Such was the romance of the road. And Allison was all about romance.

Dave massaged his temples. "I knew it was crazy to let Rayanne manipulate me, and even crazier to try to buy her off."

"But she took the money—which seems like more proof she hasn't changed and isn't really interested in Allison. And paying her gave you time to think."

"Yeah, but I haven't *used* that time. I don't have a plan."

"You will." I slithered from my chair and onto his lap. "*We* will."

"You're willing to stay with me? After all that?"

I delivered a kiss that made my answer clear. "I am unless you've got other revelations worse than this one."

"This was it." He returned the kiss, holding me so close I felt like I was wearing his shirt. "I messed up bad. I don't want to mess up again. Not this time. Not with you."

"Good. I don't want to mess up either." I held up the yellow pad and pointed to my loan payment. "I have enough student debt to finance an expedition to Mars. I'll still be paying on it when my Social Security kicks in."

Dave waved that aside as if I said I owed $50 in parking fines. "You needed that degree. When you get a teaching job you'll pay down the principal and be out from under it in a few years."

Not exactly true.

But exactly what I needed to hear.

I delivered another kiss and he passed it back. "Are we good?"

"We're more than good. But if a situation arises where we don't agree, then we discuss, we negotiate, or we find someone to mediate. Arresting me is *not* an option."

The next morning the footprint story hit the paper. Front page. Four pictures. Two sidebars. One explained who—or what—Bigfoot was for the benefit of anyone who only seconds ago moved to the Pacific Northwest. The other profiled Gnome Guy. I discovered he'd spent his entire adult life chasing sightings of creatures that might or might not be Bigfoot in all 50 states and several foreign countries.

I never thought of chasing Bigfoot as a way to see the world. Talk about missed opportunities. Of course, those opportunities came with the company of Gnome Guy.

Admitting I was woefully behind on Bigfoot news and related travel opportunities, I vowed to watch more videos posted on the Internet. Then I grabbed a piece of toast, and headed for work an hour ahead of time so I wouldn't miss the opening acts of the media circus.

The circus, however, was already underway. Five TV trucks packed the parking lot in front of the shop. Dozens of cars lined both sides of the road for blocks in either direction. Fortunately, someone had cordoned off an area for employees, so I had space to wedge my car in beside Doug's—after blowing my horn to create a lane through the crowd.

And I mean crowd.

A hundred people or more milled along the edge of the lot watching reporters preparing to give live reports. More were busily snapping pictures of the footprints under the watchful eye of Larry's mother. Others were having their photos taken with Gnome Guy, buying T-shirts from the heaps in the bed of his truck, and getting his autograph on plaster casts that looked like giant white feet.

I thought of Dave's claim about the odds of encountering Gnome Guy again. He'd turned up twice since Dave made the prediction. Were my odds of stumbling into a murder case—or stumbling upon Bigfoot—also improving?

Trying not to think about that, I elbowed my way to the office door. Doug opened it far enough for me to squeeze through.

"What a zoo. Good thing Larry and I camped here all night. People started showing up long before dawn. Some were still in their slippers and bathrobes and whatnot."

"Whatnot?"

"Don't ask. Some people should wear more clothing to bed—a *lot* more clothing." He pointed to Gnome Guy. "You know, if we could get on this Bigfoot marketing bandwagon, we'd make a fortune."

"We could make T-shirts of our own," I joked. "Like a cartoon of Bigfoot lifting a car so Larry could change the tire. Or Bigfoot driving up in a pickup with a dragging muffler."

"Genius." Doug hugged me so hard air whooshed from my lungs. "You're a genius."

"I was kidding," I gasped.

"I'm not. It's a great idea." He set a stack of flyers on my desk and yanked his phone from his pocket. "I'll call Gladdy."

Gladiola Gardiner—and no, I'm not making up her name—is the Captain Meriwether High School drawing instructor. The woman is so eccentric she wears rubber boots year-round, but she's talented and a heck of a motivator. Even kids who can't manage a straight line with a ruler emerge from her class with amazing portfolios. "Didn't she take off to Shetland to study weaving?"

"Darn it! She did. Do you know anyone who can draw?"

I considered sketches Paulette did for her interior-design ideas, then cancelled the thought. Not because I doubted Paulette's ability, but because she was likely to be insulted if we asked her to sketch Bigfoot. Besides, she had enough on her plate today. With Allison in tow, she was headed for a furniture shop on the far side of Portland.

"It doesn't have to be fancy," Doug said, "just fast and good."

84

"What about that kid who's always sitting in the hall near the library before school?"

"The one who did that great caricature of Big Chill prodding teachers to sign their contracts? The one where she had devil horns and a pitchfork?"

Big Chill, the high school's head secretary, feigned outrage when copies of the sketch circulated, but I knew for a fact she secured the original for $20 and had it framed. "That's the kid."

"Is he fast? I want to get rolling on these an hour ago."

"He did that sketch in about five minutes."

"Great. What's his name? Maybe the registrar is working today and I can get a phone number."

I stashed my purse in the bottom drawer of the desk. "Uh, I don't know his last name. His first is Corbett. No, wait, Corbin. Or maybe Corwin."

Doug shot me a scalding you're-no-help glance.

"Josh might know. I've seen them talking in the cafeteria."

I headed for the restroom to wash out my coffee mug.

"Call Josh." Doug stepped into my path. "Then coffee."

Talk about a man with a plan.

I set the mug on the desk, dug my phone from my purse, and keyed in Josh's number. In a few seconds, I heard his voice. "I'm slaving for the king of crappy cuisine all day. Leave a message."

"Josh, this is Barbara Reed. Call me when you get a chance. It's important."

Doug trailed me as I resumed my mission to stoke my caffeine-craving brain and body. "When do you think he'll call?"

"It could be a while." I sloshed water into my mug to clean it. "They can't bring their phones into the restaurant, so he keeps it in his car. They have to park on the street, and they get only the minimum allowed time for breaks. Sometimes he can't find a parking spot closer than three blocks away, so even if he runs to his car, he—"

"Go over there." Doug turned off the water.

I clutched my mug. "To Krammee's?"

"No, to Afghanistan."

"Good." I shouldered past him. "I'd be more likely to live to tell about a visit to Afghanistan."

Doug rolled his eyes. "Krammee's isn't that bad."

"Compared to what? Would you eat their food?"

"Well, no, but—"

"I rest my case." I poured coffee, added salted caramel creamer, and glugged down half the cup.

Doug gave up on arguing and ordering and adopted the expression of an orphaned child peering through the window of a bakery. "If I could get hold of the kid, get a sketch, and get it to one of those quickie T-shirt places, we could be selling shirts by the middle of the afternoon."

He pointed through the window behind my desk to the shop where Larry, Mark, and Denny were hard at work despite the chaos outside the open bay doors. "Larry could get the business paid off sooner. He could sock more money into his savings account. He and my sister could get married before I'm so old I'll need a walker to get down the aisle."

"I didn't realize the best man walks down the aisle."

"When the wedding's over he does. Or, in my case, he turns cartwheels." Doug clutched his head. "The Sunday-dinner conversations about veils and bouquets and candles are driving me crazy. Two more discussions of the

86

pros and cons of seed pearls and another argument about the guest list, and my permanent address will be Around the Bend."

"What can I say?" I finished the coffee and got my purse. "After all, you're the one who suggested this *incredible* job opportunity. You were instrumental in placing me where I could interface with a renowned Bigfoot ex—"

"Sarcasm noted." Doug opened the door. "Sacrifice noted. I'll buy your lunch tomorrow."

"Mexican?" I bargained. "From my favorite place, *Vaya Con Queso*?"

"Yes and yes."

"Then color me out of here."

CHAPTER 10

To call Krammee's an eyesore would be like calling Mt. Everest a hill. Krammee's was the eyesore by which all others were measured and found to be not sore enough.

The parking lot had last been paved around the time pavement was invented, and the landscaping appeared to have taken a hit from a herd of hungry goats. Then there was the building itself. Once a service station, it looked like it had been rehabbed by the angry ex-wife of the lowest bidder, then painted with cans of color scavenged from yard sales and applied by a troop of gorillas.

(For the record, I realize I'm prone to exaggerate and embellish, but this time I'm actually toning down my description.)

I left my car at the far edge of the lot and picked my way to the entrance, hoping I wouldn't sprain an ankle in a chuckhole. The door opened under protest, hinges squealing, and the scents of hot grease and cold fries surrounded me like a posse bent on vigilante justice. The soles of my sandals slid, stuck, and slid again.

I told myself not to look down, and approached the counter like a high-wire walker, arms out to the sides for balance. That kept me on my feet, but drew stares from Krammee's patrons—four teenagers at a corner table, two young men in work boots stuffing their pockets with catsup and mustard packets, and an ageless guy with yellowed teeth and hair to match reading the menu board posted above the counter and clutching a squashed cigarette like it was a winning lottery ticket.

Two teenage girls slouched behind the counter chatting with each other, one combing hair dyed almost white, the other using an emery board to sharpen nails painted traffic-cone orange. A manicure scissors and a bottle of polish sat beside the cash register.

If my gag reflex hadn't already been in overdrive, this personal grooming in close proximity to food would have done the trick. Because I suspected I might be accused of overstatement when I told the tale of my visit to Krammee's, I snapped off a shot on my cell before they saw me. For good measure I clicked a few more—an overflowing trash can, a puddle of something by the soda dispenser, and a napkin holder without a single napkin.

The girls wore shirts like the one Josh peeled off a few nights ago. Theirs were tight enough to make it apparent they'd skipped past the brassiere drawer when they dressed—if indeed bras were *ever* part of their wardrobe. I wondered if the lack of underwear was a marketing ploy, a matter of choice, or a violation of health and safety rules. I made a mental note to ask Josh later.

When I was within a yard of the counter, their lips lifted in vampire-like smiles and their yellow-brown eyes scoped me the way a predator studies prey for signs of fear or weakness. "Welcome to Krammee's," they chanted. "How may we help you?"

Their snarky tone and chilly gazes implied they had little interest in doing anything beyond asking the stock question.

I straightened my shoulders and used my sternest substitute-teacher voice. "I need to talk with Josh. It's urgent."

They glanced at each other and then smiled—this time with enthusiasm. "Oh, gosh, no talking for Josh," the one on my left sang out. She laid the comb on the counter beside a display of cookies with venomous pink icing. A name badge pinned upside down above her right breast indicated her name was Manhattan. "Josh is a very busy boy."

Peering past them, I spotted Josh in the far reaches of the restaurant. Knees bent, spine bowed, he was lugging an enormous sack of frozen fries into a walk-in freezer. "It will only take a minute."

"Time is money. Don't you know that?" The twin on my right shook a freshly manicured finger and raised her voice. Her badge had broken from its pin, but by the process of elimination, I pegged her as Brooklyn. "If Josh doesn't work, Daddy fires the jerk."

Josh turned my way, flushed, grimaced, and shrugged.

"If he punched in, his time belongs to Krammee's," Manhattan said. "Every single second."

"When does he get a break?"

"He was late clocking in." Brooklyn smiled, tucked her hair—dyed yellow and orange—behind her ears, and rasped the emery board against her thumbnail. "No time off until his lunch break at 2:30."

"Could I talk to him from here? While he works?" I raised my voice to a near shout. "He's the only one who knows how to get hold of the kid at Captain Meriwether who does the caricatures."

The twins shook their heads, turned to face each other, and chorused, "Too bad. So sad."

Josh shot me an okay sign, mimed scribbling something, and jerked a thumb toward the rear of the building.

I hitched my purse higher on my shoulder. "Well, I'm glad I could bring joy into your limited little lives by giving you an opportunity to display your lack of flexibility and humanity. I wish you all the best with your grooming and food contamination activities."

I spun on one heel—easy to do given the slick condition of the floor—and plowed into a tall, thick-bodied man. He wore chestnut brown loafers with dimes in the penny slots, a pair of khaki slacks, a Krammee's uniform shirt, and a scowl. I recognized him from photos in the newspaper. Woodrow Krammer.

He took my arm as if to steady me, but his grip said "control." "You got a problem?" He had a dense accent that made me think of gangster movies. Smart money said that was intentional.

"Nope. No problem." I attempted to pull free. "I'm leaving."

His grip tightened. "Without your order?"

I leaned into the grip, but it didn't relax a single millimeter. "I didn't order."

"Why not?"

Because I don't have a stomach pump handy.

"I, uh, I'm on a diet. You don't have anything I'm allowed to eat."

"I post a menu at the door," he growled. "So picky eaters don't come in and waste my employees' time."

"She didn't even look at the menu," Manhattan snitched.

"All she wanted to do was talk to Josh," Brooklyn added.

"But I didn't." I jerked loose, knowing I'd have bruises to show for it later. "And if I find out you penalize him, I'll get everyone I know to come by twice a day and document unsanitary conditions. Not to mention safety violations."

And wouldn't the Committee love that assignment? Within an hour Jim would have them organized with enough determination and precision to make a military commander green with envy. "And I'll be at the health department turning in complaints so often the director will think I work there."

"Ooooh," the girls chorused. "We're soooo scared."

I headed for the door, trailing the young men with their condiment packets.

"Shut up, you two," Woodrow Krammer snapped. "Get to work. I don't pay you to stand around."

"You don't pay us enough to do much else," Manhattan sniped.

"You don't even pay us enough to wear these lame shirts," Brooklyn complained.

"I told you to shut up," he shouted. "And get that crap off the counter. You'll work for what I decide until you make good on what I laid out for your lawyer."

I recalled what Dave told me about their illegal activities and wondered what the latest brush with the law was about. The Krammee twins might be bad apples, but that could be because the family tree had rot at the core.

The teens at the corner table cast sidelong glances, but didn't stir from their seats. If they came here often, this drama might be business as usual. The ageless guy also seemed oblivious. He'd parked the cigarette behind one ear and was sorting through a handful of change.

No telling how the twins would torment him.

Waving a five, I lured him to the door and out to the parking lot. "Go somewhere else and buy something edible."

He snatched the bill and shuffled off without a word of thanks.

My limited faith in human nature confirmed once again, I tritty-trotted past a gleaming luxury car I assumed belonged to the King of Kram, and around to the rear of the restaurant.

Like the auto repair shop, Krammee's backed up to a greenbelt. Although my knowledge of Reckless River geography left much room for improvement, I bet it was the same greenbelt. And like the auto repair shop's, Krammee's rear lot wasn't paved—unless you counted a layer of flattened pop cans, paper bags, and splintered plastic containers. Reeking trash bins flanked a gray metal door. It was closed and, I discovered when I pulled at the handle, locked.

I was about to knock when I spied a fresh white paper bag with a name written on it with squirts of mustard.

Yesss!

Whipping out my phone, I called Doug. "Corcoran McGuckin."

"Thanks."

I dropped my phone in my purse as the rear door swung open and Woodrow Krammer loomed over me. "You!"

"Me," I confirmed, determined I wouldn't be intimidated—or at least not show that I was.

"You trying to make me mad?"

"Nope. You seem to have that handled."

He scowled. "You trying to talk to that kid?"

"On the contrary. Your daughters—lovely and helpful creatures that they are—made it abundantly clear non-business conversations are restricted to break periods."

I wadded the bag, smearing Josh's message. "I stepped in a puddle of mustard by your door. Fortunately I noticed there was plenty of trash lying around to clean the mess off my sandal. I'll be happy to dispose of it in the correct manner if you'll open one of those trash cans for me."

Krammer's scowl deepened, then gave way to puzzled disbelief as if I'd asked him to remove his own appendix with a set of chopsticks.

"I'll take care of it." Dragging a bulging trash sack, Josh eased alongside Krammer. He opened the sack to reveal stuff best left to your imagination. "Toss it in here."

"Thank you, Josh. Nice meeting you, Mr. Krammer. It's a shame your daughters don't appreciate you."

With a flick of the wrist, I disposed of the evidence of Josh's "crime" and scampered away.

By the end of the afternoon, Doug was hawking T-shirts in a variety of sizes and colors and available in two designs. One featured a caricature of Bigfoot using vines to pull a truck into Start 'er Up Auto Repair. Another design included a true-to-size outline of a footprint, the date, and the words "Bigfoot steps out in Reckless River, Washington." At $20 each for adult sizes and less for kids' shirts, we were set to make a tidy profit.

I made a call to Mrs. Ballantine, then shot a few pictures and zipped them along with a bit of information to a friend who can't imagine what life was like before social media. She slathered pictures around cyberspace using phrases like "limited offer" and "don't miss out."

That's all it took.

T-shirts sold like those proverbial hotcakes, making me wonder how rapid sales were described before hotcakes were around.

At closing time cars were lined up waiting for space in the lot. Dozens of callers burned up the phone line begging me to stay open until they could get across town, see the prints, and buy a shirt.

Larry sent Mark and Denny home and hung with us until Mrs. Ballantine swooped down and ordered him to get some sleep. Then, with Sybil and Verna assisting, they sold shirts until dark while Doug placed additional orders and I fielded phone calls and set shirts aside.

The next day's sales were every bit as hot—until early afternoon when the wind shifted and clouds tumbled across the sky. Despite the canopy Doug erected over the prints, the resulting wind-driven downpour wiped out all evidence of our visitor.

"The rain's here to dampen the Fourth," Doug said with a laugh. "Like usual."

True. It seemed it almost always rained on or just before the Fourth of July. Shortly afterward, the summer drought began. Except for an occasional shower, if the usual weather patterns held, Reckless River days would be dry until September.

"Good thing we snapped pictures." Larry handed me a square of white paper that reeked of the meatball and onion sandwich he'd wolfed down for lunch. Notations and numbers spiraled among the grease stains. I squinted and shook my head as I transferred them to the blanks on a computer form. I admired him for making good use of scratch paper, but this was getting a shade old, especially when the scent clung to my hands.

"And it's a good thing we made those plaster casts," Doug agreed. "The shelves should be here in an hour or so. Want to set up the display tomorrow?"

"Whatever works for you," Larry said.

"What shelves?" I asked. "What display?"

Doug grinned. "How would you like a new job title? Museum Curator?"

Chapter 11

"Curator?" I plugged another number into a space on the spreadsheet. "Sounds like more work, more interruptions, and more aggravation."

"Exactly." Doug grinned as if I'd mentioned benefits instead of drawbacks. "Plus you'd have the opportunity to meet interesting people."

"Like clones of Gnome Guy?"

"People of all ages. From all over the country."

Talk about a spin doctor. Doug could sell snow-removal machinery in Key West.

I slotted in the final number, ran a tally, and turned the screen so Larry could see. "I'd say I'm thrilled, but even in your present Pollyanna-like mood, you'd realize I was lying. So, please, dispense with the preliminaries and tell me about your latest scheme. Spare none of the tawdry and degrading details."

"Sarcasm bounces off me like bullets off Superman." Doug thrust out his chest. "Imagine I'm standing on a mountaintop. Imagine a cape rippling behind me."

Larry turned a thumb up and I saved the bill and sent the form to the printer. "Imagine me slamming that cape in the door on my way out of here to find a new job."

"What would I do without you?" Larry's face turned the color of library paste. "You can't quit."

I sighed, wadded the meatball sub wrapper, and tossed it in the trash can. "You're right. I can't. I need the money. And I don't relish the torture of looking for work— and maybe ending up in a dump like Krammee's. So tell me about this display-slash-museum-slash-opportunity."

"It won't take up *all* that much room or be *all* that much work," Larry mumbled as he slipped through the door to the garage. "It was kind of Mrs. Ballantine's idea."

"Aha. That means none of us can veto the scheme, no matter how wacky it is." I poked Doug's chest with the eraser end of a pencil. "Not even you and your imaginary cape can triumph over her."

Doug rolled his eyes, but then conceded the point. "Dave got it right when he called her a force of nature. I hope I have that much energy when I'm half her age."

"Who knows when you'll reach *that* mark. Mrs. Ballantine avoids admitting her age the way I avoid my ex-husband."

"Late 60's?" he guessed. "Early 70s?"

"I dare you to ask."

Doug thought it over for about four seconds. "Pass."

"Smart guy. Now tell me what's not going to take up too much room."

"Mostly shelves. For T-shirts and plaster casts and photos and whatnot."

"Whatnot? The last time you used that word you were referring to sleep apparel and you told me not to ask what you meant."

"This time it means souvenirs. Maybe Bigfoot dolls, masks, key chains, coffee mugs, pens. You know, stuff like that."

"And all this stuff is going where?"

He pointed at the two customer chairs and the tiny table between them where I'd placed the coffeepot. "There."

"And where will our customers sit?"

"Around behind the shop. Under the big canopy Mrs. B ordered. On the plastic chairs she ordered." He studied the boxes of paperwork I hadn't gotten around to sorting and culling yet. "We'll have to find a place for those boxes. And push your desk back."

"Back where?"

"Closer to the wall. A few inches. You'll still be able to get in the chair if you—"

"Go on a diet?"

He raised his hands. "Hey, I didn't say that. But you might have to, you know—"

"Suck in my gut?"

Hands still in the air, he retreated two steps. "Uh, yeah. Uh, not that you have a gut. I only meant—"

"I get it. I'll squeeze. What about the coffeepot and creamer and cups?"

He frowned and surveyed the limited space.

"Sounds like a problem for Mrs. Ballantine to handle," I suggested. "Anyway, we shouldn't have a coffeepot in here. Someone might soak a plaster cast or stain a T-shirt."

"Good thinking." He headed for the garage. "I see the delivery truck coming. I'm glad you're on board with this."

If by "on board" he meant "counting the days until school started and I could return to substitute teaching" then, yeah, my feet were firmly planted on the deck of the good ship *Make-a-Buck*.

With one thing and another—and another after that— it was Saturday evening before Josh and I crossed paths again. Paulette, Penelope, Dave, and I were under a canopy on the deck with Mrs. B and Dario O'Brien. We were sipping frothy drinks and nibbling at offerings included in a spread of appetizers sizeable enough to quell the hunger pangs of a college football team. Mrs. B often said her second biggest fear was running out of food before her guests ran out of room. Her biggest fear remained a mystery, but I suspected it involved a global shortage of pearls.

She lolled in a lounge chair with Cheese Puff in her lap, dressed in gray slacks, lavender blouse, and a fluffy shawl a few shades darker. But even a casual outfit usually called for pearls—if only in the form of earrings or a ring. When there was serious business at hand, she'd break out a double or triple strand. Tonight she wore a single strand—although it measured two feet long and consisted of baroque pearls the size of malted milk balls.

Despite a relentless drizzle that chilled the air, Dario wore a Hawaiian shirt in shades of screaming orange and toxic pink, a pair of dark green shorts, and yellow flip-flops nearly large enough for Bigfoot. When he wasn't headed for an evening out with Mrs. Ballantine, Dario reverted to what Paulette referred to—in a cautious whisper Dario couldn't overhear—as "Goon Gear" or "Gorilla Garb."

Dario seemed to enjoy playing the Hollywood version of a Las Vegas hood, but I often wondered how much of that was acting. His background was as mysterious as

Mrs. Ballantine's age, and Dave said it was best to leave it that way. He treated Dario's references to crimes and criminals as colorful conversation, rather than oblique confessions a police officer would feel obligated to follow up on.

Paulette wasn't put off by Dario's past—real or fictional—but his leisure wardrobe made her eyes cross. When she'd joined us, she took a chair as far from his as possible, even though that raised the risk of drizzle dampening her hairdo and taking the starch out of the long green shirt she wore over a pair of beige linen slacks.

Penelope, however, sat beside him. She'd inoculated herself against Dario's drapery through her involvement with my sister, the queen of cargo pants and extra-large message T-shirts.

Perhaps because my sister hadn't checked in, Penelope was on her third drink. In an effort to make her smile, Dario was regaling us with Allison's exploits behind the wheel of the beater vehicle he'd bought for driving lessons. Allison had yet to pass the learner's permit test, so her driving was limited to a development site where construction had been halted due to the recession.

"So, there's this tree. Same place it's always been. Way at the edge of the graded area." A muscle twitched beneath Dario's left eye, providing evidence that even talking about Allison's driving set off his facial tic. "And every time she starts up I say, 'Watch out for that tree.' And every time—"

"Shhhhh," Mrs. Ballantine hissed. "She's coming."

Dario faked a cough and raised his voice. "Every time you make those little wieners in that cherry and mustard sauce, Muriel, I get even more nuts about you." He lifted

Mrs. B's hand to his lips as Allison and Josh came through the door from my condo.

"Good save," Dave breathed.

"Yeah," I agreed, "but I wanted to hear more about the tree."

Allison didn't share details of her driving lessons beyond complaining about the age and condition of the vehicle, her fear the lack of air conditioning was causing her sweat glands to pump harder, and her larger fear that some of her friends might see her. From what I'd gleaned hearing Dario's descriptions—discounting 15% for exaggeration in the name of humor—it appeared we were a long way from a license, increased insurance fees, and escalating demands for a car of her own. That was a relief to me, *and* our budget—the budget that might take another $500 hit before we came up with a plan to shake off Rayanne.

"Little cucumber sandwiches," Allison trilled. "And shrimp. And tiny cheesecakes."

She dashed to the snack table without so much as a finger flip of acknowledgement. Josh, however, worked his way among us, greeting and chatting in a polished way that made me fear he might consider a career in politics.

"Hey, Ms. Reed," he said when he got to me. "Mr. Krammer sure was honked off. After you left he kept asking who you were and what you wanted."

"And you said . . .?"

"That you were from the high school checking on kids who were falling behind in their classes because they had problems at home and you needed help finding a kid who moved."

The kid had fancier footwork than Fred Astaire. "Good thinking."

We exchanged high-fives and he hustled to the snack table where Allison balanced a mounded plate in one hand while stuffing her mouth with the other.

"It's wonderful she has such a healthy appetite. So many girls her age starve themselves and mistreat their bodies." Mrs. B beamed at Allison, then turned to me fast enough to give herself whiplash. "What's this about Woodrow Krammer? Why is he mad at you?"

"It's nothing. I went to Krammee's to—"

Mrs. B aimed a bejeweled finger at my nose. "Woodrow Krammer is not a man to trifle with."

"I wasn't trifling." Well, not all that much. "I—"

"He's nasty," Paulette said. "Vindictive. Scary."

Penelope nodded. "I wouldn't work for him unless you held an electric screwdriver to my head and I knew it had a full charge."

"See?" Mrs. B twisted her rope of pearls. "He's not a man to cross."

"I didn't cross him." At least not all that far. "I wanted to talk with Josh—"

"Why didn't you tell me this?" Dave gripped my wrist.

"Because there's nothing to tell. All I did was—"

"Who is this guy?" Dario stuffed a mini quiche in his mouth, sending bits of crust cascading across his shirt. "Want I should pay him a visit?"

"Stop! All of you stop right now." I jerked free of Dave's grip and made a time-out sign with my hands. When they were quiet—a state they didn't achieve without as much grumbling as your average awakening volcano—I told them about my visit to Krammee's.

"Threatening to go to the health department might have seemed like a smart move at the time," Dave said, "but it wasn't."

"It was like poking a tiger," Penelope agreed. "Word is the health department is about at the limit with the way Krammer rides the line. A friend at the county says they might shut Krammee's until he makes some major safety and sanitation upgrades. If he thinks you'll force them to do that sooner rather than later—"

"He might hurt you bad," Paulette said. "The man's a thug."

"See, that's why I should conversate with him. One thug to another." Dario dusted pastry crumbs from the front of his shirt. Cheese Puff jumped down to scarf them from the deck. Lola raised her head, but seemed to decide crumbs weren't worth the effort of moving from beneath Dave's chair.

Penelope and Paulette and I nodded, liking Dario's idea. Dave shook his head. "Dario, I know you mean well, and I appreciate your offer. But if you threatened Woodrow Krammer, and if he pressed charges, you—"

"A man can't press charges if he doesn't have a name or a description of the person he's pressing charges against. That's the advantage of a midnight visit without an appointment. All he'll have when I'm gone is a wet spot in his pants."

Dave grinned, shrugged, and said no more.

CHAPTER 12

Sunday evening I was on the deck again, this time to watch fireworks displays and keep an eye out for sparks in the grass and brush along the river trail.

Reckless River residents were all about celebrating the Fourth of July—even if some probably had no idea why the date was significant. Each year they raised thousands of dollars for a huge sky show put on by an organization with a fantastic safety record. And each year hundreds of private citizens with far less regard for safety—their own or that of others—set off fireworks in their neighborhoods. Many paid no attention to the legal window of time, or to what types of fireworks were allowed within city limits.

Dozens of their rockets started fires. Some did little more than scorch grass and shrubbery, but others took out trees, carports, and even homes. Jim had gone door-to-door this morning reminding condo residents that the fire department would be stretched thin, and urging them to be careful with personal celebrations and prepared to put out small blazes.

"Thank goodness for the rain." Mrs. B checked the connections on the hoses running across our joint deck, down the steps, and through the rose garden. From there they headed a few feet each way along the trail, then were coiled neatly, nozzles on top. "It dampened things down."

"And today's heat dried things up again. Except for my pits." Dario unbuttoned a Hawaiian shirt even more garish than the one he wore yesterday, flapped his arms, and fanned the matted gray hair on his chest with the newspaper. "I'm sweating beer out faster than I can pour it down my throat. I'd go inside, tip the air conditioning down, and watch the big show on TV if you hardy female fire cadets wouldn't call me a sissy."

I chuckled and clamped Cheese Puff against my chest as a sting of pops from somewhere up the trail made him tremble. Dave and Lola were on patrol at the city park where Josh and Allison had joined the throng waiting for official rockets to launch and window-rattling explosions to begin. That left me with a four-legged bundle of nerve endings wrapped in a special shirt Mrs. B bought. The ad claimed it was guaranteed to keep him calm. So far the ad seemed to be all hype. The shirt was having exactly no effect and, as Mrs. B lamented, even with the addition of a rhinestone-studded collar, the outfit wasn't stylish.

"Maybe we should slip him a Mickey," Dario said.

"Believe me, the idea crossed my mind a few times since breakfast when I heard the first pops and bangs. Fireworks aren't cheap and you can't get the full effect in daylight. You'd think they'd wait until dark."

"Especially if they're setting off illegal stuff. Harder for cops to find them after dark."

"Well, the little prince will be fine on my lap." Mrs. B slipped into her usual chair, tucked her necklace—pearls alternating with sapphires and rubies in honor of the day—into the neckline of her red blouse and stretched out her arms. Cheese Puff wiggled from my grasp and made himself comfortable, rucking up her blouse and leaving a cluster of orange hairs on her white slacks. Mrs. B rewarded his efforts with a kiss planted between his ears and a full minute of oogy-googy baby talk that made Dario roll his eyes, drain his beer in three long swallows, and reach into the ice-filled cooler for another.

Jim passed by on the trail and raised a hand in greeting. He wore a helmet with a light on the front, and carried a flashlight large enough to serve as a weapon or, should a game break out, a baseball bat. His belt sported an assortment of loops and sheaths and was loaded with paraphernalia. I spotted a cell phone, a knife, a small fire extinguisher, and a set of handcuffs. Undoubtedly there was more I couldn't see. Like pepper spray. And possibly a gun. A silver whistle the size of a lemon hung on a chain around his neck.

"How loud is that thing?" Dario asked.

Jim lifted the whistle to his lips and shrilled a long note. Cheese Puff howled and hid beneath Mrs. B's blouse. Dario nodded approval. "I should be able to hear it from the end of the complex."

"That's the idea." Jim patted his pockets and marched off.

"Are you expecting trouble beyond a few jerks with illegal fireworks?" I asked.

"I'm always expecting trouble," Dario said in his rasping voice. "That's why I'm still alive."

Mrs. B ran her fingertips along his arm in a way that let him know she was glad he was. Dario, tough guy that he pretended to be, purred like a kitten.

Darkness fell and rockets rose from the park, spraying the sky with streamers of color. Dull percussions pounded

107

the humid air and echoed off the condo walls. More rockets screamed up from boats on the river and from parking lots and open areas along the trail. Mrs. B kept up a steady narration for Cheese Puff who peered from beneath her blouse now and then and blinked at the sky. I speculated about the profit margin on fireworks, the amount the average family spent, and the impact on their budgets. Dario eased his lounge chair into a near horizontal position and snoozed.

The big show ended with a final barrage of rockets that rode ribbons of silver and gold higher and higher until they burst, setting spidery streamers of color free on the black sky. Finance forgotten, I let loose an involuntary "Ooooohhhhh," and heard Mrs. B do the same.

When the last spark faded, Mrs. B clapped Cheese Puff's front paws together. "That's it for another year."

He yawned, but cut it short when a rocket shrieked up somewhere behind the complex. With a yip, he burrowed beneath her blouse once again.

Dario chuckled, then levered himself from his chair with a series of grunts and a few pops from his knee joints. "Think I'll make a pit stop and then find Jim and walk with him until these fools shut it down for the night."

"Take one of those flashlights." Mrs. B pointed at a collection on the table behind us. "They're not as powerful as Jim's, but they'll keep you from tripping where roots have buckled the trail."

Dario kissed her, buttoned his shirt, picked up a flashlight, and went into her condo. I glanced at the door to my unit, considered the effort involved in getting up and doing all that should be done before I went to bed, and stayed where I was. The air was cooling, a faint breeze coming down the river through the Columbia Gorge fanned my hair, stars spangled the sky, and two inches of a rummy drink remained in my glass.

"When you get to be my age," Mrs. B said in a low voice, "you treasure nights like this. You treasure them for beauty and friendship and shared experiences." She sniffed and blotted her eyes on a napkin. "And you treasure them because you don't know how many more will be written in your book."

I nodded, wondering what would be written in my book. My wondering shifted to the present and a boat festooned with twinkling lights. It appeared to be drifting with the current, sliding closer and closer to the bank. A dozen young men and women clustered in the stern, reeling with the pitch of the boat and with what I suspected was a great deal of alcohol. Two or three held candles. Another struck a match. Laughing and jostling each other, they leaned over a cluster of rockets.

I wiggled to the edge of my chair for a better look. "Are those fools going to set off fireworks this close to the bank?"

"I believe they are." Mrs. B leaned forward, drawing a whine of annoyance from Cheese Puff. "And I don't see anyone at the wheel."

"Great." I stood on legs numb from sitting and wobbly from my rummy drink. Mrs. B had a lot of talents, but the art of making a drink light on liquor wasn't among them. "I'd better turn the water on in case we need it."

"And I'll put Cheese Puff inside where he'll be safe."

She stood, earning an annoyed yip from the Puffster, and closed him in her condo, then tapped over in high-heeled blue sandals to check on my progress with the faucets. Dario had checked them earlier in the evening, apparently using all his power to turn off the one on my side of the deck. I couldn't get it to budge.

"Should I get a wrench?" she offered.

Unwilling to admit defeat, I sat, put both hands on the faucet, and leaned. The small wheel turned and water gushed into the hose. "Got it."

Mrs. B extended a hand to help me to my feet, then pointed at the boat. "They're going to hit the rocks or pilings if someone doesn't take the wheel."

A thud and shrill screams punctuated her sentence. The boat shuddered, spun, and tilted, flinging men and women to the deck. Candles flared and fell. A fuse sparked. Then another. A rocket shot into the trees and exploded in the leafy canopy with a burst of green and gold.

I pulled Mrs. B behind the glider swing, hoping canvas, cushions, and a metal frame would stop a rocket. We peered over the top, Mrs. B's hand gripping mine.

Shoving and screaming, the crowd on the boat rushed for the bow. Another rocket arced from the stern, clearing the trees, skimming inches from the roof of the condo complex, and sailing toward the parking lot and the street beyond.

Mrs. B gasped. "I hope Dario and Jim see that coming."

"They're probably headed this way. They must have heard the screams and explosions."

On board the boat, a man broke from the stampede and took the wheel. The boat shuddered, spun, and slammed against something under the water with a hollow boom. It tilted again and another rocket went off.

Sizzling across the river trail, it plowed into the sloping garden of the condo on the other side of Mrs. B's.

110

"Oh, no," she moaned. "Not the savanna."

While our units featured a scatter of rose bushes surrounded by bark mulch, previous owners of this one had planted tall clumps of ornamental grasses. The current owners hadn't trimmed those clumps for months and were on an extended vacation in Canada. The grass, level with my head, was dry and feathery.

"Maybe the rocket buried itself in the ground." I crossed my fingers. "Maybe it's out." I peered at the stern of the boat, but saw no more sparks. "I think it was the last one."

I started to stand, but Mrs. B caught the hem of my T-shirt. "Stay down until those fools get that boat under control and out of here and we're sure nothing else is coming our way."

It was at least five long minutes before the boat, after thumping and scraping, made it into the channel and headed up the river.

By that time, a fat twist of smoke rose from the tall grass.

CHAPTER 13

"Call Dario and Jim," I told Mrs. B. "I'll start spraying the fire."

I raced across the deck, opened the gate, and hurtled down the wooden steps and through the narrow sloping rose garden. Fortunately Mrs. B had coiled the hose right where I needed it, a few feet from the flames licking at a clump of drooping yellow grass. That breeze from the river I'd been so thankful for was stronger now and coming in bursts. Even in the dim light cast by antique-look globes along the trail, I could see the blaze spreading glowing orange tentacles toward other clumps, and sending up swelling puffs of smoke.

Grasping the nozzle, I aimed at the flames and squeezed the handle. Water spurted forth. Flames writhed, spitting and surging. Grass sizzled and crackled. Smoke swirled down the short slope and rolled over me.

"They're coming." Mrs. B's sandals tapped across the deck. "I'll get the other hose."

Smoke rose like a thunderhead and enveloped me.

My eyes watered. My nose ran. My throat burned.

I coughed, closed my eyes, and turned my face toward the river.

Mrs. B screamed.

Something slammed into me.

The hose flew from my hand. Momentum carried me to the far side of the trail. My knees struck the low stone wall bordering the asphalt and I belly-flopped across it. Air whooshed from my lungs.

Mrs. B screamed again.

Feet pounded, running toward me.

Other feet slapped asphalt, running away.

Men's voices shouted orders.

Water hissed against flame.

I wheezed, managed only a shallow breath.

Then Mrs. B was patting my back and raising my arms.

Air filled my lungs. I slid from the wall and leaned against it.

Jim, a nozzle in each hand, fought the creeping fire, smoke and steam washing over him like a gray tide.

Mrs. B took my hands and helped me to my feet. "Let's get inside. You've breathed enough of this."

I wobbled toward the deck, wiping my streaming eyes on the sleeves of my T-shirt. "Where's Dario?"

"Chasing the thing that came out of the tall grass."

"Thing?" The hair on the nape of my neck prickled. "What thing?"

"The thing that knocked you down. Didn't you see it?"

"No. I had my eyes closed because of the smoke. What did it look like?"

"Like a furry refrigerator with legs and arms." Mrs. B gasped and clutched my arm. "You don't think it was—?"

"If I believed in Bigfoot, I'd say that was him." Dario emerged from a billow of smoke. "Or something as big and hairy as Bigfoot is supposed to be."

He relieved Jim of a hose and worked the top of the slope. "Sucker can run. Not what I expected from seeing that old video."

"Yeah, the critter in the video seemed like he was kind of mincing along." Jim turned his nozzle to the spray setting and aimed it up, creating artificial rain.

"He must have been holed up under the deck," Dario said. "He had good cover with the grass and plenty of water with the river right there."

"Food, too," Jim agreed. "People are always throwing bread for the birds or leaving stuff out after they barbecue."

"I bet that's where that bag of chips went on Tuesday. And the rest of the can of cashews." Mrs. B patted my arm. "You had such a hard day at the repair shop. I was certain you needed them and forgot to tell me."

A safe guess. Hard day or not, there was seldom a time when I didn't "need" cashews. But I always let Mrs. B know if I "borrowed" from her supply. And I absolutely always mentioned when that supply was running low so she could stock up.

Until this moment I'd had a live-and-let-live attitude toward Bigfoot. But if I found out he was making off with "my" cashews, I'd reconsider the policy in a heartbeat.

"We've about got it whipped!" Dario attacked a stubborn pocket of flame at the base of a hummock, creating clouds of steam and smoke.

I closed my eyes and tugged at the neckline of my T-shirt, pulling it over my nose and mouth.

And that's when Mrs. B screamed once more.

"He's back," Jim shouted.

I opened my eyes. A figure loomed in the smog.

"I'll get him this time." Dario threw down his hose and rushed the creature, hitting it at the knees with a flying tackle.

Jim followed and piled on.

They rolled along the trail in a smoke-shrouded tangle of arms, legs, and suitcases.

Suitcases?

Just as my brain registered the anomaly, the creature let loose with a string of male-bashing profanity.

The voice was as deep as I imagined Bigfoot's might be, but the language made it clear this was no forest-dwelling creature. This was, in fact, a creature who in all likelihood hoped never to set foot in a forest again. This was—

"Iz?" Mrs. B called.

"Iz?" Dario and Jim echoed.

The trio disengaged and got to their respective feet. "We, uh, thought you were—"

Dario elbowed Jim before he said "Bigfoot" and made the situation worse. "We thought you were the person who set the fire."

Dario and Jim brushed off Iz's suitcases while my sister shook dirt from her cargo shorts and the T-shirt that read: My Way or No Way.

"You're back," I said as I caught the faint scent of skunk.

"Trust you to have a firm grasp of the obvious," Iz snarled.

Mrs. B patted my arm, a signal for me not to engage. "And how was San Francisco, Iz?"

"As it always is. Light years ahead of Reckless River."

115

And yet you're here.

Dario picked up a hose and picked up on my thought. "So what brings you to *this* vicinity again?"

Jim, adjusting the nozzle of the other hose to create a thin stream of water, cut to the chase. "And why are you hauling your suitcases? Why didn't you take them to Penelope's?"

Even in the dim light from the lamps along the trail I had no trouble seeing Iz glower. Between the white skin around her compressed lips and the bright red of the rest of her face, it was possible pilots of passing planes could spot her.

Mrs. B, in a voice sweeter than imitation maple syrup, saved Iz the embarrassment of answering. "It's quite late and I'm sure Penelope has to be at work early in the morning. It's thoughtful of you, Iz, not to disturb her. And since Dave will be coming in with Allison and Lola, and I expect they'll make quite a bit of noise, perhaps you'd get more rest if you slept on my sofa instead of Barbara's."

Dario growled, but Mrs. B wasn't fazed. "It's not as comfortable as your bed at Penelope's, but it's only for one night, right?"

I faked a cough—something that came easy given the lingering smoke and my sister's woodland perfume—and hid a grin.

Iz's lips compressed again, harder. The white area spread, making her look like a circus clown on a bad hair day. I read her body language as signs she'd A) intended to crash with me, B) intended to stay for more than a single night, and C) been painted into a corner by Mrs. Ballantine. "Thanks," she muttered.

"I'll get us all nightcaps." Mrs. B trotted up the steps and into her condo. Cheese Puff slipped out as she slipped in, racing through the gate and to the trail where he skidded to a halt, bared his tiny teeth, and snarled at my sister.

"Shut up, you overgrown rat."

Coming from Iz, that comment was almost kind. Generally she contended my dog was a waste of oxygen and should be tossed in the river, mostly because he was male and, in her words, "too small to be a real dog and good for anything."

He'd never cared much for her, either. He made his point by lifting his leg and squirting the path through the rose garden that Iz would have to follow to reach the deck.

Confident that Cheese Puff could hold his own, I went to give Mrs. B a hand with her concoction, a mix of brandy and vanilla ice cream tossed in the blender with ice cubes. Once she whipped it into submission, we poured the thick mixture into cocktail glasses, and topped it with chocolate shavings and liberal squirts of whipped cream from a can.

"It's all organic, Iz." Mrs. B handed my sister a brimming glass and gestured to a seat at the outdoor table. "With only a hint of brandy."

Having seen the ingredients, I knew both statements were bald-faced lies. But since Iz only talked the organic talk while eating and drinking across the spectrum, I let it ride and watched her guzzle her drink and hold her glass out for a second.

After they rolled up the hoses, Jim trundled one suitcase up the steps and Dario dragged the other two bags—huffing to make a statement about their weight. Iz frowned, but withheld caustic remarks. She owed them for standing guard when her life was threatened last month.

I could tell she hated having to bite back a slew of snarky comments—she wore that choleric clown face again—and for a fleeting moment I felt almost sorry for her. Then I decided that holding in corrosive comments was good practice for her campaign to win Penelope back. And why else would she be here if that wasn't her objective? I wished I could be a fly on the wall when skunk woman had to eat crow to make amends to the chipmunk.

The wildlife mentioned in that last sentence convinced me I'd reached my limit on Mrs. B's bartending blends and risked a massive hangover if I didn't quit. Right now. I set my glass on the table and pushed it to the center.

"Do you think that fire will flare up again?" Mrs. B asked.

"I don't know. Grass isn't my specialty. Now if you asked about arson in a warehouse . . ." Dario grabbed a couple of cocktail napkins and wiped cream from his upper lip. "What do you think, Jim?"

"I think it's a nice night to be under the stars," Jim said. "I'll haul a lounge chair to the edge of the deck and sleep out here to make sure it doesn't rekindle."

Despite the late night, I woke up earlier than usual, crawled from beneath Dave's arm, showered, and carried my coffee outside.

Jim and Dario, armed with steaming mugs, were on the trail inspecting the fire damage.

"Your sister snores," Dario reported by way of a conversation starter.

"Should have used earplugs," Jim suggested.

"Then I wouldn't have heard you if that hairball with legs turned up and you yelled for help."

Jim chuckled. "If I was in enough trouble that I had to call for help, it would probably be too late."

They clinked coffee cups in a male-bonding moment, then returned to their inspection of the grassy area. Several hummocks were charred to the ground and others were scorched and flattened. Bark mulch and soil, washed loose by the water, lay in snaking ridges on the slope and fanned out on the trail.

"Water wiped out all the footprints," Dario told me.

"But see that." Jim pointed to the lattice that screened the area beneath the deck.

"The piece that's cockeyed?" I asked.

"Right. He pried it loose but left one nail in so it would swing aside and he could get under there. Made a bed out of towels. Probably stole them from the pool area. People are always flinging them over the railing to dry and forgetting them."

Dario snapped his fingers. "I bet he's been using the pool as a giant bathtub. That's why the cleaning guy's been complaining about more long hair in the filter than last summer."

And that explained why Bernina Burke delivered memos to all residents suggesting that if our hair was more than a few inches long we voluntarily wear bathing caps or she would take up the issue with the condo board. Wait until Bernina found out that the hair clumps were coming from—

I flashed on Dave's prediction that the odds of running into Gnome Guy again were about the same as getting involved in another murder case or finding Bigfoot using the pool as a bathtub. I'd definitely run into Gnome Guy again. And now there was evidence that Bigfoot had been in the pool. Did that mean . . . ?

I shuddered. Being involved in a murder case might sound exciting to you, but I'd had enough of that a few weeks ago when I almost ended up shot and stuffed under a bush along the river trail. If it hadn't been for my ex-husband's incompetence and a well-aimed blow with a bag of garbage, I'd be worm food.

I swallowed a slug of coffee, and told myself I hadn't seen Bigfoot using the pool, so it didn't count.

"I'll get a rake and a broom to clear the debris off the trail, and bring a couple of trash bags," Jim said. "Figured we'd cart the towels and other stuff to the bins."

"What other stuff," I asked.

"A couple of empty soda bottles, paper bags, a box of food scraps." Jim grimaced. "Looks like he scavenged most of it from trash cans at fast food places."

"Wonder why the dogs didn't smell the food and sniff around the lattice," Dario mused. "Or why they didn't bark."

"Lola only barks when she sniffs drugs or there's danger," I said. "And Cheese Puff mostly barks at my sister, or when he's annoyed." Which was at least once a day. "But it seems odd they didn't work their way in there to investigate."

"Maybe he wasn't living under there long," Jim speculated. "Or maybe the rain killed some of the odor. And lots of times you take the dogs out the door to the parking lot."

True. And lately, because of Monster Mutt, when I did take them across the deck to the trail, we went downriver unless Dave was along. Each day the huge dog came farther along the trail from the condo above ours, and it no longer backed off when I yelled for it to go home. The last time it stared at Cheese Puff and licked drool from its lips. In a rare show of good sense, Cheese Puff didn't snarl, saving his attitude for the next dog he encountered, a young dachshund securely on a leash.

I hadn't mentioned the incident to Bernina Burke because I knew she wouldn't consider licking drool to be overtly menacing behavior. But then, she hadn't been there. Until she saw the dog in action or even feared for her own safety, Bernina would continue to do nothing.

"I don't know about you two," Dario said, "but I'm against telling anyone what we saw last night. This guy's long gone. No sense in inviting the media circus to set up here."

"I'll vote with you," I said. A vote against the media was a vote against having Gnome Guy stomping around my condo. Although I wouldn't mind seeing him go head-to-head with Bernina Burke in a surliness skirmish. Speaking of that particular devil. "What about Bernina? Shouldn't we tell her?"

Dario shook his head. "Only if you want to spend the next week in a state of red alert."

"Yeah," Jim agreed. "She'll call in the police. Then she'll try to ding us all for increased fees to pay for security guards or extra lighting or a higher fence around the pool."

And she'd do that *after* she tried to find a way to blame me, maybe suggesting I gave Bigfoot a lift here from the auto repair shop. Bernina's infatuation with my ex-husband was fading and she was becoming more of a people person thanks to a mix of ego bolstering and tough talk from Mrs. B, but if she could find a way to blame me for something, she would. Suffice it to say that we'd never do each other's hair before heading off for a girls' night out. "Works for me. But what if he appears again?"

"He won't," Jim said. "Not after last night's noise and fire and smoke. If that was Bigfoot—and I'm not saying it was—he's on his way to the deep woods."

"My money says he's a long way from Reckless River," Dario said, "and still running."

Chapter 14

As prognosticators, Jim and Dario turned out to be right up there with the guys who said the stock market would never crash or World War I would end all global conflict. But I wouldn't have figured that out so fast if I hadn't been curious about three things I noticed behind the auto repair shop.

The first was a dark gray car, a long, low, luxury vehicle that seemed vaguely familiar. One rear door hung open and a few inches of wine-red upholstery appeared damp, perhaps with dew.

It didn't seem odd to find a car here. The outer door to my office/museum had a drop slot where customers could leave their keys if they brought cars in before we were open. But it *was* odd this customer would bring a car so new to Larry's shop and not to the Reckless River dealer displayed on the license plate mount. And it was even more peculiar that the owner of an expensive car hadn't locked up, or at least closed the door.

Stranger still were the parallel grooves in the dirt. They ran from the open door past the picnic table and into the grass.

Drag marks?

Was that blood, not dew, on the upholstery? And in the dirt between the drag marks?

I forced a laugh. A loud laugh.

Cawing, a flock of crows rose from the swale.

A snippet of information filed deep in my mind popped out. I remembered that a flock of crows was called a murder.

Then I remembered Dave's prediction.

My stomach rolled and flipped. Despite a temperature already into the 80s, my toes and fingers grew cold and numb.

Most of the nerves in my body were now firing off messages like this: "Turn around, you fool. Run, you idiot. Stop dithering, you dolt. Call the cops, you complete imbecile."

But a few voyeuristic brain cells, undaunted by name-calling, urged me to tiptoe to the top of the slope and peer into the tall grass. "A quick peek," they urged. "Only for a second. It's probably nothing."

I'd managed to lift one icy foot when Larry rolled into the lot and stopped with a squeal of brakes that brought a cacophony of cries from the crows.

"Sorry I'm late," he called as he vaulted out. "Who left the car?"

"I don't know."

"Wasn't there a note with the keys?"

"I haven't gone inside to look, but I have a feeling there won't be keys or a note." I pointed to the gouges in the dirt.

Larry stared for a moment, then sucked in a breath. "You think that . . . ?" He peered at the tall grass and then at the crows, now ensconced on the upper branches of the tallest poplar. They cocked their heads to check on us and then on whatever was in the high grass. Color leached from his cheeks and he dry swallowed. "Should we call the police? Or check it out first?"

His quavering voice and emphasis on the first question made it clear he didn't want to venture into the swale any more than I did. "I don't want to destroy evidence. Maybe we should get up on the picnic table and see if we spot anything."

"Good idea." Larry offered a hand. "I'll hold you steady."

"Me? You're taller."

"But you know what to look for."

Sheesh.

Stumble across one murder victim and some people think you're an expert.

I grasped Larry's hand and stepped on the bench seat and then to the table. It sagged and swayed like an old horse and I gripped Larry's hand tighter. Unfortunately, from that bent-over-hand-gripping position of relative stability, I couldn't see either diddly or squat.

Releasing my hold, I inched to the center of the table and straightened. To kill time, I took off my glasses and wiped the lenses on my T-shirt, blinked a few times, seated the frame on my nose, and shoved my hair behind my ears.

"What do you see?" Larry's voice was thin and brittle.

I used my finger as a pointer to follow the path of the drag marks. That path wasn't long. "I see a pair of shoes."

"Shoes." Larry let out a long sigh. "That's all?"

"I wish."

Those shoes were blood spattered chestnut brown loafers with scuffed toes, pointed in such a way that I could see the shiny dimes in the penny slots. Worse, those shoes were almost certainly on a pair of feet belonging to Woodrow Krammer.

Not for a single second did I think he was sleeping off too many Independence Day toasts.

I bent to reach for Larry's hand and spotted something I hadn't noticed when I was on the ground.

In the dirt beside the driver's door, next to the open rear door, and straddling the groove marks, were faint footprints. The heel marks pointed toward the greenbelt. The prints angled outward from the heel, the way your foot might if you were walking backwards, knees bent, dragging something heavy.

And the prints were long and wide.

Really long and wide.

My discovery was bound to give Detective Charles Atwell a major-league headache and a case of sour stomach that would stick with him for a month.

Pulling my cell phone from my pocket, I snapped a few shots. Then, without waiting for Larry to offer a hand, I jumped from the table. "I'll call the police. Put up a barricade so no one drives in here and disturbs the crime scene."

"Crime scene?"

"Right. Oh, and you might want to raise the price on all the Bigfoot paraphernalia in the mini museum. And then brace yourself for an onslaught of media like this town has never seen."

"Why?"

I jerked a thumb toward the swale. "Because the man who founded Krammee's is dead in the swale. And from the footprints that go with the drag marks, it looks like Bigfoot was the one who put him there."

Larry's eyes bugged out. His mouth formed an *O*.

"Scout's honor." I raised my right hand and saluted.

Larry's lips pooched in and out for a few seconds, but he didn't ask about the total of merit badges I'd racked up, so I didn't have to admit it was a number lower than one. He blinked and pointed to the car. "How do you think Bigfoot learned to drive?"

My turn to do the poochy-lips thing.

I studied the tracks by the driver's door. Had Bigfoot driven Krammer's car? Did Bigfoot have a license? Had he ever gotten a ticket? Who carried his insurance? Did he prefer an automatic or a stick shift? What about bumper stickers?

I slapped my cheeks to clear my head, but another question popped in. If Bigfoot hadn't been behind the wheel, who had? Had Krammer driven here for some reason and been attacked when he got out of the car? Or had Bigfoot been a passenger?

I checked for tracks on that side of the car and saw nothing. My head was starting to spin. I slapped my cheeks again.

Larry did the same, then trotted around the side of the shop, leaving me the dubious pleasure of talking with the man who, only six months ago, grilled me like one of Krammee's burgers while investigating the murders of Henry Stoddard and Jessica Flint. Thanks to said grilling—which he stretched through several interviews— the number for Detective Charles Atwell's direct line was etched on my brain.

I reminded myself that the past was the past and reminded myself that Atwell was Dave's buddy. Finally, I punched the sequence. While his phone rang, I picked up a few pebbles to keep the crows in their tree, and sat at the picnic table.

"Atwell," he growled with the warmth and charm of a hungry grizzly bear.

"Good morning," I said, doubting it would be when I hung up.

"Barbara Reed." Atwell's tone warmed, but not more than half a degree. Besides the little matter of once being a murder suspect, we have other unpleasantness in our past involving my sister, my friends, and my dog. Let's say that homicide investigations had been a lot less off-the-wall before I came along, and Atwell preferred it that way. "Calling to ask me to keep your ex-husband in jail for the rest of his life or lock up your sister for a decade because she's a public nuisance?"

Dandy ideas. Both, unfortunately, not within his power.

Two crows swooped from their tree and sailed low over the grass. I flung a couple of pebbles and they returned to their branches. "Uh, no. I called because . . . you see I . . . well, there's a . . . when I got to work I—"

"I haven't got all day. Spit it out."

"There's a body behind the auto repair shop."

Atwell released a few expletives best left deleted.

"I didn't go near him. I climbed on a picnic table to get a look. But I'm pretty sure it's Woodrow Krammer, the guy who owns Krammee's."

Atwell upped the expletive ante. His vocabulary wasn't vast, but if there was a competition for spontaneous swearing, judges would award him major points for style and creativity. Who knew a four-letter verb could be transformed into a noun, an adjective, *and* an adverb while joined by hyphens to a series of other words?

Given that Atwell had blood pressure issues and was already wound up, I decided not to mention the Bigfoot prints. Let him draw his own conclusions.

"There's a car here, too. I'm pretty sure it's Krammer's. And there are drag marks. I bet the killer brought Krammer in the car and—"

"Leave the investigating and theorizing to experts. Wait for me inside the shop."

"Um, okay. But the crows will be all over the body again if I go inside."

In a half-hearted way, Atwell released a few more expletives aimed at Krammer, crows, the paperwork he was still doing on the last homicide, and the fact that some people couldn't seem to turn around without tripping over bodies.

That last part wasn't true. Technically, this was only the second body I'd discovered, and I hadn't tripped over either of them. But attempting to set the record straight at the moment would be a dumb move right up there with sawing off a limb while sitting on it.

"Stay where you are," he ordered in a resigned voice. "Keep the crows away. But don't touch anything."

That last sentence stung. Did he think I'd check Krammer's pockets for hamburger coupons or pry the dimes from his loafers?

I flung another pebble and called Dave. His phone rang five times before he answered. "Hffffllah."

"Get your head out from under the pillow. I need you."

"Huh? Who's this?"

Have I mentioned that Dave isn't a morning person? If he's had plenty of sleep, he's merely sluggish. But after a late night, he wakes up in stages. The first stage is characterized by what I consider stupid questions.

"This is Barbara, the woman who lives with you, the woman who's not beside you right now in the second floor bedroom of the condo we share."

I've found it's best to be specific—extremely specific—and never rush the waking-up process.

"Barbara," he repeated with a yawn. "Where are you?"

"I'm at the auto shop where I intended to spend the day dealing with customers thrilled to the core by Larry's estimates. Instead, I've arranged to rendezvous with your good friend, Detective Charles Atwell."

"Chuck? You're meeting Chuck?"

"Right."

He yawned again. "Why?"

Ah, his brain synapses were starting to fire.

"Because there's a dead body behind the shop."

"Crap."

Okay, *now* he was awake and grasping the situation.

"I'm pretty sure it's Woodrow Krammer."

"Double crap."

Lest you think Dave doesn't swear, the fact is he could match Atwell any day of the week—if he wasn't trying to set a good example for his daughter. Granted, Allison was probably asleep and wouldn't hear, but Dave believed an off-again-on-again approach wouldn't help him break the blasphemy habit.

"Tell me you didn't find him," Dave begged.

"Okay, but I'd be lying."

He groaned. "I was afraid of that. What did Chuck say?"

I flung another pebble. "He said he was delighted, perhaps approaching overjoyed, or verging on ecstatic."

He snorted. "I bet. Be there in ten minutes. Fifteen at the most."

NO SUBSTITUTE FOR MYTH

And, now that he was awake, I knew he would.

So I sat there, tossing pebbles and thinking about Woodrow Krammer. Putting aside the theory that Bigfoot killed him, drove him here, and dragged his body into the swale, I considered other suspects—namely Dario O'Brien. After hearing of my encounter with Krammer, he'd offered to pay a midnight visit. Had he paid that visit last night after we finished our nightcaps? Had verbal threats led to physical violence?

I cast my mind over the evening and recalled Mrs. B inviting my sister to camp on her sofa. That put her in line with both exits from the condo. But as Dario pointed out, Iz snored with the intensity of a spawning tornado. Dario could have danced past her wearing tap shoes and corduroy pants while playing an accordion. As for Mrs. B, she usually went to bed with Sinatra on a bedside CD player and a sleep mask over her eyes.

As I was making a mental list of things I needed to know—the exact time of Krammer's death, whether Iz read or watched TV before she fell asleep, and what time Mrs. B turned out the light and snapped on Sinatra—Detective Atwell arrived.

With a jerk of his thumb, he ordered me to get inside and stay there.

Fine with me. There was a bag of miniature chocolate bars in the top drawer of my desk and I needed one the way a fish needs water.

Pausing for only a second to admire the Bigfoot displays in a glass-fronted cabinet flanked by racks of plaster footprint casts, T-shirts, ball caps, and stuffed toys, I provisioned myself with a couple of dark chocolate chunks. Nibbling, I sidled into the tiny restroom, stood on the toilet cover, and peered out the window. Atwell was already on the picnic table, shading his eyes and scanning the swale. He made a quarter turn and studied the car and the gouges in the dirt.

Larry wedged a stool beside the toilet and hauled himself up. "Has he seen those footprints yet?"

"No. But I think he's about to."

Atwell balanced at the edge of the table, shaded his eyes with both hands, and bent forward.

Larry and I held our breaths.

Atwell shook his head, rubbed his eyes with his knuckles, and studied the ground once more. His shoulders slumped and his lips moved, spewing what I guessed was a fresh batch of profanity.

"I wonder what he's thinking," Larry said.

I hadn't spent so much "quality time" with Detective Atwell for nothing. "He's thinking he doesn't want the media to know about those footprints."

"Oh." Larry fidgeted on the stool and gripped the windowsill to keep his balance. "Then I guess he'll be mad when he finds out I called the reporter who was here last week."

Chapter 15

I allowed myself a tiny smile. Atwell was in for it now. "Mad doesn't begin to cover it. In fact, there isn't a word in the dictionary to cover the state of fury he'll achieve."

Larry pulled his phone from his pocket. "I'll call Stewart and tell him . . . uh . . . I'll tell him I looked again and . . . uh, it must have been a shadow."

I laughed. "Pathetic."

"CPR dummy?" Larry ventured.

"Wearing loafers?" I patted Larry's shoulder. "It's out of your hands now. All you can do is say you didn't realize calling the media would create problems. Then hang your head and let Atwell bellow until he's out of breath. Then order more T-shirts and coffee mugs and stuff."

Larry jumped from the stool and hustled into the office to survey the racks of paraphernalia. "Do you think thongs would sell? Doug thought they'd be money-losers, but Mark and Denny would definitely buy them for their girlfriends."

Thongs?

Well, why not?

"Buy a few and test the market," I called. "You can always give them away as gifts if they don't sell." Maybe I'd find one with Bigfoot and a skunk strolling through the forest and present it to Iz for her birthday. Anonymously, of course.

Atwell climbed off the table. I retreated to my desk and shooed Larry into the garage where he opened the bay doors and got busy looking busy—for about five minutes. That's how long it took Atwell to announce he was shutting the place down.

"It's a crime scene. The whole place, including your cars. Do whatever you need to close this place, then clear out so we can work it."

Doug arrived and launched an argument about free enterprise. Atwell, in turn, suggested Doug was interfering with a police investigation and indicated there would be penalties. Doug considered those penalties and backed off. Having seen that coming, I'd already called customers scheduled for today and offered a vague excuse about a city project that forced us to close temporarily. No one was happy, but most rescheduled when I promised a five-percent discount.

After warning me not to talk about what I'd seen—a warning he failed to apply to Larry who was closing the bay doors at the time he delivered it—Atwell got out of our faces. Pretending to sort papers and check supplies, we took our time obeying the clear-out order.

A crime scene team was taping off the rear lot when Dave arrived with Lola at his heels. He waved as he walked past the office door, called that he'd return in a few, and went around the side. From my post at the restroom window, I watched as Atwell greeted him, arms moving with stiff gestures, pointing toward my car, the picnic table, and the drag marks. Dave shrugged and spread his hands, perhaps indicating that the location of the body at my place of employment was purely coincidental and in no way my fault.

Atwell scowled, said some things I decided to be glad I couldn't hear, and made a few more robotic moves.

Dave signaled Lola to sit, walked with Atwell to the picnic table, peered at the gouges and footprints, and shook his head.

Atwell kicked the table. Twice.

Dave made a time-out sign with his hands, pointed to the prints and the swale, then collected Lola, and called for me to meet him in the car.

Atwell kicked the table once more, then dug out his cell phone.

"Lola's trained to sniff out drugs," Dave said when we were headed for home. "Not follow a scent trail."

Lola flopped on the rear seat and grunted agreement.

"Atwell didn't know that?"

"He knew, but he was trying to get around calling for Sergeant Bender and his dog. Missoula's a German Shepherd and the best tracker in the region, but Chuck and Bender have a personality conflict that goes way back."

I zipped my lips. This wasn't a good time to mention that Atwell could have a personality conflict with inanimate objects, even those without significant personality, like slices of untoasted generic white bread and glops of unsalted mashed potatoes. Besides, Dave knew all that. And he remained friends with Atwell in spite of it.

Speaking of what Dave knew—he'd been there when Dario offered to have a thug-to-thug talk with Woodrow

Krammer. Should I bring that up, or assume he remembered?

Dave glanced at Lola. "No offense, girl, but I'd rather have Missoula along if I caught up with whatever left those tracks and it turned on me. Missoula's got more jaw power."

Clearly not insulted, Lola thumped her tail.

"After I drop you and Lola at home, I'll help search the area."

"*With* your gun, right?"

"You bet. I may be foolhardy, but I'm not stupid. What are your plans?"

"Catch up on my sleep. Swim. Sweep the deck." I stretched. "Not necessarily in that order."

"Before this came down I'd counted on having the morning off to supervise Allison." He shot me a pleading glance. "Would you mind checking her current events notebook?"

I suppressed a whine. If there was anything *in* the notebook, it would likely need more than checking. "Only if you make it up to me under cover of darkness."

He leered. "Can I make it up to you twice?"

I mock sighed. "If you must."

"Oh, I must. I definitely must."

I shivered with anticipation as he pulled into the condo complex, careful to adhere to the speed limit as we passed Bernina Burke's office. No point in poking the dragon. "I have no idea how long Chuck will want me around, so expect me when you see me."

He pulled me close and gave me a kiss that made my toes tingle. "Hard as it will be for you to keep quiet about this, please do me a huge favor and don't tell anyone about Woodrow Krammer until Chuck releases information to the media. Okay?"

I laid a finger across my lips, suspecting that even now Atwell was besieged by the media in the shape of a slouching Stan Stewart. "I won't say a word until it hits the news."

He thanked me with another kiss and took off before the thought about Dario as a suspect floated into my brain again. Lola watched him drive away, gazed at me in a way that made it clear I was no Dave but better than nothing, and trotted to the condo door.

Even before I turned the key, I heard Allison screeching with rage. When I opened the door, Cheese Puff leaped into my arms and stuck his head into the sleeve of my T-shirt. Lola twined around my legs, whimpering.

"Don't even pretend you're lecturing me because you care how I'm doing the laundry," Allison shrieked.

The recipient of the verbal barrage responded in a lower voice—so low I couldn't make out who was speaking. I dropped my purse on my desk, closed Cheese Puff and Lola in the office, slipped off my sandals, and tiptoed along the hallway.

"You're picking at me because you like to push people around."

"I'm not pick—"

"Liar," Allison screamed. "You're a lying liar, Iz."

Ah. That explained Allison's eruption. My sister was the queen of spleen, the princess of provocation, the duchess of displeasure. Even world-renowned pacifists might snap at Iz in full-throttle scold mode. And Allison was no pacifist.

"You never say anything nice. You pick at everyone. Me. Barbara. My dad. Pick, pick, pick. All the time."

I eased along the wall and peeked around the corner. Wearing the bikini she donned for sunbathing, Allison stood by the washer, a wad of clothing—blacks, whites, and an assortment of colors—in her arms. Iz reached for a pair of bright blue shorts. "If you dump all that in the same load, the colors will bleed."

Allison pulled the shorts from Iz's grip. "For your information I was going to wash them in cold water."

"They won't get clean in cold water."

"They will so. I checked and there aren't any grease stains. They're just sweaty. And what do you know about clothes anyway? All you ever wear are baggy sweats like the ones you have on. Or cargo pants and T-shirts saying nasty things. And I bet Penelope does *your* wash."

To my knowledge, Iz owned a pair of black slacks and at least one tailored blouse, so score only half a point for Allison on the wardrobe shots. But my money was also on Penelope doing the wash. Iz talked the talk about pitching in with chores, but when it came to walking the walk, she usually took a hike—even if only to the bathroom for an extended stay.

I should know. Before Iz met Penelope, she spent many long days camping at my place, eating like famine was forecast, leaving dirty dishes in every room, and kicking her clothes into the corner by the washer.

By the time Iz got her lips unfurled for a comeback, the kid was on a new topic. "You know what? Everyone knows you were stupid to leave Penelope in Wyoming. She was the only one who really liked you. She was the only one who didn't put up with you because you're family or kind of family or we feel sorry for you."

Iz clenched her fists. "I'm a nationally known figure! Why would anyone feel—?"

"Because you're pushy and bossy and lazy and you think you know it all but underneath you know you don't and you have hardly any *real* friends. Except Penelope. And you went and messed that up over a stupid skunk and I hope you smell from it for the next year."

Allison dumped the load of wash into the machine and slammed the lid. "I'm done talking to you. And I'm *really* done listening. The next thing you say should be to Penelope and it should be 'I'm sorry.'"

With that, Allison flounced out to the deck, headed for the lounge chair she favored for catching rays.

Iz didn't move.

I didn't either, even though a big part of me wanted to leap out of hiding and shout a stale cornball saying like "Out of the mouths of babes."

Iz sniffed, raised her right arm, and wiped tears from her cheeks with the sleeve of her sweatshirt.

Crud!

The last thing I wanted was to feel sorry for my sister. But I did. Allison was right about Iz being pushy and bossy and a know-it-all. But the kid was also on the money about Iz having few friends. The fact that Iz was crying proved she knew that, and it hurt.

I wanted to console her, but that would be admitting I witnessed what went down. That would embarrass and humiliate Iz. And those emotions, I knew from long experience, would make her tee off on me. I'd had my fill in years gone by, thank you very much, so I played dumb and crept to the office.

Cheese Puff and Lola peered out from their refuge in the kneehole of my desk. "How's my little orange mutt?" I asked in a loud voice as I slipped my sandals on. "I'm home early and Lola's with me. Want to go for a walk?"

By the time I reached the kitchen—my canine companions lagging well behind—Iz was poking through the refrigerator. Seeing her preparing to graze on my provisions whittled away at the sympathy I felt, so I reminded myself she stepped in and raised me when my parents checked out emotionally. She hadn't exactly nurtured, hadn't doled out more than a few hugs, but she kept me fed and in good health.

Recalling the day she beat up a predatory boy who tried to pull down my underpants, I summoned feelings that, while not exactly warm, were at least room temperature. "Hey, Iz." I forced a laugh. "Don't tell me there's more to choose from in my kitchen than at Mrs. B's."

"I won't." She slammed the refrigerator door, rattling bottles and jars. "Because it wouldn't be true."

Cheese Puff yipped and led Lola in a retreat to the office.

I hid a grin. The tears were gone. Iz was in fighting form once again.

"I don't know why I thought that for once you might have prepared something healthy," Iz stormed. "Something that isn't processed and pre-cooked and devoid of all taste and nutrition."

Translation: Something that met the standards of her latest diet—probably a diet she'd glommed on to in San Francisco. If the past was any indicator of the present, she'd have followed that diet to the letter for a day, possibly two. For the next month she'd preach it while secretly gorging on forbidden fruit. Finally, she'd renounce it and move on to the next fad.

For a moment I considered borrowing Mrs. B's car, trekking to the store, and making something to Iz's specifications. Then I noticed her suitcases stacked beside the sofa—stacked in a way that said "I'll be staying here for a few days."

No. No. No. No. No.

Forget food. Forget sympathy and warmth. And forget the time she beat up the bully. The rest of *that* story was she hated his guts, had been looking for an excuse to knock out a few of his teeth, and relished every minute of the fight.

I squared my shoulders and stiffened my spine. Desperate times called for desperate measures. "There's plenty of tasty and nutritious food in the refrigerator. There's pulled pork and barbecue sauce."

Translation: Bull, meet red flag.

I didn't know what foods were included in the latest diet, but I had memorized a short list of foods Iz didn't like or usually wouldn't eat, even when she wasn't on a diet, and even when no one was looking.

"Pork?" she raged. "Barbecue sauce? You call that healthy?"

"Well, there's other stuff, too." Gambling that she wouldn't check the shelves, I named off foods usually on her no-eat list. "Macaroni and jalapeno cheese, coleslaw with lots of mayonnaise and onion, rhubarb pie, and deviled eggs with horseradish."

Iz scowled, snatched up the grocery pad and a pencil, and marched to the dining room table. "You know I can't eat any of that. You'll have to go to the store. An organic grocery store, not the cut-rate place where you buy those puffed cheese snacks you're so fond of."

She pulled out a chair, sat, and licked the tip of the pencil. "I'll make a list and we'll go over it together so you understand my dietary requirements."

No. No. No. No. No. And no yet again.

I scoped out the suitcases once more and realized their presence meant that Mrs. B had given Iz the gate— although undoubtedly in a kind and caring way. With that door closed, Iz was low on sleepover options. Jim, Verna, Sybil, and other members of the Committee probably dreamed up excuses within two minutes of meeting my sister for the first time. Paulette, although her home had two guest rooms, would rather pluck every hair from her head with a tweezers than invite Iz to stay in either of them. Theirs wasn't an oil and water relationship, it was more like baking soda and vinegar. Explosive.

So that left me.

And Penelope.

My first instinct was to hit and hit hard, to tell Iz I overheard what Allison said, and inform her the kid made some good points.

But that would not only result in a shouting match, it would also dredge up the debt of childhood. And, although I felt as if I'd repaid it a hundred times over in the years since, I knew I'd always feel obligated.

A calm and rational approach wouldn't work either. Iz would interpret it as weakness and I'd be forced into the shouting match I wanted to avoid.

Appealing to her higher nature? Well, that might work. If she had one.

Making a case that Dave and I needed space and time to grow our relationship—space that was already at a premium thanks to Allison, Lola, Cheese Puff, and the demands of our jobs? Nope. Iz liked Dave slightly better than deceased Albert and divorced Jake, which was to say, not much, seeing as how Dave carried a Y chromosome.

No, the only way to get Iz out of my condo was to take a page from Mrs. Ballantine's playbook, and resort to psychological warfare. Once I twisted her mind to make her think I was on her side, it would take only a tiny final twist to make her think my ideas were hers.

Don't get me wrong. My sister is no dummy and she's been known to resort to this kind of thing herself. But she has a blind spot. And it's a huge blind spot, a blind spot big enough for me to high step through leading a marching band with at least 75 trombones.

CHAPTER 16

I pulled out a chair opposite Iz, sat, and contrived a sugary, sympathetic tone. "I'm sorry the trip to Wyoming didn't go well. The thing with the skunk, though, that was a practical joke, right?"

Iz didn't look up, but her pencil paused in the middle of the word "broccoli."

Aha.

She hadn't considered that someone might have messed with her for a laugh.

Why not?

Because when they were passing out senses of humor, she was in another line demanding an extra helping of ego.

While she was mentally reviewing the skunk incident, I gave her something else to think about. "Penelope should have realized what was happening. She should have confronted the people leading the totem exercise. She should have made it clear the skunk thing was not only not funny, but ill-conceived *and* a risk to the future of their operation. After all, you're not just anyone, you're a national figure."

Iz nodded.

"At the very least, Penelope should have walked out with you."

I manufactured a lung-clearing sigh. "But that's all water under the bridge. At least this time, with this relationship, you didn't—"

Iz smacked the pencil against the table. "Didn't what?"

Thank goodness she stopped me. I'd almost said "didn't get dumped like before." I'd almost sloshed gasoline on the conversation and lit a match.

Iz had been dumped in a big way at least twice. Her official versions of those breakups, however, were far different from what I'd gleaned from unguarded comments and, in one case, a police report. "Didn't get too committed to Penelope before you realized you're all wrong for each other."

Iz picked up the pencil and wrote "organic Brazil nuts" on the list.

"Completely wrong," I continued. "Total opposites. I mean, she's *nothing* like you. She has a regular job. She owns a house. She irons her shirts."

I said that last bit in the same tone I'd use for "She kicks puppies."

Iz didn't look up as she wrote "Fresh. Check to be sure."

I rolled on, adopting a conspiratorial tone. "But all that is no big deal compared to the other stuff."

Iz underlined the last bit about checking the Brazil nuts. "Other stuff? What other stuff?"

All right. I had her attention. Now to attack her weak spot. If there was one thing Iz prided herself on the absolute most, it was being a unique and powerful self-made individual. An icon. "I mean the way Penelope has

145

been changing you, molding you into someone you're not. Everybody sees it."

(For the record, Penelope had never once suggested Iz so much as toss out a worn toothbrush or try a new brand of potato chip. Penelope is an eyes-open/no-expectations kind of person who accepts my sister as she is. Sure, she reserves the right to chuckle at some of Iz's foibles, but in a kindhearted and loving way—not like I was prone to do. Still, over the past few months Iz had changed in subtle ways. She no longer wore her hair in a Mohawk, she'd expanded her wardrobe, and once or twice she'd even expressed appreciation.)

I reached across the table and patted Iz's hand. "Trust me. You're better off without Penelope."

I waited five seconds and drew in a breath as if I'd experienced a jolt of mental lightning. "You know what? I'll bet she was part of that skunk joke. Maybe it was even her idea."

Iz smacked the pencil on the table again. "Penelope would never do something like that!"

I kept up the pressure. "Maybe. Maybe not. How well do you really know her? You've been together for only a few months and part of that time you were protesting or getting arrested or getting shot or recovering from getting shot. That didn't leave much time for figuring out what she was all about when she wasn't being your right-hand woman or nurse."

"And you're an expert on relationships?" Iz snapped the pencil in half. "Jake's living proof that *you* didn't take time to learn *anything* about *him* before racing down the aisle."

I hung my head, not in shame, but to hide a smile. As I knew she would, Iz took that as a sign she'd made a direct hit.

"I'll have you know," she said in a booming voice, "that Penelope is the kindest and most caring person on the planet. And I haven't changed. You're wrong about that, too."

She stood, kicked her chair over, and stalked to her suitcases, the slight scent of skunk trailing her. "I don't know why I put up with you. I don't know why I think the next time we have a conversation you'll be sane and rational instead of a babbling idiot."

I kept my head down and pressed my fists against my lips to contain my mirth.

"Don't bother to get up. And don't offer to give me a ride. After your attack on Penelope, I don't want to spend one more minute in your presence. I'll call a cab."

With the grace of a squid mounting a skateboard, Iz shouldered her backpack and gripped her suitcases.

Not trusting myself to speak without joyful cackling, I waved one hand in what I hoped she'd mistake for a lifeless, hopeless, farewell salute. Then I waited.

A suitcase thudded in the hall. Iz cursed. The door whacked against the wall. A suitcase scraped across the threshold. The door slammed.

I counted to 20, then kicked off my sandals and scurried along the hallway. Hunkering behind the door, I peered through the narrow window beside it. Iz had her phone to her ear and her suitcases in a jumble at the curb.

Perfect.

I snatched my purse from the office, dug out my phone, and punched in Penelope's number.

She picked up after five rings, the thwack of hammers and the whine of saws in the background. "Barbara? Tell me you heard from Iz!"

"Heard her. Seen her. Argued with her. In other words, relationship as usual. I hope you want her back, because she's outside right now calling a cab to take her to your house."

Penelope gasped. "Really? She's coming home to me?"

"There are a lot of things I might fib about, Penelope, but the impending arrival of my sister isn't one of them. Nor is the fact that she carries with her a faint but cloying odor of skunk."

I peeped out the window as Iz put her phone in her pocket. "I think the cab is on the way. This is your last chance to move and leave no forwarding address."

Penelope didn't laugh. Instead, she sniffed and said in a wistful voice, "I wish I wasn't in the middle of a job so I could be there to meet her."

I kept my lips zipped and didn't inform Penelope that Iz would survive. In fact, she'd likely take advantage of being alone in the house to snack away the afternoon.

"I thought after what happened and the way she left . . . well, you know how proud she is, how important it is for her to be right."

"I know that better than anyone. And I'm not ashamed to say that I used that knowledge to steer her back to you. I told her you two are all wrong for each other."

"But I don't think we're—"

"I said that so she'd want to prove me wrong."

"Oh."

"Then I suggested the skunk thing was a practical joke and hinted you might have been behind it. I know that's harsh—and certainly not true—but she leaped to your defense and kicked her suitcases to the street."

"You're a genius!"

I patted myself on the back. "Don't let her hear you say that. She thinks I don't have a single brain cell in my head."

"Well I think you're brilliant. I'm going to give you a big hug and buy you a year's supply of cheesy snacks."

Spoken like a woman who had no idea of the extent of my addiction. "The hug will be more than enough, Penelope. Besides, it has no calories."

I disconnected and got busy spreading the news to Allison ("Thank Gawd she's gone."), Mrs. B ("Penelope is such a dear."), Dario ("Penelope should have her head examined."), and members of the Committee.

After I erased a message from Jake that came in while I was next door, I got busy making a pre-lunch snack (potato chips, hummus, and two baby carrots) to sustain me before opening the pink three-ring binder Dave bought for current events. The idea was that Allison would cut a news story from the paper at least four days a week, staple it on a page, and write a paragraph of complete sentences explaining why the story was important to the world or community, and what it meant to her.

To my total lack of surprise, Allison spent hours decorating the notebook cover with nail polish, glitter, and photos of Josh. I expected to find nothing beyond that, but discovered one article. It was the story of the first set of huge footprints behind Start 'er Up Auto Repair, and Allison had folded it so all I saw was Gnome Guy. Way to make my day. On the opposite side of the page she'd written: "Bigfoot could be in Reckless River. I don't care, but I'm glad my feet aren't that huge. I'd never find cute shoes."

As you can guess, I was thrilled beyond words to note she was taking this assignment seriously. What would she write after seeing a story about Woodrow Krammer's murder and the footprints found at the scene? "Bigfoot bumps off Krammee's owner. Food might improve."

Rummaging through the newspaper recycling heap, I accumulated a stack of local news sections and highlighted a dozen stories that could have an impact on our lives: gasoline prices, a proposed tax hike, coal and oil shipments, and a new supermarket opening not far away. Unlike Iz, Allison was generally shrewd enough to skip around my attempts at manipulation, so I stacked the clippings beside the notebook and took the direct approach.

"Your father intends to review your current events notebook when he gets home," I said as I led the dogs past her lounge chair. "Unless you like being grounded, you should get busy."

"But I'm covered with oil," she whined. "I'll get stains all over the notebook."

"Coincidentally, soap removes oil and there's a room upstairs with a big bar of soap by the thing called a sink. And another bar in the shower. Besides, you've been out in the sun long enough."

Allison groaned and muttered that Dave and I were mean and didn't love her and yada, yada, yada. For a few seconds I felt pangs of concern. If Allison's long-lost mother turned up and tried to reconnect with the child she abandoned, she wouldn't have a history of "being mean" and therefore might seem more attractive.

I put that thought aside, checked to make sure Monster Mutt wasn't in sight, and opened the gate to the rose garden. Every bush was badly in need of pruning. Not that there were all that many—only a quartet in my area—but these were huge and healthy bushes. Fat yellow and red blooms released showers of petals as I passed, and a thorn raked my elbow.

Jim and Dario were at work in the burned-over area, trimming tall grass to within a few inches of the ground and raking charred bark mulch. "Checking to make sure nothing is smoldering," Jim said. "Supposed to be hot and windy this afternoon. Don't want this to rekindle."

Dario loaded scorched mulch in a black plastic garbage bag. "I bought some heavy-duty wire to reinforce the lattice in case that thing returns."

I eyed the area beneath Mrs. B's deck and my own. "What about the other decks?"

"With the slope of the ground, there are only three high enough to give him a comfortable shelter. He'd have to crawl through the rose bushes to get under yours or Muriel's. This deck is farthest from the dogs and had the most cover." Jim chopped at another hummock of tall grass. "Until now."

Lola and Cheese Puff sniffed their way up the slope to where the lattice hung askew, and poked their heads through the opening. "Get away from there," I ordered. "Come."

Lola raised her head, glanced my way, and appeared to consider my command. Cheese Puff slipped through the gap and under the deck.

"He's okay," Jim said. "There's no broken glass and we got all the towels and food out."

151

Knowing it was in vain, I called for Cheese Puff to come. As if to console me, Lola trudged to my side and licked my wrist. Dario tied off the trash bag and growled out a threat to tell Mrs. Ballantine. That did it. Cheese Puff emerged, head high and prancing in his self-important little way.

"I guess we missed whatever this is." Dario scooped him up and pried an object from his jaws. "A punch card."

I'd seen a poster advertising punch cards like this while I was talking with the Krammee twins. I wondered if they'd been informed of their father's death, wondered how they reacted when they got the news. I tried to work up a sense of sorrow for his death and their loss, but what I'd seen of Woodrow Krammer I hadn't liked. And the same went for Brooklyn and Manhattan. I decided to confess my lack of grief and regret to Mrs. Ballantine later—after the news of Krammer's death became public and I was free to talk.

I pointed to the logo in the corner of the card and watched Dario. If he killed Woodrow Krammer, I might see a flicker in his eyes or some other tell. If I did, I'd report it to Dave when I reminded him about Dario's threat. "It's a freebie card. At Krammee's. It's good for ten orders of fries. You get one if you spend $50.00 or more on burgers. Then you show it when you order and they punch it every time they give you free fries."

Dario gave no sign of being rattled when I mentioned Krammee's, so I hit it again. "Fifty bucks is a lot to spend on burgers, especially at a cut-rate restaurant like Krammee's."

Nothing. But then, if Dario was even 10% of the thug he let on, he'd have years of practice pretending disinterested innocence. Or perhaps he thought about

152

disposing of someone like Woodrow Krammer the way most of us think about taking out the garbage—something insignificant you did so you could get on with the rest of the day, and something you could erase from your mind once the task was done.

"It's got three punches left." Dario handed Cheese Puff to me and untied the trash bag. "That's three bouts of indigestion I can prevent if I toss it."

"Why would Bigfoot have a punch card?" Jim asked. "I thought he ate nuts and roots and berries."

"Or hunted down forest creatures and killed them with his furry fingers." Dario examined the grubby rectangle of white cardboard. "Do you suppose he found this? Or bought it?"

"You can't buy them anywhere except Krammee's," I said, watching Dario again.

Not a hint of a reaction.

"And your point is?" Jim asked.

"That thing we saw was huge. Someone would notice if he strolled up to the counter."

"Not if everyone in the place is a teenager," Dario said. "Like Allison, the girl who doesn't notice the only tree in the lot where we practice driving."

"They're not all like Allison. You'd be surprised how observant some of them can be." For example, the day I wore mismatched socks to sub in U.S. History, half the kids in each class spotted my fashion fumble as they came in the door.

Jim shrugged. "Okay, maybe they noticed that he was an XXXLT, but would they be likely to tell anyone except other teenagers?"

He had me there. "Maybe not."

"Okay," Dario said. "Let's go with 'found it' and let's suppose he uses the greenbelt as a highway. It links our condos, the auto repair shop, and Krammee's. So maybe someone dropped this card in the Krammee's parking lot and he picked it up."

"I'll buy that," Jim said. "Except I wonder *why* he picked it up. Taking towels from the pool, that makes sense. They're soft and maybe he's seen people drying themselves or lying on them. But that card is nothing more than a worthless scrap of paper unless you understand how to use it to get food."

"Hmmm." Dario studied the card once more. "Maybe he saw someone exchange it for a bag of fries and picked up on the concept of trade and barter."

"All right, I'll give him credit for the ability to reason that out. But we're back to him walking up to the counter and being seen," Jim said.

"Does Krammee's have a drive-up window?" Dario asked me.

"I don't remember seeing one. But maybe."

"If it does, and he was lurking nearby, maybe that's where he saw the exchange. And maybe that's where he redeemed the card."

"And that brings us around to someone noticing him," I said.

"Maybe the lighting is poor at the drive-up," Jim suggested. "Maybe he stood off to one side."

I set Cheese Puff down, snapped on his leash, and led the dogs west and away from Monster Mutt's territory. "I'll let you two hash that over. I'm going for a walk."

I strolled away, relieved that neither of them asked why I was home so early.

CHAPTER 17

When I returned, Josh was sitting on the deck catching rays, his Krammee's shirt crumpled at his feet. He seemed broader and bulkier than he had a few months ago. Lugging sacks of fries and mopping floors at Krammee's seemed to be having a physical effect.

"Allison's taking a shower," he said. "Is it okay if we go to a movie after she finishes the laundry and her current events project?"

"Fine with me." I unhooked leashes and the dogs darted inside. "But I thought you were working all day."

"I was supposed to be." He shrugged. "But I got fired."

"Fired?" I dropped into the chair beside him. "Because of me? Because I came to talk to you?"

Josh shook his head, his fine hair lifting and settling with the motion. "Chill, Ms. Reed. It has nothing to do with you" He lowered his voice. "Mr. Krammer got killed last night."

Uh oh.

If Josh knew, and if he told Allison, then the proverbial cat was not only out of the bag, but also scampering around social media sites. In which case, my promise to Dave was null and void.

"They told me not to tell anyone." Josh leaned closer. "But I figured that doesn't mean you, because you probably already know because you're, like, always in the middle of the crime stuff that happens."

Now *that* was something to put on my resume. Every school in the state wants to hire a teacher who was always in the middle of "crime stuff that happens."

Not.

"Uh, yeah. I know Krammer was killed." Despite Josh's ringing endorsement of my talent—or lack of talent—I refrained from painting myself into the picture as the one who discovered Krammer's body. "His body was dumped behind the auto repair shop and the police shut it down for the day. Did they close Krammee's too?"

"Yeah. For two days. Maybe more. Tomorrow they're gonna have guys going through everything, even the garbage." Josh mimed gagging himself. "It's bad enough to open those bins to throw stuff in. I sure wouldn't want to pull stuff out. Especially when it's so hot."

I nodded agreement, then did a double take worthy of a cartoon character. "Wait a minute. If the place is shut down for only a few days, why were you fired?"

"Because after the cops got our names and addresses and stuff, Brooklyn and Manhattan said they're in charge." He kicked the Krammee's shirt. "They told me I made everybody else look bad, so I had to get out and never come back."

I swallowed three or four X-rated comments. "I hope they paid you all you were due. If they didn't, I'll see about—"

"Mr. Krammer wrote the checks. They don't even know how. But it's cool." Josh pulled a roll of bills from the pocket of his khaki slacks. "They didn't let me stick around to find the rake I bought to break up the ice in the soda machine, but they handed me a bunch of money from the safe."

Sheesh.

Some secure financial system. Krammer's feral daughters didn't know how to write checks, but they knew the combination to the safe. I gave Krammee's a week before business flatlined. Unless, like some speculated, it was a money-laundering operation or a front of some sort. "And you're okay with this?"

"Totally." He riffled the roll of bills. "I got a month's pay that I don't have to work for."

I didn't mention that a few movie and dinner dates with Allison would put a huge crater in his cash. "Want some lunch while you're waiting for Allison?"

"I'm good. Took a sack of burgers and a bunch of fries on the way out. I'm bummed about my rake, though. I always left it on top of the soda machine, but it wasn't there. My mom could have used it in her garden. Hers is old and rusty." He stood. "I'll hit Mrs. B's until Allison is ready. I have an idea for a number for her routine, sort of Lawrence Welk meets Warren Zevon."

"Interesting," I said in the most neutral tone I could manage while trying to imagine "Werewolves Of London" as a polka.

He ambled to Mrs. B's door, knocked, exchanged a fist bump with Dario, and disappeared from view.

Part of me wanted to zip in after him and see what Mrs. B thought of his idea, but most of me wanted lunch.

As usual, the "Chow! Now!" campaign launched by my fat cells triumphed.

After a cream cheese and olive sandwich, I made a grocery list—Iz had a valid point about the nutritional value of the contents of the refrigerator—and a list of errands to be run when Detective Atwell allowed me to retrieve my car from the crime scene. Allison clattered upstairs and down again, hauling laundry and sighing deeply each time she passed. Sighs turned to swearing when she discovered shredded tissue stuck to everything in the washer tub.

"I checked the pockets like you told me," she wailed. "I know I did."

I doubted her claim, but figured this lesson would stay with her far longer than my words of caution. "Most of that should come off in the dryer. You'll have to clean the lint trap more often than usual, though."

A blank look told me she'd forgotten the lint trap part of the laundry routine. Amazed the dryer hadn't overheated or caught fire, I pointed to the trap, waited until I saw her grasp the handle and pull out the screen, then went to the office to surf the Internet for information about Bigfoot.

Well aware that "information" and "accurate information" weren't necessarily the same, I winnowed out much of what I came across—shaky videos taken from an extreme distance, indistinct footprints in mud or snow, and shots of Bigfoot at a ball game, eating pizza, or being sworn in to Congress along with two aliens and the ghost of Thomas Jefferson. I read about Skamania County's Bigfoot Ordinance, the Bigfoot trap in the Siskiyou

National Forest, the museum and study center in Willow Creek, California, and sightings hither, thither, and yon.

I bookmarked a few sites, got out a yellow pad, and jotted bits of lore—hair samples with DNA that allegedly didn't match any other creatures, footprints with dermal ridges, and theories about sleeping habits, stench, and stride.

When Allison called to tell me she was ready, I checked the status of the laundry and the current events notebook. Both were in satisfactory shape—if you stood at a distance and squinted while blanking out the concept of minimal standards. The laundry was washed and dried, but folded like origami. The news articles were stapled to pages with little regard for alignment and the comments were less analytical than they were self-centered or sarcastic.

For a few seconds I found myself warming to the idea of Allison's mother reclaiming her. Then I recalled my own aversion to chores as a child, reminded myself this had been Dave's idea, and sent her off with Josh. After a few moments spent refolding my T-shirts and ignoring the others, I went to the pool.

Clad in flowered swimsuit cover ups, Verna and Sybil were leaving when I arrived. "That big dog's outside the fence," Sybil said.

"Monster Mutt? The one from up the way?"

"Yes. He's dug a foxhole in the bark mulch under a rhododendron." Verna pointed to the far side of the pool area.

"He kept looking at us and slavering." Sybil shuddered. "I'm afraid he's going to bite someone. Or maul a child. Bernina says she's going to have a talk with the owner, but—"

"We don't believe that for a minute. Everyone's scared he'll sue for every penny they have." Verna patted the capacious leather purse that seldom left her side. "Jim's looking into the laws, though, and Muriel says she'll hire the best lawyer around, and Dario—"

"Says some dark night that dog might disappear." Sybil snapped her fingers. "Without a trace."

"I told him we didn't want the dog dead," Verna added, "just gone."

"And he said he knew a guy who knew a guy." Sybil frowned. "I have no idea what that means."

"It means we shouldn't ask who any of those guys are," Verna said. "Now let's leave Barbara to enjoy the water. If she can with that beast watching her every move."

Good point. I was self-conscious enough in a bathing suit when I was alone in the dark.

I set my gear on a low plastic table and walked to the far side of the pool. Sure enough, Monster Mutt had dug deep into the cool earth, doing no favors to the root structure of the rhododendrons. One bush canted against the fence and the leaves of another appeared gray and brittle. The beast raised his head and stared at me with malevolent eyes that reminded me of the Krammee twins. "Your days on this property are numbered," I warned him. "The Committee is on it. And when the Committee is on it, things happen."

Not always things that were *supposed* to happen. But Monster Mutt didn't need to know that.

I set my glasses on a low table and then, keeping my back to him, I did a lazy sidestroke in the tepid water and thought about what I'd read on the various sites I'd trolled. Theories about Bigfoot abounded, but most boiled down to a few basic assumptions—these creatures were rare, tended to be cautious, fled from humans, and lived in areas where their need for protein could be satisfied.

If that was true, what was this particular Bigfoot doing in the heart of Reckless River? Was he—or she—disoriented? Searching for a mate? Driven by hunger to the city and its thousands of garbage cans?

Possibly. But why would a creature billed as cautious and elusive pick such a busy place to den up? People jogged and walked along the river trail from sunup until long after sundown. Residents visited from deck to deck. Cheese Puff and Lola and a platoon of other dogs must have trotted within a few yards of him.

I shivered, got my feet on the bottom, and gripped the wall. One report claimed Bigfoot would tear into threatening dogs.

Given his miniscule size, Cheese Puff was hardly threatening. And Lola was mellow—unless one of us was in danger. I hoped Jim and Dario were right and the creature wouldn't return. But, as I squinted and glanced around the pool area, I saw the appeal of hanging out here—an abandoned towel, an outdoor shower, lounge chairs, umbrellas, and a trash can. There was even a toilet and sink in a small room behind the pool gear storage area. Maybe the creature had figured out how to flush. Maybe it had figured out a lot of other things, adapted to city life, and thought of this as its territory.

Territory?

Some reports claimed Bigfoot might stalk or harass humans entering what it perceived as its domain. Had the creature considered the garbage area behind Krammee's its domain? Had Woodrow Krammer found it rummaging through a bin and tried to chase it off?

I could visual a brief chase, a grappling fight, a dead burger magnate. What I *couldn't* visualize was Bigfoot getting behind the wheel of Krammer's car and driving to the auto repair shop to dump the body.

In fact, I couldn't visualize anyone—anyone who thought it through—doing that. What was the point of moving a body if you weren't going to hide both it and the vehicle you used to move it? Why take the risk of driving the body to another location—a spot no more private than the first?

If Woodrow Krammer was killed behind Krammee's, why not drag his body into the greenbelt from there? And why dump him behind the auto repair shop? Why not in a more remote area? Or in the river?

I pushed off from the wall and did another lap, thinking about the process of dragging a body. Closing my eyes, I brought up a mental image of those footprints I'd spotted. The distance from the toe of one print to the heel of the next was close to a yard. And the distance the tracks were offset from each other was far more than a foot.

Some of the Bigfoot sites contended the stride was longer and the footprints more in a single line than the ones I saw this morning. But if Bigfoot was walking backwards and dragging a 200-pound man, his stride might be significantly shorter and he might broaden his stance for better balance and more power.

Arrggghhh.

If I kept on like this, I'd soon be conferring with Gnome Guy.

I turned a somersault to clear my mind, but again returned to the image of Bigfoot behind the wheel. With enough supportive arguments and a frothy drink to grease the skids in my brain, I *might* buy the idea of him grasping the purpose of the Krammee's punch card by watching through a window as someone used it. But driving was more complicated—even with an automatic shift and power steering. There were intersections, signs, and traffic lights.

And then there were the tiny details of driving, like fitting the key in the slot. A creature with hands that matched the feet that left those prints might have trouble holding a key. And what about adjusting the seat and mirrors? Clicking his seatbelt? Tuning the radio?

I flipped to the other side and stroked on through the warm water, wondering about Bigfoot's top-ten song list. "Wooly Bully" sprang to mind. So did "Catch Us If You Can" and "I Like Big Butts." Would crime scene technicians check to see if he messed with the radio preset buttons on Krammer's car?

Okay, I'd crossed the line between speculation and hallucination. But the fact remained—if Bigfoot was as hairy as conventional wisdom indicated, and if he'd been in that car, there should be plenty of evidence.

And if it wasn't Bigfoot in the car, if it was, say, Dario wearing oversized rubber feet, there should be evidence of that, too.

But why would Dario go to so much trouble—so much pointless trouble—to move the body? And why would he take a chance on leaving evidence behind? He'd been clear about paying Krammer a visit at a time when there would be no witnesses. Surely if he'd killed Krammer he wouldn't risk running into someone afterward—especially if he was wearing rubber feet.

Unless Dario, who knew we knew he was a professional, had gone to ridiculous lengths to point the finger of suspicion away.

Arrggghhh to the tenth power.

My brain cells were tying themselves in knots and my theories were getting more convoluted and preposterous by the minute. At this rate even Gnome Guy would suggest I seek help from a mental health expert.

I turned another somersault and resorted to a tried-and-true technique for driving everything else out of my brain—counting all the different brands and types of cheesy snacks I'd ever devoured.

It was well after dark when Dave returned, pulled off his muddy shoes, and flung himself on the sofa with a sigh that sounded like a hot air balloon deflating.

"I haven't seen anything on the TV news or the Internet." I handed him a beer. "That's good, right?"

He drank half the bottle before he came up for air. "Chuck leaned on the editor to hold the story for the morning edition. Leaned on everyone else to keep it off social media. I'm amazed the Krammee twins went along. They seemed less than impressed with his badge."

Dave drank more beer. "But about five minutes after the paper lands on Reckless River doorsteps, the TV trucks will roll and the media barrage will begin. Every reporter in the country will want in on it. Every Bigfoot hunter, too."

And there were a lot of them. I knew that from my afternoon of research at the computer. Some hunted with cameras. Others hunted with guns. Add public excitement, stir in fear, whip in media hype, and it was a recipe for disaster.

The floor heaved.

My stomach did the same.

Someone could get hurt. Or killed.

I clutched at the back of the sofa and slumped across the armrest. "Did . . . did Missoula find a trail?"

"Yeah, when Sergeant Bender finally let him put his nose in the grass to sniff. Like I said, Chuck got on the wrong side of Bender. It will be a cold day in hell before they kiss and make up."

Dave finished his beer. "Bender took his sweet time getting to the scene, but Missoula followed someone—or something—about a mile this way along the greenbelt to a wide pond. That's where whomever—or whatever—they were trailing went into the water. Missoula tried to follow, but Bender pulled him off."

"Because of the water?"

"Officially because they were losing the light. Bender said it was too dangerous to go on."

"And unofficially?"

"Chuck wanted him to keep going and move faster. Called Bender a coward."

"That Atwell, what a people person."

"Yeah, if the department had a works-and-plays-well-with-others award, Chuck wouldn't win it. Anyway, Bender said Chuck was welcome to wade in if he wanted to, but only idiots would go into the night after a creature with claws like the ones that tore out Woodrow Krammer's throat."

CHAPTER 18

My stomach flipped and I slapped a hand over my mouth.

I'd seen the blood on Woodrow Krammer's shoes, but I hadn't considered its source or the nature of his wound. I hadn't wanted to. "Tore out his throat?"

"Ripped it wide open. Down to the spine. Ripped up his face and arms, too."

The room spun. I closed my eyes and thanked my lucky stars that when I perched on the picnic table, I saw only Woodrow Krammer's feet.

Then I did a quick mental review of the pictures I'd studied on the Internet. Did those Bigfoot creatures have claws? Claw marks hadn't been part of the footprints we found last week, but maybe Bigfoot didn't have claws on his feet, or maybe he could retract them like a cat. And not seeing marks on footprints certainly didn't mean his *hands* were clawless.

The claw angle—at least in my mind—took Dario off the list of suspects. Strangulation or a bullet in the back of the head seemed more his style. Unless—and I returned to the image of Dario donning huge rubber feet and dragging

Krammer's body—his intention had been to cast suspicion on Bigfoot.

If Dario didn't do it, was Bigfoot the killer?

Up until this moment I'd thought of the creature as fairly harmless. Sure, his size made him a little scary. And the fact that no one *really* knew much fed that fear. And there *were* a few reports that mentioned death and destruction. But despite that, I'd considered Bigfoot to be fascinating, even a source of entertainment.

There was nothing entertaining about claws capable of ripping a throat open—claws that apparently *had* ripped a throat open.

"They've got officers on the bridges that cross over the greenbelt, and more guys going door to door in neighborhoods nearby. They're urging people to turn on outside lights, lock doors and windows, and call 911 if they see or hear anything odd."

"I hope they brought in more 911 operators. Some people have a loose definition of 'odd.' Your daughter, for instance."

A smile flickered across Dave's face and he patted my hand. "They'll bring in more dogs and troops tomorrow. Probably put a chopper up. He won't get away. Don't worry."

The odd thing was that, despite the stomach flips, I wasn't all that worried about the creature remaining on the loose and hurting others. I was far more worried about others getting between Bigfoot and a bullet.

Mostly I was confused. And any way I examined this whole mess, the more confused I became.

If Bigfoot had stuffed Krammer's body in the car and driven it to the auto repair shop, then he was far above the level of simple forest creature in a whole lot of mental and physical ways. A simple forest creature might have attacked Krammer, but then most likely dashed.

Or dined.

Perhaps that explained the injuries to Krammer's face and chest.

(For the record, in case you think I'm making light of Krammer's death, I don't think he deserved to die, and certainly not the way he did. But I wonder if John Donne would have thought twice about using the word "diminishes" if he'd had a run-in with Woodrow Krammer before he wrote his poem about the tolling bell and no man being an island.)

I got another beer for Dave, lifted his feet, and squeezed onto the end of the sofa. "Has Atwell called in a Bigfoot expert to check those footprints to make sure they're not fakes?"

Dave snorted beer through his nose. "Are you listening to yourself? Are you aware you used the words 'Bigfoot expert' in that sentence?"

I did a quick mental replay. "Um, yeah."

"And you don't find that odd?"

A week ago I might have, but after listening to Gnome Guy expound on the points he felt indicated authenticity and my afternoon of research, my previously firm opinions were wobbling. Recognizing that, however, didn't mean I wanted to admit it.

So, time to change the subject. "The Krammee twins fired Josh."

Dave tipped a thumb up. "That's a positive career move."

"Yeah, he's not in mourning. He and Allison are out spending some of his severance pay. The girls gave him a wad of cash from the safe. Josh said they didn't know how to write a check."

"But they can get into the safe." Dave rolled his eyes. "The company accountant will love that. Or maybe not. Paying in cash could be business as usual for Krammee's if rumors are true. What's Josh planning to do now?"

"Hang out with Allison. Work on songs for Mrs. B for when she's on *Still Got That Strut.*"

Dave rolled his eyes again. "She's never going to do that show."

"Of course she is. She'll sign the contract as soon as she finds the right music and choreographs a number. And then Dario will get the wheels rolling."

"The wheels won't roll if the brakes are locked."

"Thank you, Mr. Words to Live By. She's been practicing routines every day."

"And changing her mind about them every other day."

"Well, yeah. She wants it to be right. She was famous in her day. Why wouldn't she want to be on the show?"

"Because she was famous in her day. This isn't that day."

"You're the king of pithy sayings tonight, aren't you?"

He saluted me with the beer bottle. "As confident as she seems, I think she's afraid of returning to Vegas—no matter how good she looks for her age."

True again. I was starting to get seriously annoyed with Dave for making me rethink. But then he checked his watch and said those magic words. "Allison won't be home until curfew. If we took the dogs out for a quick trot right now, we'd have plenty of time to spend upstairs."

Every nerve ending in my body tingled. Still, the man had mocked me—sort of. "Upstairs doing what?"

"You were at a crime scene this morning. I think a trained police officer should conduct a search to make certain no evidence was transferred to your body."

"What kind of a search?"

"A strip search. A thorough and time-consuming strip search."

I shivered. "Will you need special equipment?"

He leered. "*All* my equipment is special."

Dave was up before dawn and off with Lola at first light, but not before tossing the paper on the bed beside me and muttering that Chuck Atwell must be spitting nails.

When I rubbed sleep from my eyes, I saw an enormous headline: BIGFOOT SUSPECTED OF MURDER.

Before I read my way to the second page, Larry called to tell me to forget about coming to work—police had ordered the shop shut down for another day.

"What about our cars?"

"Still being processed. But even if you had wheels, you'd have to park half a mile from here. There are reporters and photographers and sightseers everywhere. Doug maxed out his credit card ordering more paraphernalia to sell when we open again."

Imagining Doug shopping for all things Bigfoot, I drifted to sleep, my mind awash with the merchandizing I'd spotted yesterday. In addition to mugs and T-shirts and hats, I'd come across lights, key chains, shot glasses, garden statues, bumper stickers, watches, and even business cards and a driver's license.

With that image in my mind, I settled into a dream about Dario passing the driving-lessons torch to Bigfoot. A hairy creature with what most contended was significant body odor would raise Allison's drama output to new levels. It might also speed up the learning process. Not that we were anxious to have her on the road.

I woke up, smiling, and glanced at the clock. 8:27.

Practically noon—at least to someone accustomed to crawling out at 5:30 in order to make it to a high school subbing assignment before 7:00.

Throwing on a T-shirt, shorts, and flip-flops, I raked my fingers through my hair and hustled downstairs with the paper in my hand and Cheese Puff close behind. I poured a cup of coffee—thick and slightly burnt after simmering in the pot since Dave made it—and clicked on the TV to find Gnome Guy in full cry, demanding to study both the footprints and the body.

"Any fool knows Bigfoot would have snapped Woodrow Krammer's neck instead of tearing it open," he told an aging male reporter with a comb-over lifting in the breeze to reveal a shiny bald spot.

Not good. And I don't mean the bald spot. The fact that Gnome Guy knew about the wound indicated a leak from Detective Atwell's team.

I didn't envy Dave.

And I didn't envy myself if Dave was foolish enough to admit he told me how Krammer died. Atwell wouldn't believe I hadn't blabbed to the immediate world.

Gnome Guy's interview gave way to video of the park where last week the newspaper reported a sighting of something that might have been Bigfoot. A young reporter with puffy blond hair strolled into view talking with a woman leading a black Cocker Spaniel and gesturing at a stand of trees. So much for that woman's earlier desire to remain anonymous.

171

An artist's sketch of Bigfoot popped up next.

Cheese Puff whined, ran to the TV, stood on his hind legs, placed his front paws on the image, and wagged his tail.

Odd.

Usually Cheese Puff paid no attention to the television unless someone set a plate of cookies beside it or a dog barked as part of a program. "You know that guy?"

Cheese Puff whined and pawed at the screen. The image was replaced by grainy film shot from such a distance the creature in the forest was nothing more than a dark blur. Cheese Puff growled until the video gave way to an interview with Detective Charles Atwell. Then he growled louder.

"I know he's Dave's buddy," I told Cheese Puff, "but I feel the same way. He's not a people person. He's not a dog person either." I clicked off the TV and opened the door to the deck. "Let's check the great outdoors."

It was a sparkler of a day. Clear blue sky. Light breeze rippling the river. Aromas of bacon, toasting bread, and fresh coffee.

I gravitated toward the source of those aromas, goodies Mrs. B and Dario were setting out for breakfast—fruit salad, bagels, cream cheese, and coffee that smelled a heck of a lot better than the sludge in my cup.

"Now I know why you were home early yesterday." Dario tapped the newspaper in the center of the table.

"I'll get a plate and cup and you can tell us all about it," Mrs. B called. "And I have a special treat for the little prince—once he takes care of business."

As if he understood his assignment, Cheese Puff raced to the gate. I trotted behind, peered up the trail to make sure Monster Mutt was nowhere in sight, and opened the latch. Cheese Puff watered a rose bush, left a deposit beside another, and raced for the steps. By that time Mrs. B had placed a silk cushion on a chair for him, set his special plate—with his picture in the center and initials in gold repeating around the rim—beside hers, and was dicing rare roast beef plucked from a white doggie bag.

Dario glanced at me and rolled his eyes. "I shelled out $47 for that last night. And put up with the world's snootiest waiter. Guy had a stick so far up his butt it made a bump on his head. Full as I was, I would have used a spoon handle to stuff my gullet if I knew that meat would be a mutt's breakfast instead of my lunch."

"Now, Dario." Mrs. B settled Cheese Puff on the cushion and pushed the chair closer to the table. "The little prince deserves a treat now and then."

"If it was only now and then I wouldn't complain. But it's now, then, and every minute in between."

Cheese Puff smirked and gobbled a tiny chunk of beef.

"Better get used to playing second fiddle or find another orchestra." I patted Dario's head, filled my cup with coffee from a silver pot, and poured cream from a crystal pitcher. "Have you seen any signs that our huge and hairy friend returned to his lair beneath the deck? Dave says the tracking dog trailed him along the greenbelt in this direction before they called off the search for the night."

Dario nodded toward the condo next door. "I checked this morning. No prints. The wire was in place."

"TV reporters think he's bottled up around that marshy pond." Mrs. B sat and spread a napkin on her lap. "But he could have slipped past the officers on guard during the night."

"If I was on guard I'd let him pass," Dario said. "And hand him a civic improvement award for bumping off Woodrow Krammer."

"Now, Dario." Mrs. B tapped a silver spoon on the rim of her cup. "Of course you don't mean that."

But we all knew he did.

Dario didn't answer, and in a moment Mrs. B squeezed his hand and moved the conversation along. "Well, I'm certainly glad you and Jim fixed it so that creature won't be lurking under my deck."

"Oh." I reached for half of an onion bagel toasted to perfection. "Did you reinforce the lattice behind the rose gardens after all?"

"We did Muriel's part. Then we ran out of wire. And time. I'm flying to Vegas this afternoon and Jim's got commitments. The dogs will be a deterrent."

He cast a glance at Cheese Puff. "Or at least Lola will. Hairy as that creature is, he'll avoid the thorns on your overgrown rose bushes."

Given that they were now considered a safety feature, I scrapped my plan to prune the roses today.

Well, to be honest, it wasn't exactly a plan. It was more of a seed of a fleeting thought. A really dry and shriveled seed that might sprout after about, say, 40 days and nights of rain.

"Oh, by the way, dear," Mrs. B said, "Jake called last night."

At the mention of my ex-husband's name, Cheese Puff growled and snapped his tiny teeth.

CHAPTER 19

"How much money did Jake want?" I asked.

Cheese Puff growled again. Given his size, it wasn't a sound that would terrify anything larger than a hamster or perhaps an anemic squirrel, but I gave him a pat on the head for trying.

"I don't believe that came up. We had a nice chat about the changes he's making in his life."

I slathered cream cheese on my bagel and plugged my mouth with a huge bite. While I chewed, I tried not to think too hard about the student debt that wouldn't be quite as gigantic if Jake hadn't siphoned off my savings.

Dario executed yet another eye roll, the implication being Mrs. B was far more forgiving of Jake than any human should be.

"Jake's doing very well in jail. He's teaching classes on finance and physical education and how to use social media to find employment. He tells me he's practically one of the staff."

And I'm practically a size four.

I stuffed my mouth once more and chewed in what might be taken for a thoughtful manner by someone extremely nearsighted. The way Mrs. B aimed her forefinger like the barrel of a gun told me she wasn't fooled and knew I was mentally dissing my ex.

"The reason he called is that he has something important to discuss with you."

Jake's idea of important usually hinged on the benefit to him—never mind how it might adversely affect others. "Did he tell you what that something is?"

"No."

"And you didn't try to wheedle it out of him?"

She blushed. Meaning she wheedled, but he didn't cave. "He told me twice that it's very important."

"Ah, *very* important. Well, that's certainly specific."

Mrs. B jabbed the finger in my direction. "He's been trying to reach you for days but you don't return his calls."

Spoken as if he could take my call day or night. As if he had a phone in the pocket of whatever fashionable garments they doled out in jail. If those garments even had pockets.

I swallowed and centered the remaining chunk of bagel on my plate. "And why does he think I haven't called? Because I lost his number? Forgot how to punch it in? Had my fingers removed?"

Mrs. B chopped her hand at me, rings sparkling. "Haven't we talked about taking such a negative approach to life? Jake has learned a good many lessons in the past few months and he's had a lot of time for self-examination. He wants to be a better person. He's trying. People change, you know."

Did they? Or was that another myth?

Tough call.

It all depended on how you defined the word "change" and whether you were talking about an alteration in core character, or about minor or cosmetic adjustments. It also hung on whether you meant change for the better.

Some people, like the leopard in that old saying, couldn't change their spots. Jake went into jail a charming, fast-talking con artist. Proof he hadn't changed was the glib claim he was "practically one of the staff."

"It was me," Dario muttered, "I'd call Jake the day he and I were the last living creatures on earth and I was hungry."

I choked on a laugh. Mrs. B glowered at both of us. Cheese Puff seized opportunity and pawed at a pat of butter on her plate. His effort left claw marks that made me think of Woodrow Krammer's throat. My appetite went south.

I finished the coffee, but wrapped the remains of the bagel in a napkin to go. Cheese Puff tagged along into our condo, belching with satisfaction as he leaped into his favorite chair and snuggled into the gap between the cushion and the side. Facing up to chores, I got to work scrubbing the sink and emptying the dishwasher. I'd about worked up to unwrapping the bagel when the phone rang.

Jake?

I checked the tiny screen on the answering machine.

Not Jake.

But almost as bad. It was Aston Marsden, the Captain Meriwether High School history teacher who spent his free time dressing as a mountain man and taking part in historical reenactments.

It being summer, Aston wouldn't be calling to ask me to cover his classes. That left two possibilities. One, he wanted me to take part in a reenactment wearing something I suspected would be hot and uncomfortable or, worse yet, skimpy and demeaning. Two, despite his involvement with fellow teacher Brenda Waring and despite my involvement with Dave, he had romantic intentions. He'd recently expressed those by telling me how well I'd fill out a revealing reenactment costume.

"In your dreams," I told the phone. "There's no way I'll play a camp follower! Especially if you're in the camp I'm following."

I backed away from the phone, letting the machine pick it up, the machine with Dave's voice telling callers to leave a message for us.

"Got that, Aston? The key word is 'us.' As in Dave and me. Us. A couple."

The prompt ended, the beep did its thing, and Aston spoke. "Tell your boyfriend to tell the other cops they're wasting their time with dogs. There's only one man who can find Bigfoot if he's hiding in that greenbelt, and that's me."

"Because when you're in character you smell like him?" I asked the machine.

"I'm doing a presentation over in Yakima, but I'll be home tonight. I know what Bigfoot will eat and where he'll find it," Aston went on.

I gagged, remembering some of the things Aston brought for lunch when he was "eating in character."

"So tell the cops if they want—"

Curiosity trumped revulsion and I picked up the phone. "Good morning, Aston."

"They haven't found that critter yet," he said without preamble. "And they won't. Not the way they're going at it. If it's even Bigfoot they're chasing."

"You don't think it is?"

"Hell, I don't know. Don't even know if I believe Bigfoot exists. Could be a cougar killed that guy. And they haven't let an expert get close to those tracks to see if they're fakes, so my jury's still out."

He coughed and cleared his throat. "Sorry, too much dirt in the eggs."

Silly me, I almost asked what the *correct* amount of dirt might be.

"But if it *is* Bigfoot and they want to find him in that brush, and bring him in without a lot of folks getting hurt, then I'm the guy to do it."

As opposed to every other Bigfoot hunter on the face of the earth. "Why you?"

"I have the tools and I have the talent. I know what he'd look for in the way of hiding places and I have the patience to watch and wait. I don't mind sleeping rough and I can scavenge wild foods and make a meal of what the land presents."

Aston coughed again and pounded his chest. "Tell your boyfriend I'm the man he wants. Tell him if they keep botching this job I'll go out there on my own and show them how it's done. Hell, I've a good mind to do that anyway."

"Won't that be dangerous? I mean, there are dozens of police officers out there with guns. You might get in the line of fire."

"Never happen. I have eyes like a hawk, ears like a bat, and a nose like a bear."

And an odor like all three combined with a dead sturgeon.

"You know what, damn it, I'm going out there. And I'm going dark. So you keep quiet."

"What does 'going dark' mean?"

"It means no flashlight, no cell phone, no contact with the outside, and no one knows I'm there."

Not my idea of a good time. "What if you get hurt?"

"Never happen."

For a few moments after he disconnected I considered calling him. Then I settled for ignoring the parts about keeping quiet and no one knowing, and wrote a note for Dave.

When I was finished, I wrote a question I wanted the answer to: Why not let Gnome Guy look at the tracks?

If it was possible to be an expert on a creature that might not exist, then Gnome Guy was it. What did they have to lose by letting him take a peek?

I jotted down another question: How sure were they that Missoula had trailed whatever killed Woodrow Krammer and not another creature that wandered through the crime scene?

I mean, it wasn't like they had a pair of boxers they were sure belonged to Bigfoot because they got them from his dirty clothes hamper. What if, for example, a coyote drawn to the blood, had been about to munch on Krammer as I drove up? What if a stray dog or cat or raccoon had wandered by and retreated when I arrived?

To expand on that, what if another creature—a human creature—had killed Krammer in a way that wasn't immediately evident? And what if yet another creature—of the non-human variety—made the gruesome wounds?

I plugged Dario into the "human creature" slot. He could have choked Krammer. Or snapped his neck. The wounds could have obscured the cause of death until the medical examiner took a close look.

That led to another question: When would the autopsy results be available?

180

Having worked as a radio producer, I knew that it could be days or even weeks before reporters got their hands on the complete report. But I also knew Detective Atwell would get the pertinent details a whole lot sooner. And Dave was Atwell's friend.

Not that Dave would spill all the details to me—especially details Atwell wanted held back from the public. But Dave's poker face would never play in Vegas, and his reaction to carefully phrased questions often told me all I wanted to know.

And on the topic of Vegas, Dario was headed there later today. Perhaps I should call Dave and remind him about Dario's threat before the plane took off. On the other hand, Dave was involved in a search right now and wouldn't appreciate an interruption. And Dave was a professional law enforcement agent. Surely he remembered the threat and had already considered Dario and crossed him off the suspect list or passed the theory on to Atwell.

CHAPTER 20

While I was pondering all that, Allison dragged herself downstairs, hair wet from the shower, but makeup in place. She poured a glass of juice, leaving a trail of orange droplets on the counter. "How come you're not at work?"

The question stood as evidence that Josh had kept his lips zipped about the murder. I decided not to clue her in—after all, she was supposed to read the paper—and deflected the question with one of my own. "What are your plans for the day?"

"I was supposed to learn how to fry chicken and make biscuits and stuff, but Verna and Sybil changed their minds for some reason."

"Some reason" being fear for their personal safety and a desire to avoid a call to 911. Frying chicken meant hot grease in close proximity to stove burners. Baking biscuits meant another episode with the oven. Both were fraught with peril. "So Plan B is . . .?"

Allison shrugged. "Hang out with Josh."

"Where?"

"Around."

"Around where?"

"Just around."

"Around here?"

"Maybe. Or maybe we'll go someplace."

"Like where?"

"I don't know. Someplace that isn't here."

Since we hadn't succeeded in setting a specific geographical area for hanging around, I moved on to activities to be pursued. "What would you and Josh be doing?"

"Stuff."

"What kind of stuff?"

"You know, stuff."

If this conversation was designed to wear me down, it was succeeding. My stomach rumbled and I eyed the remains of my bagel once more. Tiny fissures in the drying cream cheese made me reconsider for the final time and I pushed it to the back of the counter. Perhaps later I'd take it to the river and feed it to the first duck that bobbed by.

I went to my default setting. "Call your father and see what he thinks."

Allison pouted and went to her default setting. "Seriously? You can't say it's okay for me to hang with Josh?"

In theory, I could. Dave had ceded that power, telling me to trust my instincts. I trusted Josh to make far wiser decisions than Allison and I knew Dave had explained to him exactly which body part he'd forfeit if hormones took them too far. But Allison had pushed me into a corner, so it was time to push in return. "Not unless I have more information. Specific information."

Allison huffed and stomped and then heated up a breakfast pastry characterized by purple filling and pink icing with sprinkles. Feeling virtuous because I hadn't been responsible for purchasing whatever it was, and doing my best to ignore both drama and aroma, I made myself comfortable on the sofa and gave the lead story and sidebars another read.

Allison flopped beside me, picked up the remote, then craned her neck to study the paper. "Hey, that's Krammee's. And those are the Krammee twins, the skanks who fired Josh."

She yanked the paper from my hands and brought it close to her face. "They're sooooo ugly. They have eyes like those wild pigs that live in the desert. And their hair— Hey, why are they in the paper?"

"Their father was killed the night before last."

"Wow! Does Josh know?"

Uh oh. Quicksand ahead. If I said "yes," I'd drop Josh in it, and Allison would berate him for not sharing the secret. If I said "no," sooner or later Allison was bound to realize I'd lied and berate me as well. If previous castigations were a gauge for future rebukes, I'd be hearing about this for weeks to come.

The best course around certain doom was to veer off into a detour. "Someone dumped his body behind the auto repair shop."

Allison's eyes widened. "Did you get to see it?"

Asked with breathy eagerness as if that would allow her to overlook several of my flaws.

I hesitated for a few seconds, thinking an increase in my worth might balance the value of a long-lost mother should that LLM turn up as threatened. Then I went with the truth. "Only his feet."

"That's all?"

"Sorry to disappoint, but that's it." I made a mental note to replay this conversation for Dave and ask whether

184

Allison's interest was normal and fed by TV, movies, and novels, or something we should be concerned about. "And his shoes."

Allison blew air between her lips, implying I was as worthless as an expired movie coupon, then snatched the paper from my hands. "I'm gonna use this for my current event."

When Dave hatched this scheme he'd mentioned world leaders, historical context, and human rights, but if murder and mayhem got Allison interested in reading the paper, I'd go with it. "Okay, but don't cut it up until I'm finished reading."

That earned me an eye roll, but Allison moved on to the comics and scrunched up on the opposite end of the sofa. I kept a wary eye on her as I skimmed through world and national news, aware that at any moment she might resume the wheedling. When she tossed the paper aside and glanced at the clock, I tensed. But before she opened her mouth, there was a knock at the door.

Allison bounced to a standing position, jumped over the arm of the sofa, and raced down the hall.

"Apparently she and Josh made plans to hang out before clearing it with me," I informed Cheese Puff.

He gave me a look that implied I was too stupid to live if I thought otherwise, and burrowed deeper into his cushion crevasse.

Allison's footsteps returned to the living room at a slower pace, accompanied by the tapping of heels. Definitely not Josh.

I craned my neck and saw Paulette, decked out in a lime green dress and matching sandals, and sporting pink sunglasses with lenses as large as dessert plates. To top it

185

off, she wore a multi-colored broad-brimmed sun hat that could only be described as "adorable."

"I came to get the scoop, the whole scoop, and nothing but the scoop." She tossed the sunglasses and hat on the end table and headed for the refrigerator. "As soon as I get something cold and sparkling and devoid of calories."

Unlike mine, Paulette's fat cells didn't cry out constantly for carbs, salt, and sugar. Or, if they did, she was far better at ignoring those cries. In a moment she had a pineapple-coconut flavored beverage in a can that went well with her outfit. After brushing and fluffing the cushion on which Allison had been curled, she sat and kicked off her sandals.

"The story in the paper doesn't say, but I'll bet my manicure budget you found the body." She waved her fingers, exhibiting sculpted nails painted a pearly pink with lime green dots, evidence that her manicure budget was a heck of a lot bigger than mine.

(For the record, that allotment is the same as what I set aside for one-of-a-kind designer outfits—zero.)

"So, what's the *real* story behind everything on the news?"

Where should I begin? What should I include? More to the point, what should I leave out?

Before I could decide, the phone rang.

"It's Dad." Allison scooped up the receiver, listened for about two seconds, then tossed it to me.

I caught it on the first bounce off the arm of the sofa. "Hel—"

"What did I do to deserve this?" Dave raged. "I never kicked a kitten. I never took candy from a baby. I hardly ever jaywalk. I never once—"

"Calm down." I used my substitute teacher voice. "Take a breath. Speak slowly. What are you talking about?"

Paulette leaned close. So did Allison. I tipped the phone away from my ear to share his tirade.

"Her! I'm talking about her."

Paulette winced. Allison made some kind of complicated sign with her fingers. I felt a headache clamp my brain like a pair of giant barbecue tongs. There were billions of women on this planet but—not counting Rayanne—only one who could make Dave froth like a rabid dog.

"As if this wasn't already enough of a circus with reporters and Bigfoot hunters and every Tom, Dick, and Harry who has nothing better to do," he fumed. "As if there wasn't already enough potential for someone to get hurt. As if everyone on the force doesn't know she's—"

"My sister. I get it. What's she done now?"

"The usual. Protesting. Picketing. Stirring up her band of followers."

What Iz did best. But what could she find to demonstrate about in the hunt for the creature that may—or may not—be responsible for the death of Woodrow Krammer? A creature that might not even exist.

"Smear," Dave said.

"Smear?"

"That's her latest organization. Stop Making Erroneous Assumptions Right Now." He choked out a laugh. "I guess the 'Now' is silent. Unlike your sister."

True. With her booming voice and amazing vocal cord endurance, Iz saved money on public address systems. "I'm afraid to ask, but I can't help myself—what is it she feels those erroneous assumptions are being made about?"

"Bigfoot, I assume. But that might be an erroneous assumption on my part."

If Dave could make two jokes in a row, lame as they might be, his stress level was dropping. "I'm sorry."

"For what? You can't help it that she's your sister."

Paulette nodded agreement. Allison frowned as if she wasn't so sure.

"But it's my fault she got together with Penelope again. She might have returned to San Francisco if I'd booted her out."

"As if you owned boots big enough for that job. Uh oh. Chuck spotted Iz. Gotta run."

Allison carried the phone to its cradle. "Are we going over there to see Iz?"

"Nope." I reached for the remote, clicked on the TV, and muted the sound. "The last thing your father needs is us getting in the way."

"In the way of what?"

"In the way of him keeping a low profile," Paulette said. "Until the police department recovers from the mess Dick McBain made in the few days he was in charge, your father needs to stay as far under the radar as he can. And having his daughter taking part in a protest wouldn't help."

"But—"

Paulette raised her hand in a stop signal. "Hot as it is and much as you hate to sweat, I know you don't want to march. So it must be all about the cameras."

Allison pouted. "I want to be interviewed. I want to be on TV. It's not fair. I bet the Krammee twins are gonna be on TV."

Talk about comparing apples and oranges. Or penguins and potatoes. And talk about a waste of breath if I tried to explain the difference between being interviewed as a protester vs. being interviewed as the daughter of a murder victim. All Allison cared about was being on camera. "We're not going down there or anywhere today. I don't have a car."

Paulette raised perfect eyebrows.

"I parked in the crime scene before I knew that's what it was. The car's being checked over. Knowing Detective Atwell, he'll hang on to it for a week."

"Maybe longer." Paulette pointed to the TV screen and the image of my sister holding a picket sign aloft and leading a string of women along the shoulder of the road that passed Start 'er Up Auto Repair. She seemed larger than life in a screaming yellow T-shirt with a drawing of Bigfoot on the front. "Much longer. Since Iz turned up."

Compared to the way he felt about Iz, Atwell's feelings for me were warm and fuzzy.

Allison leaned toward the screen. "Is the Bigfoot on her T-shirt carrying a purse?"

"Yes. And it has a bow in its hair." Paulette laughed. "That must be what Iz means by erroneous assumptions—assuming the creature they're chasing is male."

My headache swelled. My stomach knotted. Trust my sister to make gender a major issue. And trust her to find a way to paint herself into the foreground.

Allison flopped on the carpet in front of the TV. "I don't get it."

"That's because there's not much to get," Paulette said. "This is another way for Iz to grab some headlines."

"So it doesn't matter if Bigfoot is a boy or a girl?"

I shot Paulette a you-started-this-conversation-so-you-can-finish-it look. She tapped a finger against her lips and gave it a go. "Obviously, if Bigfoot exists and there's a viable population of, um, Bigfeet, there must be both males and females."

"And babies?" Allison asked.

For the first time in my experience, Paulette appeared flustered. Perhaps because of her lack of knowledge on this particular subject. More likely because she'd gotten a mental image of Bigfoot doing the wild thing. "Uh, yes. There would be babies."

"So, it would be worse to hurt a girl Bigfoot? And even worse if she had a baby?"

Paulette picked at a cuticle, something else I'd never seen her do before. "Why don't you ask your father when he comes home?"

Allison yawned, turned to the TV screen, and pumped up the sound as a young male reporter asked Iz what her protest was about. As my sister launched into what promised to be a long and bombastic answer, she closed her hand over his, taking control of the microphone.

"That poor reporter," Paulette said. "He doesn't stand a chance."

"Yeah, he's about to find out how a goat feels in an anaconda's coils."

"Huh?" Allison muted the sound again. "Why are you talking about goats and snakes?"

Paulette stood in one fluid motion and smoothed her dress. "I'd love to hang around all day and watch Iz storm the media, but there's an estate sale preview in Hood River. Want to ride along and get some lunch on the way?"

I thought about the drive up the scenic Columbia Gorge and lunch at some little place where Paulette would be pampered by the owner and served special items not on the menu. Then I thought about leaving Allison unsupervised. Finally, I thought of the time Paulette would spend examining furniture, paintings, knickknacks, and doodads.

Don't get me wrong, I appreciate and admire Paulette's interior design skill, but I don't share her interest. When it comes to buying stuff to sit or sleep on, eat from, or store things in, I'll pick practical ahead of pretty, functional before formal, and cheap over Chippendale.

"I see your mind working," she said. "And, yes, I will be there most of the afternoon. It's a huge house and the owners traveled a great deal."

Meaning the place was stuffed with souvenirs, some valuable, some not, and most requiring on-the-spot research to determine their value. And then there would be the haggling. As far as I knew, Paulette paid full price only to her hairdresser and manicurist and only because she feared what they might do to her hair and nails if they grew weary of dishing out discounts.

She tugged at Allison's hair. "How about you?"

Allison's thumbs stopped tapping buttons on her phone. "Huh?"

"Want to ride up to Hood River? You could watch the windsurfers while I check out the sale."

Allison glanced at her phone. "Can Josh come?"

"Sure."

"Can we get pizza?"

"As long as you don't get grease on me or my upholstery."

Allison tapped with her thumbs. "Deal. Josh is almost here. I gotta do my hair and change my clothes."

191

An activity that could take anywhere from 20 minutes to two hours. Paulette headed it off at the pass. "Do what you want, but I read in a magazine that guys like the natural-dry, tousled look."

Allison patted her hair. "Really?"

Paulette lowered her voice and shielded her mouth with her hand as if keeping a secret from me. "They think it's flirty."

Talk about manipulation. The job I did on Iz was nothing compared to this.

Allison patted her ruffled hair once more. "But I should change, right?"

Paulette gave her outfit—sleeveless pink T-shirt, blue jean shorts, pink flip-flops—the once-over. "Only if you own something cuter than what you have on. But you might grab a jacket. Maybe that blue jean one with the big zipper."

When Allison hit the top of the stairs, I shot Paulette the okay sign. "Did the article say guys like zippers?"

"What article?" She picked a strand of orange dog hair from her dress. "You forget my daughter was once a teenager." Then, settling her hat on her head, she scooped up her sunglasses and sashayed to the door, flipping me a finger wave.

In a moment Allison pounded down the stairs with the jacket, her purse, a floppy white sun hat looted from my closet, and a pair of sunglasses almost as large as Paulette's. "See you later."

She was gone with a slam of the door before I could decide if I should mention what a nice touch it would be to ask permission before borrowing.

Chapter 21

Cheese Puff heaved a faint sigh and a louder belch, extracted himself from the cushion crevasse, and sprawled belly-up. I did the same on the sofa, contemplating my sister's latest cause and whether there might be some merit to it. If the creature in the greenbelt was a female, and if she had a little one with her, that might add another dimension to Woodrow Krammer's killing—a mother protecting her young. But, male or female, if this creature was the same one who knocked me down two nights ago, it was huge and frightening.

If Iz was here right now and knew what I was thinking, she'd clock me with her picket sign. Because the creature was large and less than attractive, it wasn't necessarily dangerous. If Bigfoot appeared to be cute and cuddly, would I be frightened? If its hair was shampooed and conditioned and brushed, would that make a difference?

I'd like to believe that I'm without prejudice, but that was clearly a myth. I didn't wake up every day ready to meet the world with a mind emptied of prior perceptions. What I encountered in the past influenced how I perceived the present and to what extent I held to my previous beliefs and interpretations.

Vowing to do better, I pumped up the sound and channel surfed, but found no more live reports. I snapped off the TV, ran the vacuum and restored order to the top shelf of my closet—meaning I replaced items Allison tossed on the floor in her search for the hat she'd absconded with.

I've heard people say if you can get organized, then it's easy to stay organized. That might work for someone who lives alone and has a minimum of possessions and a maximum of shelf and drawer space. Sharing a condo with Allison and Dave, however, had turned the goal of an organized space into a mirage retreating steadily toward the horizon. To protect what remained of my mental health, I decided to focus on common space and personal space, and leave them to deal—or not deal—with their messes.

With that in mind, I shoveled Dave's shoes to his side of the closet and arranged mine in the remaining area. On a roll, I shoved loose change, rubber bands, and slips of paper to his side of the dresser and centered my jewelry box on the surface I cleared.

It wasn't a large box—big enough for a couple of bracelets, three or four necklaces, and the thin and inexpensive wedding rings I'd set aside after Albert's death and my divorce from Jake. Staring out at the river, I realized my memories of considerate, absent-minded Albert had faded like an old photograph. But my memories of lying, cheating, self-centered Jake remained in the same sharp focus as on the day I finally saw the light.

So much for that myth about absence making the heart grow fonder. It would take more than absence to make me grow fonder of Jake. It would take enough cash to cover what he siphoned from my bank account plus interest, plus a hefty sum for wasted time, plus more interest. And even then . . .

If Mrs. B was in the room and could read my thoughts, she'd tell me to stop being so negative. She'd probably even say my days with Jake weren't completely wasted because I learned about myself and what I wanted in a man.

And I suppose I had.

But was that knowledge worth the humiliation of Jake's infidelity? Worth the mountain of debt looming over me?

Certainly my experience with Jake made me a better money manager and more cautious about my relationship with Dave. Never mind that Iz was convinced I jumped into cohabitation simply because I couldn't live on my own.

As if she could!

She'd seldom gone more than a month or two without a partner. And some of her relationship failures had been—if you didn't consider the money angle—more spectacular than mine. At least *I* hadn't been left with a former lover's name tattooed on my breast. And *I* hadn't had to borrow money from my sister to have it removed.

Smiling, I bounced downstairs and clicked on the TV to catch the noon news. In a few moments Iz appeared, leading a dozen picketers along the highway. Not one of them was Penelope.

Odd.

Had they split again?

195

I told myself three times it was none of my business, but then punched Penelope's number into the phone. She answered after four rings. "Are you wondering why I'm not hiking along the highway with a picket sign?"

Was I that transparent? "Uh . . . Would you believe I thought you were sick?"

"No." She laughed. "No, I wouldn't believe that. And no, I'm not sick. What happened in Wyoming made me realize I need to hold on to my own space, hold on to who I am. I was in danger of sacrificing too much of my agenda for hers."

"That's easy to do with Iz."

"Easy to do with anyone if you're not careful."

Good point. I thought of those weekends when, fingers chilled, legs cramping, rain seeping through my jacket, I'd waited in a thicket with Albert for a glimpse of an elusive bird to add to his life list. Yes, I was thrilled when he spotted the feathered creature. I was delighted to share his joy. But, on my own, would I have been content with watching more common birds from a seat in a sunny park? You bet.

"Anyway," Penelope said, "I promised myself I'd weigh the merits of courses she sets before I follow in her wake."

"And this particular course doesn't have enough merit?"

Penelope laughed again. "What do you think?"

"I think it's more of an attempt to grab some media attention than anything else."

"Same here." She lowered her voice. "But I'll have that conversation when she's not on a protest high. Today I took the coward's way out and said I couldn't get away from the job site."

Having never held a "real" job, Iz had no experience with the obligations of a workplace. "And she accepted that?"

"It's a charity build for a family that got burned out. I played the guilt card."

And probably saved a lot of hassle. "My lips are sealed."

"I hope so," Penelope said, and signed off.

I was doing jumping jacks in water up to my shoulders when I heard the gate to the pool area open. Squinting, I saw Dave with Lola limping behind him, her right front foot wrapped in a bandage. Ignoring the rules about no pets in the pool area, he held the gate wide and ushered her inside.

"Cheese Puff went to the airport with Mrs. B," he said. "Afterward they're going shopping and taking in a movie."

"I hope it's not a movie where a dog saves the day. He's insufferable after he watches one of those."

"He's insufferable when he doesn't." Dave closed the gate and plodded my way. "Anyway, I think it's a romantic comedy at one of those living room theaters. Do you know where Allison is?"

"At an estate sale with Paulette. In Hood River."

"Let's hope she doesn't break a Chinese vase." He dropped into a chair. "I didn't want to leave Lola alone in case she chewed at the bandage. We were searching the edge of a parking lot when she stepped on a broken bottle." He patted Lola's back. "A curved piece was half buried. When she put her foot on one edge the other came up and caught her in the leg. Two wounds for the price of one."

I paddled to the steps and climbed out. Picking up my glasses from the low table where I laid my keys and cell phone, I dripped my way to an adjacent chair. "Poor girl. How bad is it?"

"Bad enough that we got the rest of the day off. But nobody carped about that because we already racked up more than our quota of way-to-go points." He stretched his legs and toed off his hiking boots. Clumps of dried mud dropped from the grooves in the tread and broke apart on the pool deck. Two strikes against him if Bernina Burke came by.

I tossed my towel over his boots, hiding that bit of evidence. Nothing I could do about Lola who sprawled in Dave's shadow. "Sorry about Iz and her demonstration."

"Not your fault."

"Was there any sign of the creature?"

"Not a hair. Not a print. Not a shadow in the brush. And until Missoula learns to talk and tells us what he scented, I'm keeping an open mind about what we might be hunting. But . . ."

"But what?"

Dave glanced over both shoulders and leaned toward me. "From what I've heard, so far there's no evidence to support the death-by-enormous-wild-creature-with-claws theory."

He was quiet for a moment and so was I. Not an easy task with every brain cell screaming, "What does *that* mean? Tell me everything you know! Tell me now! I won't blab to a soul. Honest."

And I wouldn't. Not if Dave swore me to secrecy.

Which I hoped he wouldn't. Don't ask me why, but keeping a secret because I wanted to was a heck of a lot easier than keeping a secret because someone else wanted me to.

"Chuck will shoot my lips off if he finds out I told you any of this."

I nodded eagerly and held up my right hand in a scout's salute.

Dave rolled his eyes. "You do know that two fingers is the Cub Scout salute, don't you?"

Ooops.

He chuckled and wove his fingers with mine. "Later you can tell me about what must have been a long and illustrious career in scouting. But right now, without raising either hand, promise me you won't tell anyone— not even Mrs. Ballantine."

"Promise."

He relaxed and stretched his legs again. "First, as annoying as your friend Gnome Guy may be, he *has* been all around the globe studying footprints. So Chuck finally agreed to let him have a look at the ones with the drag marks."

Dave paused to get his thoughts in order, a habit he slips into when he's in serious-discussion mode. As you might guess, that makes me crazy. I'm from the splatter-it-into-the-breeze school of conversation. Of course, that means I spend a lot of time explaining what I meant and/or apologizing for what I said, but at least I get it all out. With Dave I wonder if too much contemplation will result in thoughts being fumbled, falling into mental corners, and forgotten. I also wonder if he uses pauses to stuff things to a corner of his mind because he's not ready to share them. Like those payments to Rayanne. And Rayanne herself.

Knowing I couldn't rush him, I chewed at my lip and surveyed the pool area. Two green-and-white striped beach towels hung on the fence and a smaller burgundy one had been wadded into a makeshift pillow on one of the lounge chairs. If Bigfoot returned to the lair beneath the deck, he'd find plenty of bedding free for the taking. Fresh vegetables, too. Several of the residents had taken up container gardening and some were already giving away zucchini. And then there was whatever people left in unlocked cars.

Dave leaned forward, removed one of his socks, and tapped his instep. "The first footprints showed an arch. Not much of one, but definitely an arch. And, like you noticed, the prints weren't identical and neither was the length of the stride and depth of impressions. The prints from the latest batch were nearly flat. And, other than right and left, there were next to no variations."

"So they weren't made by real feet?"

"There were only a dozen good prints for comparison, but most likely not. Either someone strapped on a set of fake feet, or pressed plaster casts into the dirt." Dave pulled off his other sock and flexed his toes. "Probably option number two. Your buddy Gnome Guy thinks so. And when he pointed out the other marks—"

"He's not my buddy. And what 'other marks' are you talking about?"

"The marks along the sides where someone brushed away a tangle of smaller footprints. Your buddy thinks that person used a feather duster."

"He's *not* my buddy. And I bet he's not Atwell's buddy, either. Not after that analysis."

"Actually, Chuck was relieved. He never bought the Bigfoot-as-killer scenario. That was media hype."

"Is he going to set the record straight with an interview?"

"Chuck never set the record crooked. And he avoids interviews the way you avoid owning up to that secret stash of chocolate inside the empty soy milk container in the refrigerator."

My face flushed. I'd been so proud of that hiding place, and so certain Dave would never find it because he loathed soy milk. "It's not a secret stash if you know it's there."

Dave patted my head as if I was a toddler, then pulled off his T-shirt and spread his arms to the sun. "Chuck told Gnome Guy he could have the pleasure of spouting off to the microphones."

That sounded like a harebrained decision. But, after a moment of thought, I saw the benefit. Let Gnome Guy have a few more minutes of fame. Beyond his opinion that the tracks were faked and the person who faked them was smart enough to obliterate traces of his own tracks, he didn't know much. "He probably can't make things worse."

"Might even calm things down. And derail your sister's protest."

"Bonus." I smiled, imagining Gnome Guy facing off with Iz. I'd pay all my cash on hand—about $7.40, give or take a few stray pennies in the bottom of my purse—to witness that. The only thing better would be seeing video of Iz getting skunked.

I stood, splashed water from the pool to cool the deck around my chair, and slipped on an oversized T-shirt. It covered my swimsuit and allowed me to appear "decent" as Bernina Burke's latest memo to residents claimed we should be when traveling through public space between our units and the pool. "We've got to get to the TV."

"They'll play the highlights all evening." Dave yawned. "And I'm comfortable right here. This is way ahead of beating the brush."

That reminded me of Aston Marsden's call and his plan to camp out in the greenbelt and capture Bigfoot. Much as I wanted to avoid talking with him, I wished there was a way to get in touch. He needed to know that the tracks were phony. But—

"Wait a minute. What about the first set of tracks? Were those faked?"

"Your buddy Elmer doesn't think so."

I bent and stared into his eyes. "Just so you know, if you use the expression 'your buddy' one more time, you'll suffer."

"Suffer in a kinky kind of way?"

"You only wish."

"Got it. I'm finished with the buddy system."

"Good." I brushed dried mud flakes into a pile with the edge of my hand and wrapped the heap and Dave's boots in my towel. "So, if the tracks leading to Krammer's body are fake . . . ?"

"Where's the person who made them? And who was Missoula following?"

"Exactly." I added Dave's socks and shirt to the bundle.

"For all I know he was after a coyote or a cougar."

Since he brought that up, I felt obliged to fish for anything he knew about the autopsy results. "Cougars and coyotes walk on four feet. Does Atwell think Krammer was dead when he was dumped there and a predator made the wounds?"

Dave opened his mouth, then closed it again. I suspected he was pondering what he knew and how much to leak my way. I feigned lack of interest, sitting on the edge of the pool with my back to him and paddling my feet in the water while using a corner of the towel to push my cuticles to where they should be. If I ever got out of debt, I'd blow some bucks on a professional manicure.

"Okay." Dave poked me with a toe. "In the interest of not giving wildlife a bad rap, the answer to that question is 'No.'" He poked me again. "And before you ask, from what I saw of the preliminary report, they didn't find anything in the wounds to support the predator theory—no hair or skin or saliva or broken bits of claw."

I turned to face him. So much for feigning lack of interest. "Then what made the wounds?"

"Something with several sharp points equidistant from each other." Dave clawed the air with his fingers. "Like big claws, but made of metal."

I held my hands out and made claws of my own, trying to visualize what kind of instrument the killer used. A thought tickled the bottom of my mind. Then it was gone.

CHAPTER 22

"Krammer was killed elsewhere." Dave opened his hands and spread his arms to the sun once more. "There wasn't much blood where you found him and not all that much in the car. And, so far, all they've turned up at Krammee's are flagrant violations of health department codes. Plus the drugs Lola sniffed out."

"Drugs? A lot of drugs?"

"Enough to supply Reckless River users for most of the summer. Hidden in the back of the walk-in freezer under about a ton of frozen fries."

Lola raised her head and thumped her tail. I scooched across to her and scratched her ears. "So the rumors that Krammer wasn't on the level were true. He was selling more than burgers."

"Or he was storing the drugs for distribution. Krammer's wife and the twins deny any knowledge of illegal substances."

"Of course," I scoffed. "Wouldn't you?"

"Yeah, but we may have to accept their denials. Unless we find prints on the packages, or a witness to a transaction they were involved in."

"Maybe someone who worked there saw something." I gripped Dave's arm. "Maybe Josh did."

"I'd like to think he would have mentioned it if he had." Dave stretched and stood, jigging into the damp spot I'd made as the soles of his feet registered the temperature of the deck. "He's a bright kid. Observant, too."

"Maybe he saw something but didn't know what it was and didn't want to cry wolf." A darker thought crept into my mind. "Or he was afraid of what might happen to him if Krammer found out he blew the whistle."

"Possible." Dave nudged Lola's hip with his bare toes and got a grunt in return. "And considering that he needs money to buy gas and keep Allison entertained, maybe he didn't want to jeopardize his job."

"Even though it was a horrible job." I got to my feet and wadded the towel tight around Dave's boots, socks, and shirt. "Even though the Krammee twins treated him like pond scum and Woodrow Krammer threat—"

I froze, bent over the towel, my fingers spread to grip it, spread like a claw. A vision of a garden rake formed in my brain—a hand tool like the one Josh bought to break up ice cubes when the soda machine jammed.

"Are you okay?" Dave gripped my shoulder. "Did you pull a muscle?"

If he thought I could pull a muscle bending and reaching for a towel, then he must think I was in pretty pathetic physical condition. Which might mean I actually was. Which might mean I needed to get on an exercise program more radical than water aerobics, dog walking, and moving chairs around on the deck so I could sweep.

But that was an issue to take up later—much later. Right now Dave's daughter was miles away with a boy who had the motive, the means, and possibly the opportunity to kill Woodrow Krammer.

Abandoning the towel, I pointed to Dave's chair. "Sit."

"But I just stood up."

"I'm well aware of that. Sit. Now."

"I see how you've survived in high school as a substitute teacher." He sat, grinning. "And it's kind of a turn-on. Maybe we—"

"Stop talking. Listen. Josh had a metal garden rake." I made a clawing motion with my hand. "A small one. He bought it to break up ice jams in the soda machine at Krammee's. Woodrow Krammer wouldn't reimburse him because he took the initiative and didn't get approval first."

Dave's grin sagged and gave way to slack-jawed disbelief. He made a clawing motion of his own. "You think—?"

I didn't want to say what I thought. That would make it too real. "Some of those rakes have three prongs and some have more. I don't know how many prongs were on the rake Josh had."

"Had?"

"When I saw him after he got fired, he said he wanted the rake because he never got paid for it. But it wasn't where he usually left it, and the Krammee twins wouldn't let him look for it."

"And you think he made that up because he used the rake to kill Woodrow Krammer, and then got rid of it?"

"No." My legs wobbled and I sank into the chair beside Dave's. "I mean, I don't *want* to think that. Josh is such a great kid. He's funny, kind, helpful."

"Same things people say about the serial killer next door, the one that always helped lug their garbage to the street."

"I know, but I can't see Josh as a serial killer. If he killed Woodrow Krammer it must have been in self-defense. Krammer was a big, scary guy with a bad attitude, maybe he—"

"Enough speculation." Dave stood and headed for the gate to the pool area. Lola staggered to her feet and limped behind him. "I'll call Chuck and tell him about the rake. Any idea where Josh might be?"

I felt dizzy, sick. "He's . . . he's in Hood River."

Dave turned, color draining from his face. "With Allison?"

I swallowed. "And Paulette."

As if petite Paulette could stop a six-foot teenage boy who might have ripped Woodrow Krammer's throat open with a garden rake.

Another dark thought rolled through my brain. The day I'd gone to Krammee's, I'd seen Josh lugging a bag of frozen fries into the freezer. What if he was aware of the drug stash? Worse, what if Josh was involved in drug traffic? What if Krammer's death was the result of a struggle within the drug distribution network?

Dave spun toward the gate once more, calling over his shoulder. "I'll clue in Chuck and have him alert the police in Hood River. Then I'm headed up there. Keep an eye on Lola, okay?"

"Wait! What about Paulette? Should I call her?"

"No. If she freaks out it could tip him off."

Paulette was hardly the type who freaked out. Allison, on the other hand, would put herself in the center of the drama. She might even decide to get between Josh and a police officer who came for him.

I grabbed my keys and phone and raced after Dave, the concrete deck scorching my bare feet. "You might need Paulette to separate your daughter from Josh if a cop tries to take him into custody."

Dave gripped the gate and his body went limp. I knew he was visualizing what I had a second ago—and a whole lot more.

"Let's get in out of the sun." I ducked, laid his right arm across my shoulders, and half-led half-dragged him to the condo, Lola trailing behind. "Let's give this more thought."

Eyes glazed, feet dragging, Dave moved like a condemned man. As we shuffled past Bernina Burke's open office door, I launched into a loud complaint about the length of the grass. Not that I gave a flip, but I'd discovered that complaints about tasks that were her responsibility were like holding up a crucifix to ward off a vampire. As long as I kept up my phony diatribe, Bernina would remain in her lair, pretending to be too busy to raise her head as I passed.

I remembered Dave's boots and the dried mud wrapped in my towel. The downside of my little act was that when she emerged, Bernina might go hunting for violations of condo rules and regulations. With any luck, I could return and retrieve the evidence before she discovered it.

I unlocked the parking-lot door to the condo and led Dave along the hall to the living room. As we passed the office, I had another dark thought. If police took Josh into custody and questioned him about the rake and Krammer's death, Allison might see that as a betrayal.

She'd accuse Dave of not trusting Josh and, by extension, not trusting her and her choices. If Rayanne made good on her threat to contact her daughter, she might paint herself as a victim of the police, thus making herself more attractive in Allison's eyes.

Crud.

Whether Josh proved to be innocent or not would make little difference to Allison. If there was evidence Josh was involved with drug trafficking, she'd claim it was trumped up. If there was proof Josh planned the murder, she'd go into heavy denial, make excuses, maybe even offer an alibi.

An alibi!

I slid from beneath Dave's arm and gave him a shove toward the sofa. "What time did Woodrow Krammer die?"

He shook his head like a man emerging from cold, deep water. "I don't know."

"You *do* know. You saw the preliminary autopsy report."

I filled two glasses with cold water and put one in his hands. "Think. And while you're thinking, remember Josh was with Allison at the fireworks display on July 4th. And remember you all went to the park in your car because you're a cop and you could bypass the public parking snarl."

Dave stared into the depths of the glass, then brought it to his lips and drank. When he was finished, he set the glass on the coffee table with a thump and sat up straight. "Krammer died around midnight, give or take."

"How much give and how much take?" I dropped into Cheese Puff's favorite chair knowing he was off with Mrs. B and I wouldn't get doggy grief for my trespass.

"Maybe as much as an hour. They'll probably narrow that down some by the time they release the final report."

"And what time did you get home from the fireworks show?"

"I don't remember."

Neither did I. Mainly because I'd been asleep. But I *did* remember glancing at the clock while I was brushing my teeth. "It was after 12:15."

"Yeah, it took forever to get out of the lot. Then some guy stalled at a four-way stop and Josh and I had to push his car off to the side."

And after I brushed my teeth I laid out my clothes for the next day, filed a ragged fingernail, and looked out the window to check on the burned-over grass and Jim's sleeping arrangements. Tack on the process of plumping pillows and getting comfortable and it must have been 15 minutes later before I drifted off. "If I was asleep when you came in, it was after 12:30."

"You were asleep." He grinned. "Totally asleep. You were drooling on your pillow. So you would have been asleep for maybe 20 or 30 minutes."

(For the record, I deny all charges of pillow-drooling, but Dave insists I dribble when I ease toward deep sleep and the muscles in my jaw relax.)

"You're the expert, Doctor Drool Detector."

"And a good thing I am, because that lets Josh off the hook. I didn't hear him drive away until after I brushed my teeth and pried your dog out from under my pillow. That was probably after 1:00."

He sighed and flopped to a more comfortable position. "Chuck will still want to question him about the rake."

"But you can present the interview to him and Allison as a means of helping solve the case instead of being questioned as a suspect, right?"

"I can try to spin it that way. If Allison thinks I'm picking on her boyfriend, the words 'living hell' won't even begin to describe my life. And then there's Rayanne."

"I know. I thought of that."

We sighed in unison.

"We have to deal with that situation." I leaned close and laid my hand on his thigh. "We're already six days into the month. That's six days closer to the next payment."

"We could turn it over to Mrs. Ballantine," he said in a hopeful voice. "She's great at handling difficult people."

"She is. But, much as she'd relish sinking her manicured nails into Rayanne, I doubt she'd let you pass off the problem. She likes to help, but not unless she feels those she's helping have already gone the distance."

Dave groaned. "I was afraid you'd say that."

"Maybe you could talk with the counselor you and Allison are seeing."

He groaned again. "She'll tell me to man up and tell the truth."

"Same advice you give people you arrest." I stood and brushed Cheese Puff's hair from my legs. "We'll kick this can down the road to another day. Call Detective Atwell and tell him about the rake. I'm going to the pool to get your boots and the other stuff."

When I got there, however, the only trace of Dave's gear was a dusting of dried mud on the pool deck. The flip-flops I'd abandoned were also missing.

211

CHAPTER 23

Dang it.

Bernina Burke must have trucked to the pool after we passed her office and scooped up everything.

Double dang it.

And, because we'd violated at least two pool-area rules, I couldn't claim she'd taken our possessions for no reason other than a general desire to make my life miserable.

The only alternatives I could see were A) stealing back our possessions in a manner to be determined later, B) sucking it up and living without them, or C) apologizing for violating condo rules while offering tribute in the form of chocolate and gift coupons.

Apologizing was, as you might guess, a last resort. Sucking it up sucked. That left stealing.

With that in mind, I stopped by her office to do a little reconnaissance and, if possible, throw her off balance. The first rule to surviving an encounter with Bernina was to have an escape hatch, so I didn't actually enter the office, only poked my head in. Since the office space was small—a partitioned area of the living room of a one-bedroom condo—I could take it in with a sweeping glance.

Bernina glanced up from a yellow pad on which she'd been writing. "How can I help you?" she said in a tone that made it clear she didn't give a fig, but felt obligated to appear to be doing her job.

"That enormous dog from the next condo complex," I said, clocking a desk, file cabinet, two metal visitor chairs, one anemic spider plant, and a cushy executive chair, "has been digging in the landscaping outside the pool. Two of the rhododendrons are looking pretty grim. They may have to be replaced. And the mutt is getting more aggressive. He's been snarling and slavering at residents."

"I'll check on the rhododendrons when I have time. As for the dog, *I* have yet to see him exhibiting aggressive behavior."

Meaning she questioned the accuracy of others' reports. Especially mine.

She lowered her gaze and resumed writing, probably crafting yet another memo to residents proposing yet another set of draconian regulations. I made a mental note to suggest to the Committee that, since teaching Allison to cook was too dangerous, they devote their excess time to designing an expanded social life for Bernina. The more interests she had outside of the condo complex, the less time she'd spend finding ways to hassle residents.

"Checking that you were on top of things," I said in a tight voice. "Wouldn't want any plantings to die." And have residents get billed for them. "Wouldn't want any residents—or you—to be mauled by that monster."

I closed the door, giving myself a figurative gold star for including her in that sentence. Who says I'm too negative?

Dave was setting the phone down when I got to the condo. "Chuck's on the garden-rake-as-murder-weapon angle. He agrees that Josh isn't a suspect, but wants to talk with him. He's okay with doing it informally—at least for now. Josh met Chuck a couple of times at barbecues on the deck, so he shouldn't feel threatened if we talk here. Can you call Paulette and see when they're due?"

"Sure. Right after you tell me how attached you were to those boots you wore today."

"Why?"

"Because they're gone. Everything's gone—your socks and shirt and my flip-flops. I think Bernina Burke took them."

"Crap."

"I scanned her office under cover of prodding her to do something about that hell hound, but I didn't see them."

"Well, I don't have the energy to deal with her now. Let's pretend we haven't noticed they're missing."

"Works for me." Especially since I lost only a pair of worn-down flip-flops. "I'll call Paulette."

"Don't give anything away," Dave warned. "Be casual. Maybe ask if they'll be here soon because you're cooking a gourmet dinner."

I laughed. "Gourmet for me is using aged cheddar and artisan bread for grilled cheese sandwiches. Paulette knows that."

"Okay, maybe tell her you're rearranging the living room and need help."

I laughed louder and longer. "Do I look suicidal? Have you forgotten that Paulette placed every piece of furniture in this room?" All the while shaking her head over a collection of furnishings too pathetic to be described with the word "junk" and suggesting I dump everything we owned and start fresh.

Dave raised his hands in surrender. "Trying to help."

"Thanks, but I believe I can manage this."

I also believed that the best approach was the direct one. Paulette was a rip-the-bandage-off kind of woman.

I punched in her number and waited through four rings before she picked up. "How's it going?" I asked. "Finding anything you can't live without?"

"I'm finding *everything* I can't live without. What's up?"

"Are the kids with you?"

"No, they're by the river eating ice cream. Or caramel corn. Or nachos with cheese sauce. Why Allison isn't one giant pimple weighing 200 pounds is a myst—" Her tone changed from breezy to businesslike. "Why are you calling? What's wrong?"

"Nothing's wrong. But Josh might know something about the murder weapon in the Krammer investigation."

"And Detective Atwell wants to talk with him right away?"

"Yes, but Dave—"

"Doesn't want Josh to know what's up because Allison will freak out?"

No grass grew under Paulette's pampered little feet. "Exactly."

"Then it's time to stop shopping and get hopping. It seems I remembered an important meeting. Think I can get that past them?"

"Without even crossing your fingers behind your back."

"You're right. As wrapped up as they are in each other, it's hardly a challenge. See you in 90 minutes."

Eighty-nine minutes later, when Allison and Josh came through the door, Detective Charles Atwell was on the sofa. Because he was drinking iced tea and polishing off a grilled Swiss, ham, tomato, and red onion sandwich, he was in a slightly more pleasant mood than usual.

I'd hesitated before slicing the onion, pointing out onions aggravated his digestive issues as much as open homicide cases. He'd overruled me with a snarl, so I hadn't offered to bring out a box of tissues in case his alleged allergy to small dogs kicked in. I say "alleged" because I was 97% convinced he manufactured that allergy when Cheese Puff growled at him the first time they met.

Dave had prepared a lineup of sorts, searching various Internet sites for images of handheld garden rakes, printing them, and laying the pictures out on the coffee table.

"Paulette forgot she had a meeting. She'll call you later." Allison showed no interest in the array, but scoped out the bit of crust remaining on Atwell's plate and headed for the refrigerator. "I hope the macaroni and cheese isn't all gone because I'm hungry and so's Josh."

Josh shuffled his feet and flushed as he nodded to Dave.

"Nobody touched the macaroni," I assured her, knowing it was pointless to allude to the goodies she'd consumed in the course of the afternoon. "There's coleslaw to go with it."

"Ick. I hate coleslaw."

"I like it," Josh said. "It's crunchy and full of vitamins and fiber and stuff."

"Ick to the max." Allison got out the casserole dish of mac and cheese and started mounding up a plate. "If you want it so bad, you can get it yourself."

"Okay." Josh turned to me. "If that's okay with you, Ms. Reed."

"It's fine, but I'd be happy to get it for you." I pointed to Cheese Puff's chair. "Grab a seat and I'll pour you a glass of lemonade."

Josh headed for the chair, passing the display as he went. "Hey, those are garden rakes like the one I bought for the soda machine at Krammee's."

Without being prompted, he leaned over the table, his right forefinger swinging between two images before tapping one. "That's like the one I got. It had three prongs in kind of a triangle. And it had a long handle that was part metal and part wood."

Atwell smiled at Dave.

Dave smiled at me.

I tipped a thumb up and headed to the kitchen to fill a plate.

Josh sat. "Are you gonna buy a garden rake?"

"We've been doing some research to see which ones get the best reviews from gardeners. My idea was to shop around, but Barbara wants to go after the weeds in the rose garden right away." Dave nodded in my direction. "Could we rent your rake for a few days? Or maybe buy it?"

"Sure. If I still had it."

I handed Josh a glass of lemonade, then stuck his macaroni in the microwave. "That's right. I forgot you said

217

it wasn't where you usually left it and the Krammee twins wouldn't let you look for it."

Allison uttered a couple of adjectives describing the Krammee twins that earned a frown from her father. Ignoring that, she plunked her steaming plate of mac and cheese on the coffee table and sat cross-legged on the floor.

"Yeah. They said they'd looked and couldn't find it. And I never got paid for it, either." Josh gulped lemonade. "But they gave me way more than I earned when they fired me, so I'm good."

"Still, it's too bad about the rake. What do you think happened to it?"

"Maybe they wanted to keep it. I mean, it was great for busting up the ice. It was heavy for its size and the handle was long."

"When you find the right tool for a job," Atwell said, "you don't want to give it up. If someone wanted my leaf blower, they'd have to pry it from my cold, dead hands."

There were a dozen things I wanted to say to that, but I told myself not to comment.

"Maybe they lied when they said they couldn't find it," Dave said.

"They're good at lying." Allison dug into her mac and cheese like food was going out of style. Lola raised her head from where she'd flopped beside the sofa, sniffed, gave Dave a wistful look, and went back to sleep.

"And they're good at stealing," Allison added. "Only I guess not all that good because they keep getting caught."

"Well, it's too bad the rake is gone." Dave shuffled the printed images together and tapped an official-looking form at the edge of the table. "Hey, while you're here, maybe you can help me with my timecard. I know it was

218

late, but I can't remember what time we left the fireworks show. Can you?"

Allison shook her head.

"Right around midnight," Josh said. "But it took a long time to get out of the parking lot. And then we pushed the stalled car. Can you count that as working?"

"I doubt it." Dave penciled a note on the phony form. "But it never hurts to ask."

"Unless you work at Krammee's." Allison pointed her fork at Josh. "And when you ask for a better mop so the floor actually gets clean, they tell you you're wasting time."

"I noticed that hygiene and sanitation weren't at the top of the list there." I added slaw to Josh's plate and set it on the coffee table. "Do you have any idea where you might look for a job?"

"Not yet." He forked coleslaw into his mouth like a farmer pitching hay into a barn.

"Anywhere's got to be better than Krammee's. And anyone you work for will be nicer than the Krammee twins. They're evil." Allison scraped the last smear of cheese from her plate. "And lazy. They made you do all the hard work. Especially the dirty work."

"They did some of it," Josh mumbled.

"Not very much. And only when their father was watching." Allison dug her fork into the mound of macaroni on Josh's plate. "They probably killed their father so they wouldn't have to work there. And so they wouldn't have to go to that special school in New Mexico."

In the silence that followed, I imagined I heard the wheels spin in Atwell's mind. I could almost see the images click into place like they do on a slot machine right before it pays off. He locked eyes with Dave who nodded, waited a beat, then jumped into the conversation. "What special school in New Mexico?"

"The one their father said they have to go to because they keep getting into trouble," Allison said. "It's about a zillion miles from a mall."

"That far, huh?" Dave scratched his head. "How do you know all this?"

"Josh told me."

"I heard them talking." Josh ducked his head. "I wasn't trying to listen, but they kind of scream when they're mad."

Dave nodded. "And they were mad about the school?"

"Yeah. They said it's like a prison. I mean, it's *not* a prison, but kids can't leave the grounds and there are counselors watching all the time and holding group meetings every time someone breaks the rules. And there are a *lot* of rules."

"And classes start way before summer is over and they don't have weekends off," Allison said.

"And Brooklyn and Manhattan would have to live in separate units," Josh added.

"Hmmm." Dave fiddled with the phony timecard. "I've heard sometimes it's tough on twins when they're separated."

"Yeah, well, they should separate them to separate planets. Earth being not one of them." Allison abandoned Josh's macaroni, stood, and flounced to the freezer where she liberated a tub of chocolate ice cream.

"They got into Mr. Krammer's e-mail and found out the guy in charge of the school said they're bad influences on each other," Josh said. "I saw them egg each other on all the time at work."

"Egg each other on to do what?" Atwell asked, his voice sharp and insistent.

Josh didn't seem to notice the heightened interest. "Being rude to customers, pulling the seams on the bags part way open so food falls out, spitting on burgers."

Stomach roiling, I congratulated myself on never eating at Krammee's.

Atwell and Dave, meanwhile, exchanged a series of glances that seemed to check off means, motive, and opportunity. The only things missing were the murder weapon and the scene of the crime.

And I had some ideas about those.

I got two bowls from a cabinet and handed them to Allison. "There's caramel sauce and squirt cream in a can in the refrigerator. Why don't you make sundaes and take them out on the deck while I clean up?"

Dave raised his eyebrows. I rushed on before he suggested that Allison do the cleaning. "You had a long day with Paulette and I didn't have to work."

Josh brought his plate and glass to the kitchen. "I'd be glad to help."

Allison shot him a what-a-suck-up-you-are look.

I patted his shoulder, noting that I had to reach up to do it. He was as tall as Dave. "Thanks, but there's not much to it."

"Okay. But when you get a rake, I'll help you with the rose garden."

"Deal." I turned to Dave and made a clawing motion at my neck. "I have a feeling I'll have the rake we're looking for real soon. Maybe by the end of the day."

Dave's eyebrows soared, but he said nothing until Josh and Allison were on the deck and I'd closed the door. "The end of the day?"

221

"Maybe. Possibly sooner. Get me a map of Reckless River."

CHAPTER 24

Dave leaped from the sofa and headed for the door to the parking lot.

Atwell—who I thought of as Chuck pretty much only when Dave was around, and not always then—merely scowled. He was in a league of his own when it came to scowling. "What do you need a map for?"

"To figure out the spot where Brooklyn and Manhattan killed their father and dumped the garden rake they used to do it."

Atwell rolled his eyes—something else he excelled at.

I ignored him and puttered around the kitchen until Dave returned with a crinkled, coffee-stained map and spread it on the dining room table. Then I extricated a red marker pen from the collection in a chipped mug at the edge of the counter and surveyed the grid of black lines representing streets and avenues, the curves and splotches of blue that indicated streams, ponds, a lake, and the river, and the blops of green signifying parks and greenbelts. "Where did Woodrow Krammer live?"

Atwell stood, fished a small spiral notebook from the pocket of his slacks, thumbed through a few pages, and tapped a spot on the map. The grid pattern of downtown Reckless River was replaced there by curving lines indicating streets that meandered along a bluff overlooking the river.

I made an X, stifling a smug smile as I did. My theory was looking good. But it was still only a theory. If I was right, I could gloat later.

Tracing the greenbelt with my finger, I made another X where the auto repair shop stood, and a third at the site of Krammee's restaurant. From there, I drew a line to Woodrow Krammer's address.

"What time did Krammee's close on July 4th?"

Atwell consulted his notebook. "10:30. They stayed open later than usual."

"And did Krammer drive his daughters home?"

Another page flipped. "Yes. They left the restaurant right around 11:00. After they cleaned up."

Or went through the motions.

"And Mrs. Krammer . . . ?"

"Asleep, wearing earplugs because of fireworks in the neighborhood."

Bending close to the map, I moved my finger along the line I'd drawn, searching for possible routes between Krammer's home and business, searching for a likely spot for a murder.

And there it was.

Because of the greenbelt, there was no direct route from the restaurant to his home. Krammer had to zig and zag. But as he neared his exclusive neighborhood, his choices narrowed down to two routes—one direct, and one not. If Brooklyn and Manhattan were in a car with me, I'd take the direct route and put the pedal to the metal. But I'd have to hit the brake at the seldom-used railroad siding where, thanks to my perusal of the paper in search of current events for Allison, I knew the city recently installed a stop sign.

I circled the intersection with my finger. "I assume the Krammee twins say their father dropped them at home and drove off."

Atwell flipped more pages. "Allegedly he told them he had a meeting. According to his wife he often had meetings late at night."

Meaning drug deals.

"No rest for the wicked," Dave said with a laugh.

This was no time to go into it, but that smelled like another myth. I'd come across people who did rotten things all day long and still logged plenty of sack time. But maybe I was interpreting it wrong.

"Did anyone else see him drive away from his home?" I asked.

Atwell shook his head. "I, uh, haven't had the resources to scour the neighborhood yet."

Dave put his finger beside mine on the map. "You think they killed him there?"

"Or someplace similar. A place where he had to stop the car, and where they could get him out, get him away from the road, and attack him with the rake."

"The railroad right of way is pretty wide there," Dave said. "Lots of trees, too."

Atwell shook his head. "How did they get him out of the car and get him to where they could swing that rake with enough force to take him down?"

"Easy. They're arguing with him about something—maybe that school, maybe something else. It doesn't matter what. He stops at the crossing." I tapped Dave's finger. "One of them jumps out. She doesn't go far, maybe only a few yards, but she won't get in the car again. He gets mad. And then he gets out."

"And gets mauled. Their anger about the school and being separated might explain the extent of his injuries, the number of times he was struck. And with fireworks going off everywhere, no one would have heard if he called for help." Dave dug in his pocket for his keys. "Let's get out there while we've got daylight and find evidence to support this."

Atwell didn't move. "I'll buy that Krammer could have been killed that way. But why haul his body to the auto repair shop?"

"Because that's where Larry found those huge footprints a week ago," I told him.

"And the girls thought they'd frame Bigfoot? A creature that might not even exist?" Atwell smacked his forehead with the heel of his hand. "That's the craziest idea I ever heard."

"They're teenagers, Chuck," Dave said. "They don't think like you do."

"It's not like they tried to frame the Easter Bunny or the Tooth Fairy," I offered. "Bigfoot *might* exist."

"But that's beside the point," Dave added. "Look at the confusion and distraction that second set of tracks created. The manpower we put on chasing a hoax. The media. The pressure on you."

Like a carnival hypnotist, Dave swung his car keys in front of Chuck's eyes. "You. Me. Railroad. Evidence. Now."

Atwell swatted at the keys. "What about the tracks? Huh? How did they make the tracks?"

"I saw at least two guys selling plaster casts and rubber feet during the first media feeding frenzy," I volunteered.

Dave headed for the door. "I bet if you show the twins' pictures around to souvenir hawkers, someone will remember them."

Atwell groaned, then crossed to the coffee table and picked up his glass. He drank the dregs of his iced tea like it was an elixir purchased from the back of a snake oil salesman's wagon.

And then they were off, leaving Lola asleep beside the sofa, and leaving me to ignore yet another call from Jake and wrestle with one remaining question—who, or what, left the *first* set of footprints?

I had no answer the rational bit of my mind would accept when Josh and Allison left to hang at the mall and take in a movie with friends. And I had nothing when Mrs. B came in with Cheese Puff, his hair slick with oil, his stomach bloated. When she set him down, he toddled to Lola who sniffed him with interest, then licked his head.

"What happened to Lola's foot?"

"She stepped on a broken bottle. What happened to Cheese Puff?"

"He dove into the popcorn tub while I was explaining to an upstart theater manager that their rule about pets is outdated. These days *everyone* takes their pets *everywhere*."

Mrs. B punctuated that with expansive arm gestures while I carried Cheese Puff to the kitchen sink. Too full of popcorn to fight, he limited himself to hanging his head and grunting while I removed a woven blue leather collar I

227

hadn't seen before. While Lola looked on and whined in sympathy, I sprayed him with warm water.

Mrs. B knew the drill so well she'd purchased several bottles of high-quality dog shampoo for us. She considered the selection in the cabinet under the sink and handed over a bottle of pale green liquid. I glanced at the label and saw we were going with a coconut-and-lime infused fast-lathering experience.

"That self-important manager told me he doesn't make exceptions." Mrs. B fluffed her silvery hair. "Not even for widowed women like myself who otherwise would have to attend a showing alone."

I had to admire her nerve, playing the widow card as if she didn't have a dozen friends who would have gone with her. And it wouldn't matter to them if the movie was a documentary dealing with the question of whether chickens had lips.

"Didn't he realize you were wearing two strands of pearls?" I turned off the water and squirted shampoo on Cheese Puff's back. "Was it so dark in the theater he couldn't recognize what he was up against?"

"Possibly." Mrs. B fingered her necklace. "He may have mistaken them for glass beads."

I felt a pang of loss, the way a kid does when he discovers the truth about Santa. To Mrs. Ballantine, born with luminescent beauty but without a silver spoon, pearls represented the money and security she'd lacked as a child. They were symbols of power and privilege. She drew strength from them.

But Mrs. B was somewhere in the vicinity of 70. Did younger generations feel the same about pearls? Or grasp where Mrs. B was coming from? Had the manager even noticed her necklace?

"That's probably it," I said in a consoling voice. "He must have thought they were painted glass. Or plastic."

Mrs. B drew in a sharp breath at the idea of anyone thinking she'd wear plastic beads with a silk dress—a dress now stained with enough oil to fry a flounder. "He said dogs are unsanitary and disruptive."

I worked shampoo into a lather every bit as rich and thick as the label promised. "Let me guess. Right after he said that, the Puffster threw himself into the popcorn as a declaration of disdain for such an unsavory characterization of his species."

"Sarcasm doesn't become you, dear. But you're right. The little prince had no choice." Mrs. B laid a hand over her heart. "He *had* to protest."

Cheese Puff yipped his assent and shook himself, scattering clumps of lather. A few hit my face, spattering my glasses and giving me a polka dot view of the world.

"Thanks a lot." I turned the water on with my elbow and thrust him into the gush. "When it comes to protesting simply because you can, you and my sister are cut from the same cloth."

Mrs. B covered Cheese Puff's ears before I impugned his character further. "That's not at all true."

"Give me a break. A popcorn protest isn't as ridiculous as a demonstration in support of gender equity for a creature that might not exist?"

"Of course not."

She put a world of meaning into those three words, making it clear further discussion would imperil invitations to partake of frothy drinks and jumbo cashews on her side of the deck. But I'd won a victory of sorts. She'd leaped to the defense of my protesting pooch instead of my sister. And I'd gotten off with only a denial, not a lecture.

Pressing my lips together to contain a smile, I nodded. When she removed her hands, I rinsed the rest of the soap from Cheese Puff's hair.

"Do you have special towels for the little prince?" she asked in a bright but brittle voice.

Seriously?

I almost laughed, but then saw the question for what it was—an attempt to patch things up. I also saw opportunity. "I don't. I've thought of getting some, but right now the budget won't stretch that far. Use the towels from the small bathroom."

"Those pink ones with the cats on the trim?"

Her tone implied as much disbelief as if I suggested drying him with an old burlap sack or cut-rate paper towels. Since she wouldn't balk at the concept of using a guest towel on a dog, I suspected she might share my dislike for these particular bits of terrycloth. They were a shade of pink that made me think of cures for indigestion. Dave found them nauseatingly cute. "Why not?"

"You know how he feels about cats."

I pretended like I cared what the popcorn protesting pooch liked. "Maybe we could hold the towels so he doesn't see the trim."

"But they're so . . . pink." Mrs. B flicked her fingers as if banishing both color and towels. "That friend of Sybil's gave them to you, right?"

"I can't remember." I ran my hands along Cheese Puff's sides and legs, squeezing out excess water. "I got dozens of housewarming gifts at the party you gave. Verna and Sybil squabbled over how to make a list to keep them all straight, and then neither of them wrote anything down."

"That's par for their course." Mrs. B sighed. "But I bet it was that woman. If I'd realized she wanted to join the Committee so she should throw herself at Jim, I would have blackballed her. She was always bragging about getting rid of junk by regifting. Probably had those towels around since the 50s."

She gave a final flick of her fingers. "Well, she moved to California, so we don't have to worry about offending her. We'll use them on the little prince this once and then we'll trash them. Tomorrow I'll shop for something much better."

Yes!

A win-win situation. She got an excuse for shopping and I got new towels, towels I knew would be far superior in quality and tastefulness.

She trotted to the tiny powder room and returned with the kitty towels. "Close your eyes," she told Cheese Puff. "This will be over in a minute and then these ghastly things will be history."

When he was dry I plunked him on the floor and tossed the towels in the trash while Mrs. B rewarded him with one of the gourmet treats she carries in her purse at all times. Cheese Puff rewarded her with a belch worthy of a steam locomotive.

I wiped my glasses on my T-shirt. "Looks like the dive into the popcorn tub wasn't all about protest. How much did he gobble?"

"Only a few kernels." She fed two gourmet treats to Lola.

"Define 'a few.'"

"Oh, maybe a dozen. Or so."

I took that "or so" to mean far more than a dozen and headed for the door to the deck. "Outside. Let's drop some fertilizer on the rose garden."

"Watch out for that giant hound," Mrs. B cautioned.

"I will. Come on, dogs."

Lola, ever obedient, limped behind me.

Cheese Puff, seldom obedient, leaped to the sofa and rolled on the cushions until Mrs. B repeated my command.

I turned on the outside light, slid the door open, and almost tripped over Dave's boots and my flip-flops.

Had Allison and Josh brought them from the pool?

But wait. The boots and flip-flops weren't at the pool when I went to retrieve them.

Maybe Bernina Burke, having had her fun, returned them to the pool deck for Josh and Allison to find. Or brought them here to make sure I got her point and knew I had another black mark against me.

But in that case, where were Dave's socks and T-shirt? Where was my towel? Was Bernina holding those in the hope of making me grovel?

Like that would happen!

I left the flip-flops where they were, but picked up the boots and set them inside the door. Not a trace of dried mud clung to them. The soles were clean.

Bernina wouldn't have cleaned them and neither would Allison. Josh, on the other hand, might have at least knocked the dirt off.

Something else to wonder about.

But something to wonder about when I didn't have a dog that was about to explode. "Come on, you two."

Lola nudged Cheese Puff with her nose and, after another command from Mrs. B, he fell in line, waddling toward the gate through hot and humid air. I trotted ahead, squinting into the twilight to make sure the coast was clear. If Monster Mutt had dug a nest in the poolside shrubbery, how long before he came farther along the trail and camped on my steps?

The decorative lighting along the trail created a faint glow, but I saw no suspicious shadows and heard no click of claws on the asphalt trail. "Okay gang, let's go. But no dilly-dallying."

I unlatched the gate, swung it open, went down the short flight, and picked my way through the overgrown rose bushes to the trail. Grunting with the effort of descending each step, Cheese Puff followed and sidled up to the first bush he came to.

Lola limped halfway down the steps and paused, raising her muzzle to the breeze. She snorted, then growled.

"What is it, Lola?" Mrs. B asked.

I squinted into the gloom. "I don't see any—"

Snarling, Monster Mutt launched himself from behind the low wall on the far side of the trail. Claws scrabbling at asphalt, he came at me, jaws wide.

CHAPTER 25

Mrs. B screamed.

Cheese Puff yelped.

Lola barked.

I raised my arms to shield my neck and face.

Monster Mutt leaped.

I closed my eyes.

A howl split the night.

Something huge shoved me from behind, knocking me into the spiky embrace of a rose bush. Thorns ripped at my clothing and skin.

Mrs. B screamed again, a scream that gave way to a squeal and then a gasp.

Then I heard a cascade of sounds, barking, growling, yipping, whining, whimpering.

I opened my eyes to see Monster Mutt swinging from the one-handed grip of a colossal creature. The hound clawed air, the whites of his eyes gleaming in the dim light.

The creature turned my way and brushed long hair from its face with its free hand. "Hey, Ms. Reed, what do you want me to do with this dog?"

Bigfoot speaks?

And knows my name?

I levered myself up on one elbow for a better look at my humongous hero. The light was behind him, and too murky to allow me to make out his features. What I could see was a hairy chest, equally hairy arms and legs, and a pair of ratty cargo shorts. "Do I know you?"

"Yeah. Well, kinda." Monster Mutt wiggled, but was stilled with a shake that made his jaws snap. "You subbed in my calculus class once."

"At Captain Meriwether High?"

"Yeah. You probably don't remember. I always sit in the last row because no one can see over me." He ducked his head. "You didn't know anything about calculus. But you didn't hassle us, so we didn't hassle you."

That lack of hassle on both sides pretty much defined a successful day in the world of substitute teaching. "Sorry. I was never very good at math." And I've had close to 20 years of forgetting what I learned in high school and college.

Mrs. B clattered down the steps in high-heeled sandals and went to work snipping me free from my bed of thorns with the garden shears she kept in a plastic box at the edge of her deck. "When we saw you on the Fourth, we thought you were Bigfoot."

The boy laughed. "That's what my dad calls me on account of I'm up to a size 18 shoe and my feet are real wide and my toes are weird. My name's Ben. Ben Bradford. Sorry I crashed into you that night, Ms. Reed, but the smoke was getting to me."

"What's going on?" a female voice called from a unit down the way. "Is someone hurt?"

"I took a little spill on the steps," Mrs. B trilled. "I'm fine. No need for you to come out. The air is stifling."

"The heat is all in your head," the voice called. "Global warming is a myth."

A door closed with a thump and, after something mumbled under her breath, Mrs. B returned to efforts to liberate me, ignoring the thorns snagging her dress.

Monster Mutt attempted to wiggle loose again, but Ben tightened his grip and shook him harder. "Want me to let him go?"

"No," Mrs. B said. "Not here where he could hurt Cheese Puff and Lola." She pointed to the dogs sitting at the base of the steps. Neither seemed the least bit alarmed. In fact, both were wagging their tails and gazing at Ben expectantly, exactly the way they did when a treat was in store.

Craning my neck, I peered at the lattice on the side of the deck closest to Mrs. B's and, sure enough, spotted a gap. That gap, I guessed, was the new entrance to Ben's shelter. I bet that shelter contained the items missing from the pool deck.

"Do you think you could carry that beast to the parking lot at the far end of the condo complex?" Mrs. B asked.

"Sure. I'm pretty strong. And he's not as heavy as he looks." Ben flexed his free arm. "I'll take him farther if you want."

Mrs. B chuckled. "I'd like to take him to Sitka or even Siberia, but the lot will do for now."

She sliced through the final cane and helped me up. "He'll come right back if you let him loose," I warned.

"Not from where I intend to put him." She headed off along the trail with Ben in pursuit, Monster Mutt whimpering like a frightened puppy. "Get yourself cleaned up, dear, and make Ben a sandwich. Or two. We'll be a few minutes. Turn off the outside lights so no one sees us."

My mission assigned, I brushed bark mulch from my legs, saw that Cheese Puff and Lola did their duty, and ushered them inside. In a few minutes I'd changed my clothes, whipped up three ham and cheese sandwiches, and set out a couple of cans of cola. I poured a tall glass of lemonade, stationed the pitcher beside it, and opened a bag of potato chips and another of guaranteed-good-for-you oatmeal cookies.

I ate one to make sure they didn't taste like sawdust, then ate another to make sure my taste buds hadn't been mistaken. Nope, the second was as tasty as the first. I ate a third to keep the first two company. Then I rounded out the spread on the table with a jar of sweet pickles, a box of crackers, and a carton of ice cream that, by some miracle, was still a third full.

Cheese Puff and Lola, meanwhile, stood in the doorway, gazing into the darkness. When the gate creaked, they bolted across the deck. In a minute they returned, weaving themselves around and between Ben's legs. Cheese Puff's reaction to the sketch displayed on the news flashed through my brain. "You were feeding them, weren't you?"

Ben shoved long hair behind his ears and the bit of cheek visible between his eyes and scraggly beard turned crimson. "A little. When I had enough to spare."

I gestured to the table. "Well, hopefully there's more than enough here. But Cheese Puff has already exceeded the feed limit today, so please don't give him even a nibble. With all the popcorn he devoured, I'll be lucky if he doesn't barf all over the bed."

Cheese Puff sat, raised one paw, and made with the big eyes. Mrs. B's hand inched toward a sliver of ham hanging from a sandwich. I made a chopping motion. She wiggled her fingers and then pulled out a chair for Ben.

"It's only us," I told him. "Allison and Josh—I assume you know them from school—are at a movie, and Dave is off chasing evidence. Eat. You must be starving."

"Thanks." Ben sat, drained the glass of lemonade, then picked up a ham sandwich and made a third of it disappear into his mouth.

"Where did you stash the dog?" I asked Mrs. B.

She dimpled a smile. "In Bernina Burke's car."

Whoa!

"What were you thinking?"

"I was thinking the dog would be fine there for one night. We rolled the windows down a little and put a pan of water in the hatchback for him."

"I meant what were you thinking when you picked Bernina's car?"

"Oh. Well, I was thinking she should do more to protect the residents for whom she works." Mrs. B nibbled on a cookie. "I was also thinking that only a fool leaves her car unlocked. But don't worry, no one saw us."

I glanced at Ben who was roughly the size of objects that could be seen from outer space.

"I hunched over," he said. "And we stayed in the shadows."

"And I wiped away our fingerprints," Mrs. B added.

"You know that if she can't find the real culprit, Bernina will blame me. She always does."

"But she'll have so many things to deal with first." Mrs. B ticked them off on her beringed fingers. "Calling animal control to get the dog out of her car. Explaining to

238

the dog's owner why the dog was in her car. Oh, and repairing and cleaning her car."

"If that's possible. He'll probably tear up the upholstery trying to get out," Ben said. "And maybe chew the seatbelts and the steering wheel and anything not made of metal." He lowered his voice and mumbled the rest. "And, uh, dogs often tend to, uh, defecate if they're stressed."

Mrs. B snickered. "I hope she has good insurance."

Bernina was bound to find a way to punish me for this, but it might be worth it. Grinning, I went to the closet for a sack of cheesy snacks to help me fight the urge to tiptoe to the parking lot and assess the preliminary damage.

For a few minutes, we devoted ourselves to our respective meals. Ben devoured another sandwich and ate a fistful of potato chips. I crunched a bunch of those puffy, orange cheesy twists I love so much. Mrs. B, immune to the siren song of high-calorie, high-sodium, high-fat, low-nutritional-value snack food, continued to nibble the same cookie.

"So, Ben," Mrs. B said in the chipper but soothing sort of voice I imagined a nanny might use to coax a confidence from a recalcitrant child, "tell us why you've been living under the deck."

He swallowed a trio of pickle slices and slid his gaze toward me. "I got the idea in school."

I blinked.

"Really?" Mrs. B asked. "I haven't been in school in . . . well, in several years, but I can't recall taking a class that would prompt me to do such a thing."

"I guess I should have said I got the idea from a teacher," Ben amended.

And I bet I knew which teacher. The one making camp somewhere in the greenbelt even as I spoke his name. "Mr. Marsden?"

"The history teacher who had the jar of bear grease in his room?" Mrs. B pinched her delicate nose. "And created that horrible stench?"

"Uh, yeah." Ben eyed the ice cream. I took the hint and got a bowl and spoon. "He's always talking about living off the land and foraging for food and stuff out in the woods. I thought it would be fun to see if I could do it before I went off to college."

"Apparently you and I have far different ideas about what constitutes a good time," Mrs. B said.

"And a different idea of what it means to be out in the woods," I added.

"I wanted to go up on Mt. St. Helens somewhere." Ben mounded the bowl high with chocolate chip ice cream and replaced the cover on the tub. "But my parents didn't want me to go too far. In case I got hurt or something."

Mrs. B gasped and clutched both strings of pearls. "Your parents know where you are? And what you're doing?"

"Sure. They took a bunch of courses in anthropology and sociology and stuff like that when they were in college. We're all gonna write an article on living off the urban landscape. And maybe do a bunch of blogs." Ben pulled a cell phone from the right pocket of his cargo shorts. "Want to talk to them?"

"No. That won't be necessary." Mrs. B's fingers fluttered like wounded birds, then gripped the edge of the table. "I apologize. I assumed you had run away, or were homeless."

"Makes sense, considering how I look. That shower by the pool doesn't run hot and there's no soap or shampoo. And I didn't bring a comb or anything because Dad said the whole point of the experiment was to use what I found." He patted the large left pocket of his shorts. "Except we decided I should bring my phone and a jackknife and a little first-aid kit. And a toothbrush."

"Goodness, yes. You wouldn't want to use a toothbrush you found on the ground." Mrs. B grimaced. "But what about food? You didn't eat from trash cans, did you?"

"Sometimes. I mean, I pretty much had to most days. I was careful, though, I didn't eat a burger someone took a bite out of. But people throw away plenty of stuff that's still good, like boxes of cereal and stale chips. And a lot of people don't compost like they should, so I found apples and carrots and broccoli." He nodded toward the complex up the river. "The people who live in the condos up there throw away tons of good food. Once I got a whole broiled chicken still in the wrapper. Not even past the sell-by date."

"Is that how you won over Cheese Puff and Lola?" I asked.

He hung his head. "I didn't give them bones. I made sure to throw those in the trash bins where the dogs couldn't get at them."

"Thanks." I glanced at Mrs. B. "Due to the failure of certain of my neighbors to recognize the importance of his dietary restrictions, Cheese Puff has plenty of digestive issues already."

Mrs. B blushed and nibbled once more at her cookie—the same darn cookie. I began to wonder if she was human. I mean, they were guaranteed-good-for-you

241

cookies, but as my previous research had determined, they were pretty darn tasty.

I snatched one from the bag and ate it to make sure the three I devoured earlier hadn't been flukes. Nope. Number four was right up there with the first three. Maybe Mrs. B had filled up on popcorn before the protest.

I swallowed and cleared my throat. "What did you find to eat at the auto repair shop?"

"Doughnuts." Ben grinned. "They were only a little stale and still inside the box they came in, so there was no dirt on them. One was filled with custard and the other was covered with chocolate and sprinkles. They were great."

I made a mental note to tell Doug that "Bigfoot" liked his doughnut selections.

"Will you return home now that you've had a meal that wasn't, uh, foraged?" Mrs. B asked.

Ben scooped melted ice cream from the bottom of the bowl and slurped it off the spoon. "Nope. But we won't count this part of the day in the experiment."

"And now that we know where you've been sleeping?" I opened the tub of ice cream and nudged it his way. "Will you have to move your camp?"

He paused, spoon above the remaining ice cream slush. "Uh, I suppose. See, we made a couple of rules. One was that I couldn't beg for food, and another was that I had to stay out of sight as much I could. Mom was afraid if too many people saw me I'd get arrested for being a prowler or something."

"Or mistaken for Bigfoot," I said.

"Yeah." He stirred the slush, mashing a frozen lump against the side of the tub. "Dad read me the article in the paper after a woman saw me in the park. And he told me about what happened because of my footprints by the auto repair place. He and Mom got real worried when they started hunting for whoever left those prints by the dead guy. They were scared the police would find me at night or while I was sleeping and I'd get hurt, but I told them I had a safe place no one knew about."

He gazed toward the deck and his shelter. "Except that isn't true any more."

"It is if we keep it that way." Mrs. B fixed me with the full force of her sapphire gaze. "I don't see any reason for anyone else to know. If word got around and Bernina Burke found out this heroic boy was sleeping under the deck, she'd call the authorities."

"The same authorities she didn't call about the vicious dog?"

"You know Bernina operates on petty vindictiveness, dear." Mrs. B set the nibbled cookie on a napkin. "We *wanted* her to take action about the dog, and that's the kind of situation where she drags her feet. But we *don't* want her to report Ben, so of course she will. *If* she spots him."

"Is she the woman with the clipboard?" Ben asked. "The one who walks around the place sometimes in the morning and makes notes?"

"That's her," I said.

"I don't think she likes you much. Or your dogs. Her face turns red when she passes your place and her eyes kind of bulge."

"Making her even more attractive than she already is."

"Now, dear," Mrs. B cautioned, "I thought you were trying to be less negative toward Bernina."

"Says the woman who moments ago put a slavering cur in her car."

243

Mrs. B sighed. "I could argue I did that for the benefit of the residents in the complex, but I see your point."

"And I see yours. No one else needs to know Ben is under the deck. Not Dave. Not Jim. And not Dario."

Mrs. B nodded agreement, nibbled another bite from her cookie, and turned to Ben. "I'll make breakfast for you in the morning. If I do it without you literally begging for food, that will be okay, won't it?"

Sheesh.

Ben shook his head. "Thanks, but that still breaks the rules."

"What if I made breakfast for myself and accidentally went off and left it on the table outside?"

"What if you ordered an extra-large pizza," I scoffed, "and *accidentally* told them to deliver it to a hole in the lattice under the deck?"

"Now, Barbara, there's no need to be quite so sarcastic." Mrs. B's spine straightened and she lasered me with her gaze. "I was only trying to help the boy. And thank him for saving the little prince from that horrible hound."

"I appreciate it," Ben said. "Honest. But I can't break any more rules or I might as well go home to air conditioning, hot showers, and television."

All of which sounded pretty darn good to me.

Mrs. B frowned, then nodded. "Yes. I see. But when the experiment is over, you will let me treat you to something, won't you?"

"Sure." Ben spooned melted ice cream into his mouth. "But not burgers and fries, okay? And especially not at Krammee's. I've had way too many of those." He scraped the last of the ice cream from the tub. "When they close up at the end of the day, they throw away stuff they don't sell.

It's all cold and greasy and gross, but I could depend on it being there. Until they shut down, that is."

"I have a feeling they're going to stay shut down for a while," I said. "What will you do if you can't get enough to eat without breaking the rules?"

"It's an experiment. And it's *my* experiment." He pushed the empty carton to the center of the table. "So I can decide it's over whenever I want. And Mom's got a long list of chores for me waiting at home."

"When you go home, I suppose we should tell people the truth about the footprints. And end this madness with the media and Bigfoot hunters and people hawking souvenirs." Myself included, whenever the police allowed the auto repair shop and mini Bigfoot museum to reopen.

Mrs. B tapped her nails on the table. "Let's not be hasty, dear."

CHAPTER 26

"What does that mean?"

"It means let's not rush." She fingered her pearls. "Ben and his parents need time to review the data he collected during this experiment. And time to write and publish their article. Revealing the truth about the footprints right now would detract from that."

"But—"

"And imagine what the media will do to poor Ben. They may accuse him of intentionally impersonating Bigfoot. And you know how some of those reporters are— the more he denies it, the more they'll think he's lying. His picture will be all over the Internet."

Ben swallowed hard.

"So we let people go on believing Bigfoot is lurking in the greenbelt in the middle of Reckless River?"

"You know as well as I do that most people believe what they want to believe, dear. And I've found a great number prefer a shaky myth to the solid truth."

I mulled that for a moment. Then I gave in to her plan to keep the facts to ourselves. For now.

"If I'm careful and don't leave any more footprints," Ben said hopefully, "maybe everyone will lose interest."

"The media will find another story to chase in a day or two," I said. "But I don't know about the Bigfoot hunters."

Rings sparkling, Mrs. B flicked that concern aside. "Oh, someone will find another set of footprints and they'll take off for a new location." She winked. "Perhaps those prints will be near the movie theater in Portland where the officious manager asked me to leave."

I didn't ask if she planned on enlisting Ben to make the prints. After all, the less I knew, the less a trained interrogator could get out of me by threatening to lock me in a room with my sister until I talked.

Dave shook me awake a few minutes before the alarm went off the next morning and offered a giant mug of coffee and a huge grin. "We found blood, we found the rake, and we found a set of rubber feet. The Krammee twins are being fitted for designer outfits at the juvenile facility. Their mother is being treated for an attack of what they used to call the vapors."

He attempted another grin, but it morphed into a yawn. "Chuck's holding a news conference at 9:00."

I sat up and reached for the coffee. "And he'll give me credit for cracking the case?"

"Doubtful. But I'll personally see that you're rewarded." He sat beside me and nuzzled my neck. "On a daily basis."

"Starting after you've had a shower." I set my coffee on the nightstand, pushed him away, and got out of bed. "You smell like ditch water and rotting hay."

"Really?" Dave cranked his head around and sniffed one armpit. "I specifically asked for a mix of ditch water and dead possum. Chuck said that was guaranteed to turn you on."

"Given his personality and consequent lack of experience with women, I almost believe it." I headed for the bathroom. "I'm going to shower."

"Me, too." Dave stifled a yawn, pulled his T-shirt over his head, and leered at me. "We can 'discuss' the reward system while we suds each other."

Taking my cue from his yawns, I didn't wait for him in the shower. When I emerged, I found him sprawled on his back, one shoe still on. He didn't move a muscle when I worked it off and tossed the sheet over him.

Downstairs, I clicked on the TV and found the story on every local newscast, reporters live from the street outside the juvenile facility or the parking lot at Krammee's. Relieved to see they'd abandoned the auto repair shop, I slathered peanut butter on a few crackers and headed for work.

Clipboard in hand, Bernina Burke was leaving her office as I drove past. I gave her a fingertip wave and fought the desire to park a few blocks away and return to witness her discovery of Monster Mutt.

There was no sign of the media at the repair shop and, probably because of that, no sign of my sister and her posse of protesters. But that didn't mean things had returned to normal. Pickup trucks packed the street for a block on either side of the shop, and a stream of men dressed for the outback passed the building on their way to the swale. Some wore heavy belts with sheaths for knives Jim Bowie would have envied, some carried thick ropes, and others had gadgets that looked like they could deliver enough voltage to bring down a charging rhino. They greeted each other with handshaking, backslapping, and raunchy comments, then set off through the tall grass like they were headed for a fraternity reunion.

Seeing them reminded me that Aston didn't know the official law enforcement hunt was over and the woods were filling up with men on another mission. The last time I'd mentioned him to Dave I'd been informed Aston was my problem so, on the off chance he'd powered up his cell, I punched in his number. I got only a leave-a-message recording, and complied. "Aston, it's Barbara Reed. The official search is over. The tracks by the body were a hoax."

Keeping Ben's secret was tough, especially when Doug arrived with a box of doughnuts. Fortunately, we had no time to talk. I was busy booking repair jobs and selling Bigfoot T-shirts. Doug was involved showing crime buffs where Woodrow Krammer's daughters dumped his body.

I felt a little guilty and a little sad about making money off Ben's footprints, but it seemed that most of those who came to buy souvenirs were laughing at themselves, so I set aside my qualms. Maybe Mrs. B was right. Maybe people did prefer fiction to fact.

When I got home, she and Dave were on the deck with the dogs—Lola flopped in the shade of a long table set against the wall, and Cheese Puff on the glider. A tall glass pitcher filled with ice and pink liquid sweated on a table shaded by a multi-colored umbrella, and a few small bowls indicated snacks were to be had.

"Care for raspberry and lime slush with rum?" Mrs. B asked.

A question right up there with "Do you like to breathe?"

I filled a glass, sampled a few toasted almonds and a fat green olive stuffed with blue cheese, kicked off my sandals, and collapsed. "Anything exciting go on here today?"

"Bernina Burke had a meltdown. Somehow that giant mutt from up the way got into her car." Dave shook his head. "Talk about demolition. I've seen crack houses in better condition. There was nothing left of the seats but frame and springs."

"Wow." I raised my glass to cover my grin. "How did the dog get in her car?"

"Nobody seems to know. Or if they know, they're not saying."

"I bet Bernina was furious."

"That doesn't begin to cover it," Mrs. B said. "The young dog catcher was more frightened of her than of the dog. Of course, the dog was exhausted by the time he arrived, whereas Bernina was barely beginning to froth at the mouth. She wanted Dave to shoot the beast."

Dave raised his hands. "Told her I'd been leaving my gun at work ever since I found myself tempted to point it at *her*."

If I didn't already love the man, that quip would have won me over. "So what happened?"

"Well, apparently someone placed a call to an animal rescue group that goes after irresponsible owners," Mrs. B told me.

Apparently?

I hid my smile behind another sip.

"And apparently someone called the newspaper."

Undoubtedly that same someone. Someone given to wearing pearl necklaces and diamond rings. "And then?"

"Well, the animal rescue people listened to what everyone had to say. By then there were a great many residents gathered, all of whom had been menaced by the dog. Then the rescue people took the dog into their care. They agreed he was vicious, but said the fault lies with his owner. They said they'd make an example of the man."

Mrs. B polished her nails on the sleeve of a lilac silk blouse. "The owner may be ill-tempered, but he's not a complete idiot. I expect he'll realize being touted as an irresponsible pet owner won't benefit his practice, and he'll back away from a fight."

"And the dog?"

"They'll rehabilitate and train him and find a home." Dave stretched and ran a finger along the neckline of my T-shirt. "Now, how about you? Busy day at the shop?"

"Yes, but mostly because the shop is now also the Bigfoot gift emporium and a destination for every crime buff in the Northwest. They all want a peek at the spot where the Krammee twins dumped their dad."

"The ghouls will lose interest in a few days," Dave said. "And the Bigfoot hunters will be off chasing another set of tracks or clump of hair or sighting."

"I hope so." I shot a glance at Mrs. B. "Because if they're not gone in two weeks, I'm hunting for another job."

"Don't be ridiculous, dear, where can you find a job with so much excitement? And think of the dividends and commissions."

"Dividends? Commissions?"

"With all your added duties, Larry and I will be talking about restructuring your salary and giving you a percentage of souvenir sales." She twisted her long strand of pearls around her fingers and raised her voice a shade.

"It should add up to a tidy sum by the end of the summer. Unless someone comes forward and reveals those first footprints were a hoax and sales drop away."

Meaning I should keep my lips zipped.

I was caught between the rock labeled "ethics and morality" and the hard spot labeled "student loan and hush money for Rayanne."

Speaking of that.

I nudged Dave's foot with mine. "Now that things have calmed down, we need to make a plan."

"Already did." He hooked a thumb at Mrs. B. "Hot sun and cold beer and I spilled my guts."

"I only wish you'd told me sooner. Before she got her hooks so deep into your wallet." Mrs. B twisted her pearls again. "But that's water under the bridge."

"And now I have to jump off the bridge." Dave took my hand. "Mrs. Ballantine recommends telling the truth and letting Allison decide how to handle it."

My jaw dropped.

"She's growing up fast," Mrs. B said. "Once she has all the information, she'll make a wise decision."

At the risk of being branded—as usual—too negative, I swallowed my words along with most of my drink. Warmth spread to my fingers and toes and I lounged in the chair, reminding myself Dave had signed on for this plan and I couldn't be held responsible if it blew up.

Vowing to stand behind him and never utter an I-told-you-so phrase, I drained my glass. "Where is Allison?"

"At the pool with Josh." Mrs. B tapped the cell phone on the glider beside her. "I'll call them as soon as the pizzas get here."

Pizzas. Plural. As in more than one. "What kind of pizzas?"

252

"All kinds," Dave said. "Plus stuff from the bakery. That's in the refrigerator."

"Ah. Letting her see what she'll miss if she picks door number two. And Josh will also hear your confession?"

Dave shrugged. "What she decides will affect him."

"It's important that she considers all aspects of the situation, all factors involved in making a choice," Mrs. B said.

"Aspects and factors including éclairs and chocolate mousse?"

Before she could answer, the doorbell rang and she headed off to take delivery of the pizzas. Dave finished his beer, took the can to the recycling tub in the kitchen, and returned with a glass of water. Not being the one who had to keep my thoughts in order and speak without slurring my words, I poured myself a second drink.

Mrs. B called Allison, then fluttered about deploying five pizza boxes on the long table and setting places with ornate silver utensils, crystal glasses, lace napkins, and plates that probably cost $200 apiece. Every minute or so she trotted into her condo for red pepper, cola, or grated cheese. Between trips she patted Dave's shoulder and told him it would all be okay. Dave nodded in a numb way as if those words had come from a surgeon about to open his chest with a grapefruit spoon and implant a bicycle pump.

In a few minutes Josh and Allison appeared. Josh wore a plain brown T-shirt and a pair of red and brown Hawaiian swim trunks. Allison wore a blue Oxford cloth shirt over her two-piece suit—a shirt that looked suspiciously like one that had been hanging in my closet this morning. Borrowing without asking wasn't what I'd call a sign of having the ability to make wise decisions, but I uttered not a word.

"Wow. This is amazing." Josh opened the first pizza box. "The killer carnivore special! I bet there's five pounds of meat on that crust."

Lola and Cheese Puff sat up, sniffed the air, and assumed begging positions beneath the table.

Allison pouted. "I hope there's something *I* like in one of those boxes."

Josh opened the second box. "This one looks like mushrooms, artichoke hearts, and more mushrooms." Allison grabbed for a slice and Josh moved on to the third box. "And this one is bacon and tomato and spinach."

As Allison carried her slice to the table, I wondered whether Ben was in his lair under the deck listening to Josh describe the feast. Would Mrs. B—never mind the rules—see that a portion found its way to him after dark?

Dave got a single meat-laden slice and took the chair to the right of his daughter. Josh, with a slice of each offering piled on his plate, sat on her left. I went for the fourth pizza, a pesto creation with garlic and sun-dried tomatoes, and Mrs. B picked the fifth, sausage and roasted peppers.

"What's going on?" Josh poured cola into a crystal wine glass. "What's with all the special plates and glasses?"

Chapter 27

Allison glanced at the table and then from me to her father. Her eyes narrowed and her bottom lip slid into pout position once again. "Are you two getting married?"

Spoken like someone who felt she should have been consulted and asked to sign off on the plan.

I fielded the question with raised hands, arched brows, and a laugh. "Married? We're not even going to utter that word in casual conversation until you graduate from high school."

Having made that up on the spot, I realized it sounded about right. Two years was a reasonable length of time to sort out emotional and financial baggage. In two years I should have a teaching job and be making inroads on my debt. Never mind that Mrs. B's plans for me included marriage and a baby well within that period. *I* was the one who'd be taking the aisle walk and carrying said baby, and *I* was a long way from being ready for either.

"We're celebrating because your father helped Detective Atwell solve the Krammer murder case," Mrs. B said.

Allison's frown turned into a smile and her eyes sparkled when she looked at Dave. "You helped arrest those skanky Krammee twins?"

"He certainly did." Mrs. B raised her glass.

"Way to go!" Josh lifted his cola and toasted Dave. "Can I write a song about you for my rock opera?"

Dave flinched.

"Sure," I said.

Dave flinched again.

"Wait." Allison pulled her phone from the pocket of my shirt. "How come I didn't see your name in the reports?"

"Because he's not a headline-grabber." Mrs. B raised her glass again. "Your father believes teamwork is more important than taking credit."

Allison considered that with the same expression I might wear when considering a meal of fried eel with fennel sauce.

"That's cool. It's like those superheroes who keep their identities secret so they can fight crime better." Josh nudged Allison. "Don't forget that your dad works undercover. If everybody knew what he looked like, he'd never catch guys dealing drugs, right?"

Allison nodded and a dim light of admiration dawned in her eyes.

Mrs. B let out a gentle sigh.

I restrained myself from jumping up and hugging Josh.

Dave shot me a wink that I suspected conveyed his intention of demonstrating a few super powers upstairs later on.

I raised my eyebrows, all the while wondering if what was to come with his daughter would leave him feeling powerless.

When the dessert tray had been picked over and nothing remained but smears of chocolate and custard, Mrs. B brought Dave a small snifter with two inches of brandy in the bowl, ushered Josh and Allison to the glider and announced that she would clean up while I walked the dogs.

Taking my cue, I got the leashes from our condo and set off. It was a relief to open the gate without peering both ways in search of Monster Mutt. It was also a relief not to have thorns rip my skin and clothing. Someone— most likely Ben improving access to his lair—had trimmed the canes along the path and piled them neatly at the edge of the trail.

There was no way to know how long it would take Dave to tell the story and answer the questions Allison would have, so I took my time. Eventually, however, both dogs balked and turned toward home. As I trudged up the steps to the deck, I heard Allison ask, "If you didn't tell me the truth before, how do I know you're telling me the truth now?"

Uh oh.

I paused with my hand reaching for the latch of the creaky gate, the dogs whining and pushing against my legs. In the glow of the lamp beside Mrs. B's door I saw Allison huddled in the shelter of Josh's arms, an accusatory finger aimed at her father.

Dave's head drooped. "I guess you don't. I didn't tell you before because I thought you were too young to understand. But mostly I didn't tell you because I was ashamed that I did so much stupid stuff."

He raised his head. "But I was never sorry that some of that stupid stuff gave me a beautiful daughter. I love you. And I'll do anything to protect you. Except lie. From now on, I'll never lie to you again."

Allison lowered her pointing finger, but said nothing.

Dave's head drooped again.

The dogs whimpered.

A shadow wearing a string of pearls hovered inside Mrs. B's condo.

I touched the latch, but didn't open it.

Josh brushed Allison's hair aside and kissed her forehead. "When you have to write that what-I-did-over-the-summer essay, you're gonna need a lot of extra paper."

Allison snickered and kissed his chin. "Maybe you could write it for me."

"Not a chance. At least not until I know how it ends."

"You mean, what happens if my mother shows up?"

"Yeah."

Dave kept his head down.

The shadow hovered at the door of Mrs. B's condo.

The cold metal latch grew warm in my fingers.

Then Allison sat up and kicked the glider into motion. "Well, first of all, I don't think she *will* show up. I think she's just seeing how much money she can get out of Dad. But if she does knock on the door, I'll tell her she must have the wrong address because a *real* mother wouldn't sell her kid and run off to do stupid stuff—even stupider stuff than Dad did. A *real* mother would be . . . well, responsible. She'd be a *real* mother. Like Dad is a *real* father."

Dave lifted his head.

"So I'd tell her to come back after she proved she could do better." Allison bounced from the glider, perched on the arm of Dave's chair, and kissed his forehead. "I love you, Dad. You might not let me do everything I want, and you're always asking me to do stupid chores, and you don't give me as much allowance as I deserve, but you've always been there for me."

Dave wrapped her in a hug. "And I always will be."

"Besides," Allison said with a smirk, "it's not like I never lied to you."

Because of the booming Bigfoot souvenir business, Doug lobbied to open the auto repair shop on Saturday for souvenir sales, minor repairs, and estimates. Larry agreed and, thinking of my student loan and the promise of commissions, I caved and joined them.

Most of the Bigfoot hunters had departed, but a few stayed on hoping one more day would reveal fresh prints, clumps of hair, or even a sighting somewhere in the greenbelt. As for Aston Marsden, for all I knew he was still out there, stalking and scavenging.

Was I worried about him? Maybe a little. But, as I knew from the stories he regaled us with at lunch in the teachers' room, he'd gone to far more remote places alone and returned. I had no doubt he'd emerge from the Reckless River greenbelt when it suited him. Perhaps he already had.

Doug stayed busy handing out flyers and escorting visitors to the rear lot to point out where we found the original tracks. I stayed busy keeping my lips zipped about the maker of those tracks, and processing sales of Bigfoot paraphernalia.

The majority of those shelling out for T-shirts and coffee mugs either laughed at themselves as they did or assured me the tracks would turn out to be another hoax. One small boy whispered that he was sure "some guy with really big feet" left the prints, but his friends already had T-shirts, so he had to have one. When his father shrugged and forked over the money, I packed my reservations away in a dim recess of my mind.

When I got home, Dave and Allison and Josh were on the deck with Mrs. B, Dario, and the entire Cheese Puff Care and Comfort Committee. Jim and Dario had the grill fired up and the scent of searing beef and roasting vegetables filled the warm air. Hoping morsels of meat would drop, Cheese Puff and Lola sat at attention nearby.

I sagged into a chair beside Dave who was hard at work stripping husks from ears of corn. Conducting a quick head count, I came up at least three short. Paulette was off on a hot-date weekend with her airline pilot husband. But what about Penelope? And my sister? "Did someone forget to invite Iz?"

"Nope." Dave set a naked ear on a silver tray and stuffed the husks into a plastic tub. "She's not speaking to you, remember?"

"Sure, but that never kept her from a free dinner before. She shows up so she can snub me."

"Not this time, not after Penelope wondered if that might be childish behavior not worthy of her national stature."

"Have I told you lately that I'm nuts about Penelope?" I grinned and took in a deep and relaxing breath. "Is this a regular gathering of the clan or is it a special occasion?"

"Beats me. Mrs. Ballantine says she has an important announcement."

Uh oh.

So much for relaxing. Her important announcements had a way of affecting my life. Case in point, the announcement that she'd arranged for me to sell a smaller condo and purchase the one I now resided in because I'd need more room. As it turned out, Dave and I clicked, and he and Allison moved in.

A month after that, she made another announcement and prediction. I'd need still more room because Dave and I would marry and reproduce. Was she intending to push her plan for my life despite the two-year mark I set a few days ago?

"Any idea what the announcement is about?" My voice was tight and squeaky.

"Not a clue." Dave shucked the last ear of corn. "You okay? You sound like you're catching a cold."

"I'm fine," I squeaked.

"Keep saying that and you might convince yourself." He stood and picked up the tub. "I'll take the husks to the compost bin if you take the corn inside."

I'd no sooner lifted the tray than Verna took it from me and hustled off with Sybil in her wake.

"Don't skimp on the butter," Mrs. B called after them. "You can never go wrong with a little more butter."

That sounded like a culinary myth fostered by those whose fat cells, unlike mine, didn't swell at the mere mention of butter.

"I have some news." Mrs. B sidled up to me and tapped the deck three times with her high-heeled sandal. "About our friend."

"Oh." Proving I could be every bit as clandestine, I patted one bare foot on the boards twice. "What's the word?"

261

"He's home. His experiment's over. I thought we'd all go to dinner next weekend." She glanced over her shoulder. "Some place where he won't stand out."

"Like the middle of a basketball court?"

"No. I . . . oh, I see what you mean, dear. Perhaps for now I'll send him a few gift certificates to thank him for rescuing Lola and the little prince." She squeezed my arm. "And you. All of us, in fact, because I would have tried to fight off that beast."

And she would have. I was sure of that.

"That incident made me realize how fleeting life can be, and how many things I've left unsaid and undone."

Uh oh.

That definitely sounded like notice of her intention to torpedo my two-year plan.

"I found I had mixed emotions about the, uh, dog incident. So I slipped a little cash through the slot in Bernina's door last night."

A "little cash" to Mrs. B was probably enough for a good used car. But it was her money to throw around. And the size of the "donation" would make it clear it hadn't come from me, so Bernina might refrain from casting blame my way. "You were careful not to leave any prints, right?"

"Of course. I'm getting quite good at this kind of thing." She patted my arm. "But don't worry. I won't be making a career out of crime."

Good to know.

"Although it *is* exciting."

Not so good to know.

"Anyway. I have too many other projects." She smoothed her teal silk blouse and adjusted a triple string of pearls. "But I'll get into that after dinner."

When we were all stuffed and lolling in our chairs or sprawled on the deck, Mrs. B tapped a fork against a crystal glass to get our attention. "Recently I realized that I have been guilty of not following my own advice—not living life to its fullest and making the most of every opportunity. Consequently, even though the year is more than six months old, I made a few resolutions. Three, to be exact."

"Uh oh," Dave muttered.

"Ditto," I whispered. "Did you notice she's wearing a triple string of pearls?"

Mrs. B shot me a glance so sharp it could have sliced hard salami, then tapped her glass again. "First, I intend to purchase Krammee's from Mrs. Krammer. Jim and Verna and other members of the Committee are already aware of this. They've agreed to manage the restaurant if Josh will agree to show them the ropes and sign on as assistant manager."

"Whoa!" Josh leaped to his feet. "Assistant manager! Wow."

"On condition that your school work doesn't suffer," Jim told him.

"It won't." Josh put his hand over his heart. "Promise."

"I hope you're going to change the menu," Allison said.

"We're going to change everything," Verna assured her. "Especially those horrible tables and chairs. We're conferring with Paulette."

"Maybe I could work there to make money for a car." Allison slid her gaze toward her father. "Unless someone decides to buy me one."

263

Before Dave uttered a pout-inducing comment like "In your dreams," Mrs. B tapped her glass again. "My second resolution is to commit to a musical selection, commit to a routine, and commit to a date to appear on *Still Got That Strut*."

Amid a round of applause, Dario swept her into a hug followed by several lingering kisses. When they broke, she used her napkin to dab lipstick from his mouth.

Finally, she tapped her glass once more and turned her sapphire gaze my way, fingering her pearls as she did. "My third resolution is to step in when I see friends floundering and failing to do what's in their best interests."

Eeekkk.

Dave gripped my hand. "Remember, she's a force of nature. All we can do is reckon. I'm right by your side."

"You are now. But what about after we learn what she's done?"

"Still here." He laced his fingers with mine. "Always will be."

"As some of you know," Mrs. B went on, "Jake Stranahan has been calling Barbara about an urgent matter. But she refused to take those calls."

"Good for you," Jim called. "He probably wants you to send money."

"Actually, it's the other way around." Mrs. B drew a long white envelope from beneath her plate. "When they were married, Jake invested a substantial sum of Barbara's savings in a development deal I would have considered a very bad bet. As it turns out, it wasn't bad at all."

She passed the envelope to Dario. "He was trying to call you, dear, to get your advice about an offer because,

264

after all, it was your money at stake. But since you refused to talk with him, and since I've never known you to show an interest in investments, and since I made that resolution, well, I thought you wouldn't mind if I advised him."

She motioned for Dario to hand me the envelope. "I managed to negotiate more than the original offer and he got enough to repay you with interest. Quite a bit of interest. Except for a portion we set aside for taxes, Jake insisted you have every dime."

All eyes were on me as I tore open the flap and drew out a check. It had four zeroes to the left of the decimal point. It was hefty enough to pay off my student loan and then some.

Dave gasped.

I yelped with joy.

Mrs. B beamed. "Didn't I tell you Jake was changing his ways?"

Jake repaying what he looted and giving me all the profit. Iz passing on a chance to snub me. Allison setting a course that made Dave happy. If things went on this way, I'd have to rethink my stance on the question of whether leopards can change their spots.

Also by Carolyn J. Rose
No Substitute for Murder
No Substitute for Money
No Substitute for Maturity
Hemlock Lake
Through a Yellow Wood
The Devil's Tombstone
An Uncertain Refuge
Sea of Regret
A Place of Forgetting

With Michael A. Nettleton
Death at Devil's Harbor
Deception at Devil's Harbor
The Hard Karma Shuffle
The Crushed Velvet Miasma
Drum Warrior
Sucker Punches

Carolyn J. Rose is the author of the popular Subbing isn't for Sissies series (*No Substitute for Murder, No Substitute for Money, No Substitute for Maturity,* and *No Substitute for Myth*), as well as the Catskill Mountains mysteries (*Hemlock Lake, Through a Yellow Wood,* and *The Devil's Tombstone*). Other works include *An Uncertain Refuge, Sea of Regret, A Place of Forgetting,* and projects written with her husband, Mike Nettleton (*The Hard Karma Shuffle, The Crushed Velvet Miasma, Drum Warrior, Death at Devil's Harbor, Deception at Devil's Harbor,* and the short story collection *Sucker Punches*).

She grew up in New York's Catskill Mountains, graduated from the University of Arizona, logged two years in Arkansas with Volunteers in Service to America, and spent 25 years as a television news researcher, writer, producer, and assignment editor in Arkansas, New Mexico, Oregon, and Washington. She's now a substitute teacher in Vancouver, Washington. Her interests are reading, swimming, walking, gardening, and NOT cooking.

www.deadlyduomysteries.com

www.ingramcontent.com/pod-product-compliance
Lightning Source LLC
Chambersburg PA
CBHW061557170626
46811CB00001B/228